The little man spoke again. At least, his lips moved. The voice that emerged was not his. "You must take a life and add to yours. Take a life and add to yours." The voice was the embodiment of evil; its sound had a smell, its words hit like punches. The voice went on: "Every soul you send to me will mean a gift of years for you. Your life will be forever; your life will be eternity!" The voice was an obscenity, a vulgarity that splashed filth on listening ears. But suddenly Miss Finney realized she had heard a truth, a promise, a commitment.

Miss Finney screamed.

Miss Finney Kills now and then

by
Al Dempsey
and
Joseph Van Winkle

and
Sidney Levine

TOR

A TOM DOHERTY ASSOCIATES BOOK
Distributed by Pinnacle Books, New York

Miss Finney Kills Now and Then

Copyright © 1982 by Al Dempsey, Sidney Levine, and Joe Van Winkle

Based on an original screenplay by Joseph Van Winkle

All rights reserved, including the right to reproduce this book or portions thereof in any form.

A Tor Book, published by Tom Doherty Associates, Inc., 8-10 West 36th Street, New York, N.Y. 10018

First printing, February 1982

ISBN: 0-523-48008-3

Printed in the United States of America

Distributed by Pinnacle Books, 1430 Broadway, New York, N.Y. 10018

1

The old lady was disturbed by the action of the wheel-chair. She complained, "Do take it easy, Willa!"

The younger woman snapped back, "Don't worry, I know what I'm doing."

With sternness, the old lady snapped, "You will not sass me, young lady: Be careful!"

Willa, the old lady's niece, stopped short; the wheel-chair was precariously balanced on the narrow ramp that led to the front entrance of the Finney mansion. Coldly, the niece said, "You must trust me, Auntie. I've done all right by you for the past two months. Trust me."

Miss Alcorn Finney, the old lady, was terrified at the thought of the chair tumbling off the ramp; she tempered her tone: "You have done well, Willa. But *please* be careful. I could be killed in such a fall."

She waved her skinny arm toward the dropoff. It was less than two feet, but for a woman eighty-four years old, such a fall could be fatal.

"I'll take it easy," Willa answered. Old Miss Finney wished desperately that she had enough strength to twist around and see into her niece's eyes; she would like to know if Willa was truly contrite.

As they continued down the ramp, Willa said, "This is all too silly. We should simply forget the whole thing."

Miss Finney spoke emphatically, "I will not hear of it. We are going to see to this disgusting matter. We are going to get that man off my property. I will permit no

5

such vile behavior by a person in my employ."

Willa said, "I think he is in the east garden working on the marigolds."

Miss Finney seemed to be talking to herself: "My word, what a horrid state of affairs. A woman is not safe anywhere."

Willa pushed the chair around the corner of the mansion as she commented, "Really, Auntie, I think it was nothing to get upset over. He was probably drunk."

The old lady hissed, "He grabbed you, is that right?"

"Yes," Willa replied.

"And he ripped your blouse, is that right?"

"Yes."

"And he put his hand inside your bra, is that right?"

"Yes. But nothing happened."

"In my day, young lady, that was not *nothing*. When I was in my youth, such actions were considered rape. A man was lucky to get off with being hanged."

"He didn't hurt me. I told you because I thought you should know."

They moved through the grape arbor that led to the marigold garden. Miss Finney would not be put off. "That man is an animal. We gave him work when he deserved to be thrown off my property. I should never have listened to you, Willa."

The niece steered the wheelchair around a small fountain and bird feeder. She said, "I thought he would do a good job, Auntie. The gardens are in need of tending. I had no idea that he was demented. He seemed normal when he arrived last week."

Miss Finney replied, "He has been here a week too long. I am only sorry that I must pay him his wages. He is a lout."

They came out of the arbor to where the gardener was supposed to be. The only sign of him was a pile of tools and garden paraphernalia.

"Damn!" Willa spit out.

Angrily, Miss Finney demanded, "I want that person off my grounds."

Willa yelled: "Damn you, Baldwin! Where the hell are you?"

The old lady used every bit of her energy to turn toward Willa. "Watch your language, Willa Hawk! I'll have no blaspheming in this household."

Willa did not answer; she stalked away, leaving Miss Finney stranded.

The old lady called, "You come back here, Willa. Right this minute! You come back!"

Willa did not answer. She strode to the back of the mansion and disappeared around the corner.

Miss Alcorn Finney was infirm with age. She was plagued with nearly every geriatric problem known to medical science. Her mind was able, but she was incapable of physical activity other than arm movement. She fed herself; for the rest of her necessities, she was dependent on others.

Willa's walking off the way she had struck fear in her aunt's heart; the old lady could not locomote the wheelchair.

She was petrified.

"Willa!" she cried, trying to hide her fear.

"Please . . . . Pleeeeze! Come back!"

She was alone, totally alone, and her mind began to manufacture threats:

Suppose Willa did not come back. Would she die there, decaying in her wheelchair?

Suppose a storm came and lightning struck. Would she be electrocuted where she sat?

Suppose the gardener suddenly appeared. Would he put his hands on her and rape her?

The scream coming from her throat struggled for the dignity of loudness, but only an aged squeak emerged. It travelled a few feet and died.

The man who had been hired as a temporary gardener

bullied his way into her imagination. She was molested in ways that brought her to the threshold of nausea.

She called again, trembling now.

Willa came around the corner, and walked back to her aunt.

Tears triggered by gratitude and anger welled up in the old lady's eyes. Torn by conflicting emotions, she could not speak.

Calmly, unaware of her aunt's state, Willa said, "I went to his room in the stable building, Auntie. He was not there. I also checked the topiary and there was no . . . . "

Willa noticed the anguish on her aunt's face. With no pretext of remorse, Willa chided: "Now, what are you upset about? What's the matter?"

Miss Finney was struggling fiercely to speak. Finally she muttered, "Never! Ever! Leave me like that again!"

Arrogantly, Willa replied, "Now, don't be silly, Auntie. You knew where I was. You are the one who wants to see Baldwin. I certainly do not."

The old lady repeated her command.

Ignoring her aunt's distress, Willa moved behind the wheelchair and began pushing it through the grape arbor towards the front of the grounds.

"Maybe," Willa said, "maybe he is out by the front gate. We'll find him."

Miss Finney let out a gasp, followed by: "Suppose he is in the house!"

Willa stopped pushing. She walked around to face her aunt. Willa conveyed the impression that she had just realized her aunt was in a tizzy. "You're really concerned," Willa said. "You are all shook up."

Her aunt glared at her. Impatience replaced the panic in her voice. "You make light of this, Willa, but Baldwin is a menace. He might be in the house right at this moment! He might be attacking Brook!"

Willa challenged her aunt: "Now, that is silly, Auntie.

she said, "That is too funny!"

Miss Finney challenged: "It is not funny at all. Suppose that man *is* attacking Brook."

Willa gasped words between giggles. "It might just do her some good. I doubt if she's been in bed with a man since she killed her husband. A little diddle by Baldwin might just be what Brook needs."

The old lady raised a feeble hand as if to ward off the evil of the vulgar words. "Do not talk that way, Willa. You are being disgusting."

Willa did not stop laughing.

Miss Finney hissed, "Brook is a fine girl. She has been with me ten years. You are not to slur her in that manner. Get me into the house! *Now*, Willa!"

Willa was not intimidated by the scolding. To placate the old lady, she affected urgency as she pushed her back to the house. They passed through the main hallway leading to the kitchen at the back of the mansion.

As they entered the vastness of the kitchen, Miss Finney's other niece, Brook, looked up from preparing a tray of small sandwiches for their lunch.

"Find him?" Brook asked.

Her aunt let out a loud huff of relief. "Thank goodness you are safe. I was scared to death."

Brook looked at Willa, who said, "Auntie got it into her head that Baldwin might be in here with you."

Brook said, "That's silly. He's not allowed in the mansion."

Willa left her aunt midway across the white tile floor. As she approached Brook at the heavy oak worktable, Willa said, "Auntie got it in her mind that Baldwin was in here having his way with you."

Brook gave a nervous smile.

Willa came closer and continued, "Auntie thought that you might be stripped naked and spread on the table. She was thinking that you might . . . . "

"Stop that, Willa! I mean stop that NOW!" Miss

Finney's voice was not loud but carried authority.

Willa stopped talking but kept closing the distance between her and Brook. Willa radiated evil as she came within inches of Brook's face and mouthed an obscenity that offended Brook.

"Willa!" came again from Miss Finney, "You behave yourself!"

Brook cast a grateful glance at her aunt and attempted to change the subject: "There was no sign of Baldwin?"

Miss Finney answered, "None," then turned to Willa. "Now that you have started behaving yourself, you can come here and move me to the telephone at my desk. I will call the police before we have our lunch."

Willa challenged her aunt: "Now, that is silly, Auntie. There is no need to go calling the police about that childish matter." Then, turning to Brook, Willa asked, "There's no need, is there, Brook?"

Brook shook her head. She had known her cousin, Willa, for just two months, but within that time, Willa had come to exert a complete dominance over her.

Miss Finney said, "I do not really care what your views on the matter are, Willa. I am going to call the police."

Willa leaned close to Brook and whispered, "Do you want the police here? Do you want them asking how you have been doing since you killed your husband?"

Brook stiffened visibly.

Miss Finney called: "What are you two whispering about? I do declare, there is no politeness in this household nowadays."

Willa lied, "Brook was just saying that she'd just as soon the police stay away. She's afraid they might make trouble for her."

Miss Finney looked skeptical. "Is that right, Brook? Good lands, we have never had any trouble from the police in the ten years you have been here. Why should you worry?"

Brook opened her mouth to speak, but she could not

join in the lie. Willa jumped in with, "Brook is shy about it, Auntie."

Miss Finney demanded, "Why are you suddenly into all of this, Willa? What happened to Brook happened a long time ago and is nothing for us to concern ourselves about now. Just let that foolishness drop. Now wheel me to my desk so I may call the police."

Willa did not move. "We will not be calling the police about Baldwin, Auntie. I will not press charges and I am the one who was fondled. The police will not take kindly to being called out by a houseful of old maids."

"Willa," Miss Finney demanded, "Wheel me to my desk!"

Brook then saw a startling change descend upon Willa. Her smile softened, her eyes warmed, even her posture seemed less rigid. With a litheness that suggested tranquility, Willa floated across the kitchen, stopped in front of her aunt and lowered herself to eye level. In dulcet tones, she said, "I'm sorry I have upset you, Auntie. Really, my only wish is that you be happy."

Miss Finney was not moved. She glared at her niece.

Willa petitioned, "Please don't think ill of me. I don't want to cause you any trouble. I'm sure Baldwin has probably deserted us anyway. I feel horrible about causing you anxiety and I'll do anything to make it up to you."

Through the years, Miss Finney had been hardened to all kinds of personal manipulation, but the one thing she could not bear was tears. A tear suddenly appeared on Willa's cheek.

Miss Finney softened. "I understand."

Willa beamed a broad smile of relief.

Brook had watched the entire encounter with amazement. How could Willa change her own temperament, then involve Miss Finney in the metamorphosis? Fascinating. Almost mystical. Brook felt Willa's power. It was as if Willa possessed the ability to project wishes.

11

It had worked with Miss Finney; the matter of calling the police was dropped. "We will all have to be on our guard. I want that man off my property," said the old lady.

Willa added, " . . . If he has not left already . . . . "

Miss Finney smiled agreement, " . . . if he has not left already. He is probably gone."

The mood was suddenly void of tension. Brook was shocked at the change.

Willa, still in a position of supplication in front of her aunt, said, "I did not mention Baldwin in order to upset you, Auntie. I was trying to do what was right."

The old lady acknowledged the statement with a nod. Willa continued, "All I want today is for you to feel good and strong."

Miss Finney reached out a hand and stroked her niece's cheek. The old lady said, "I know that, Willa. I am a foolish old lady to let myself be so distraught. I appreciate your efforts; I am truly grateful."

Willa's head snapped towards Brook and she asked, "Are we ready to go?"

Brook was confused. She glanced at the old clock on the kitchen wall and, as she saw it was not yet noon, she said, "It is too early, Willa. I asked the rental company to have the coach here at one o'clock. That will give us plenty of time."

Willa was obviously disappointed. Brook was surprised that Willa had so completely lost track of time.

Miss Finney asked, "Are they sending Clifford as our driver?"

Brook replied, "Yes, Auntie."

The old lady gave a wistful smile and said, "That is good. You know, his brother drove my carriage for nearly thirty years. I would have hired Clifford, too, but keeping two carriage drivers seemed a bit extravagant. Besides, he could make a lot more money driving tourists around the French Quarter than he could in regular employ."

Willa said, "I think it was wise for you to get rid of all the staff, Auntie. Brook and I are doing just fine."

Miss Finney agreed, "It was a good suggestion from you, Willa. I am glad I listened to you. The way wages are going crazy, the staff salaries would have me bankrupt." All of them knew the statement about going bankrupt was an exaggeration, but, like most other people who were in the super-rich category, Miss Finney liked to poor-mouth her financial status.

Brook said, "Well, Clifford is driving us today. That is for sure."

Miss Finney seemed pleased.

Brook took the tray of finger sandwiches to the small lunching nook adjacent to the kitchen. The family only used the master dining room for the evening meals. With Miss Finney wheeled into place, Brook said, "I'm skipping lunch so that I can scoot upstairs and change."

Willa slid into the bench side of the table opposite her aunt and said, "You look just fine, Brook." Miss Finney nodded agreement.

Brook replied, "I just want to take a shower and put on a dress. I hate going out in slacks." There was an embarrassed lull; Miss Finney usually wore slack suits. Ever since her muscles had begun to atrophy, her legs had become ugly, shapeless appendages and she hid them under slacks.

Breaking the lull, Miss Finney said, "I agree with you, Brook. Slacks are for old ladies with broad bottoms and for ancient ladies with no shape left to their legs. You and Willa fail to qualify for either of those categories. So you go on up and slip into a dress. Show the world what lady-like can look like. Run along now."

Brook leaned over, squeezed her aunt's shoulders and pecked the wrinkled cheek. She was out of the kitchen in a flash. As soon as Brook had left the room, Miss Finney's expression became stern. She glared at Willa.

Sensing the hostility, Willa asked, "What's the matter, Auntie?"

Miss Finney's voice was vengeful as she said, "I will not have you playing little Miss Innocence with me, Willa. You know what is wrong." Willa did not respond. She picked up a sandwich and began to nibble. The old lady said, "You have no right to open old wounds with Brook. The accident is part of the past now."

Willa spoke as she chewed. "Accident? It was no accident. It was murder!"

Miss Finney's voice was angry as she said, "All you know about is the court ruling; you do not know the truth of the matter. I should have told you before so you would not be cruel and bring up any pain of the incident."

Willa poured them both some iced tea as Miss Finney continued, "It was twelve years ago that Brook fell in love and got married. She was living up near Shreveport at that time and she had no family guidance. Her parents had been killed when she was only seventeen. She lived alone and was an easy mark for any disreputable man. She found one. The night they were married, the vile man forced her to have sex with three of his friends. They raped her on her wedding night. When Brook and the husband were alone, he forced her to do some horrors that she has never been able to tell to anyone. All that is known is that she took a hunting knife and killed the filthy man."

Willa showed some doubts as she asked, "She stabbed him pretty well, didn't she?"

Miss Finney nodded, "Seven wounds. Each one was deep enough to be fatal; one of them nearly severed the head from the body. It was supposed to be a fairly grisly scene."

Willa asked, "Then why do you say it was not murder? If she stabbed him seven times, she meant to do what she did."

The old lady was having trouble lifting the sandwich to

her mouth. She gave up the effort and said, "The court ruled murder, but they sent her to the insane asylum. She was there for two years before I heard about the case. I arranged for her to be released to my care. Good Heavens, Willa, how can anyone consider what Brook did to be murder? The poor girl was driven to defend herself after being violated in the most horrible way possible. I do not blame her at all."

Willa looked at her aunt for a long time before replying, "I never knew it was so bad. I guess I shouldn't tease her about it."

For some reason, Miss Finney felt there was a strangeness in Willa's attitude. It was as if Willa already knew the story. But the feeling passed and Miss Finney closed with, "So we must be somewhat gentle with Brook about that part of her past, Willa. Please be considerate."

Willa promised she would.

Upstairs, Brook was being stalked by a horror that came from her memory.

The shower was invigorating. She let the hot water course over her body. She could feel the tingle of pink skin as she rubbed the nap of the towel down her arms. The shower had been a necessity; the incident with Willa had been disconcerting and she needed to pour some confidence back into her body.

Before in her life, when there had been moments of gross tension surrounding memories of her husband, Brook had been exposed to ghastly experiences. She was simply taking reasonable precautions to avoid a recurrence. She did not know why she was being subjected to the torment; she felt justified in killing the animal that had attacked her. But there was something in her mind or something in the aura around her that kept letting the horror flood back into her.

She felt a warm shower and fresh clothing would prevent the misery.

She was wrong; it lurked there with her.

She sensed the thing coming and let out a cry: "Go away!"

The command seemed to work. She was still fearful, but as she worked to get control of her emotions, she felt it had retreated.

That was when it hit. It slammed into her. The force drove her across the room. She stumbled, nearly crashed into the tub. Then, in a defense she knew was vital, she cringed down into a ball.

Hiding was critical. She could not hide.

A spear of cold, freezing like an icicle, stabbed into her groin. An explosion of frigid air burst inside her stomach. A painful blanket of raw cold enveloped her breasts, which erupted with chillblain festers.

As always, the pain was nearly unbearable. She fought to bear it. Something—she knew what it was—was trying to pry her eyes open. She grabbed at her face, trying to seal her eyes shut. She felt a gnarled thing search into her hair on the back of her hand. When it had a handful, it yanked hard, pulling her head back. Her face was ripped out of her hands, her eyes popped open.

It was there. All of it pouring at her. This was no dream, no imagination. This was horror.

The man's head was half severed and she could see the windpipe gurgling blood. A tongue flicked out of what must have been a mouth; it was difficult to tell; lips were stretched back exposing teeth that seemed to move with pain. Two hands, covered with blood, rose to the surge of blood at the throat. The hands tried to force the head back into place.

Brook felt bile rising in her throat, it was oozing into her mouth. She swallowed furiously. The form in front of her pushed down on the head one more time, but the blood kept coming. Its eyes bulged, screaming hate at Brook. One of the eyes popped out of its socket and Brook vomited.

Some force, more than just hands, began pulling at Brook. Her arms were spread flat on the floor, her legs were pulled apart. The blood mass before her began to descend onto her body.

She remembered the knife.

It was sticky with blood, but she tightened her grip and stabbed at the form. The rest of the memory tumbled into a turmoil of knife jabs, blood and gore . . . finally, gratefully . . . blackness.

She did not know how long she had been there, lying on the bathroom floor. The next thing she knew, she could hear Willa's voice calling from outside the bathroom door: "Hurry, Brook, we've got to get going. The carriage will be here in a few minutes."

Brook could hear Willa's footsteps going down the hall to the stairs. She tried to pull herself together.

2

The Finney mansion sat like a huge, white, antique cube placed on a beautifully manicured lawn. The original building had been designed by Adrien de Pauger, the planner of the old town. Later, the architect Latrobe had built the massive front entrance and gate house. Still later, Galliers had designed the stables and servant quarters at the back of the property. The main house and stables were lost in the devastating fire of 1788, but they were rebuilt according to the original plans.

The family name, Finney, seemed strange for Creoles. But the blood lines traced back to the Wild Geese of Ireland who fled their homeland after losing to the British at the Battle of the Boyne in 1690. The Irish Lords went to France and became as French as the French. The Kelly clan became Killie (Kil-lee); O'Brian became Ou'Boire and Finney became Fenois. The Fenoises did not take well to the French customs and joined the prospective colonists going to Louisiana with Le Moyne in 1718. First as commercial traders, then as cotton growers and processors, the family had business intercourse up the Mississippi and across the South. They changed the name back to Finney, but the family did not revert to Irish customs; the Finneys of New Orleans were fiercely Creole. Under strong leadership, the family business prospered and, by the time of the Louisiana Purchase in 1803, the Finneys were American at heart.

Life went well and all looked bright for generations,

but then came an error of procreation: Miss Finney's father failed to produce a male heir. Compounding his failure, Miss Finney shunned marriage, embracing celibacy following a clandestine romance during the First World War. As hopes for the future of the line diminished, so did hopes for the future of the mansion. Many of the people who knew the mansion felt it would be good for it to pass out of the Finneys' possession; it was considered to be one of the few buildings in the French Quarter better torn down than maintained; the mansion was popularly believed to be haunted. Of course, to those would-be conjurers Miss Finney said nothing; she wanted them to think the worst. The building never was haunted.

There was a more virulent curse on the Finneys. Going back over the centuries, all the way to the ancestral estates in County Dublin in the 16th century, there are records of disappearance: strange, sudden, unexplained disappearances. To earlier generations of Finneys the stories not only held credence, they produced real and lasting fear. But in the modern, sophisticated age, especially with the current head of household, they were enjoyed as harmless myths. Alcorn Finney had heard the stories of an aunt or a great uncle or a great, great, great something flitting off into nowhere, never to be seen again. Miss Finney could explain to her satisfaction each and every one: The missing ancestors had wandered too far into the swamps and lost their way, or they had fallen in love with serving maids and left New Orleans to protect the family name.

Miss Finney savored the haunted house stories; they fascinated her. Besides, for a good many years the ghost stories made the property unattractive to prospective buyers, so she was not bothered by pushy real estate salesmen. But recently, over the past ten or twelve years, there had been a new breed of buyers: the investors who would pay virtually anything for a prime piece of land.

And the Finney land was prime. It sat at the end of a

quiet cul-de-sac; it would be an incredible site for investment speculation. Miss Finney was vocal in her abhorrence of such suggestions. "No" was not a negative enough answer to such people. There were a few of the nouveau riche who had the temerity to propose buying the mansion for a personal residence. The old lady had no words in her broad vocabulary to reply to such propositions. Her silent contempt was eloquent.

The building was in superb condition. Each of the three floors above ground had a balcony decorated with classic wrought-iron grillwork. Miss Finney did not scrimp on maintenance costs. Paint was applied regularly and structural inspections were annual. The mansion was well tended.

On the first floor were the kitchen, dining room, sitting room, music salon, main parlor, ballroom and library. The library was the smallest room, and it was slightly larger than a suburban two-bedroom tract house.

The second floor held a sewing room, nursery and two master bedrooms. The bedrooms were actually large apartments that gave spacious privacy to the occupying family member. Miss Finney occupied one of the bedrooms. The rest of the floor had been closed off.

The third floor contained six suites, of which four were closed off. Brook and Willa occupied the two remaining suites.

In her rooms on the third floor, Brook dressed hurriedly so Miss Finney would not be disturbed.

It was to be, Brook felt, a silly day, but her aunt was getting older and more ill each day; she could not be long for this world.

The object of the day's outing was to visit a fortune teller. It had all begun as a round of joking during dinner a few nights before, but Willa had finally spoken of the idea seriously and set out to find a proper mystic. It was not difficult to find such a person in the French Quarter of New Orleans, but Willa had outdone herself; she came up with a man who professed not only to foretell events, but also to extend lives. When both Miss Finney and Brook had taken to teasing Willa, she became quite indignant, claiming that the clairvoyant would be a very important man in their lives. The teasing stopped only in order to avoid hurting Willa's feelings. Miss Finney did not hesitate to state she felt there was nothing to be excited about, but Willa swore there was more to it than rigmarole and hocus-pocus. Willa contended the man could cure the old lady's ills.

Brook maintained a tolerant attitude: if it helped Aunt Finney, it would be worth it.

Willa called up to Brook from the front of the house, "Hurry, Clifford is here."

Brook finished buttoning her blouse and moved to the front window. Below she saw Clifford Morton's beautiful carriage approaching the porte cochère at the entrance to the building. The black man gave a big smile as he looked up and saw Brook at the window. She waved back and turned to hurry down.

She slammed into a revolting, smelly, nauseating wall of sweat and hair. Something grabbed at the back of her head and held her face tight into the horror. She opened her mouth to scream but kinky hair jammed between her teeth, acrid drops of perspiration came against her lips and onto her tongue; she gagged, trying to keep from swallowing the putrid liquid. She reached her hands up and clawed at the blackness in front of her. She was fighting for her very life.

"Hey, easy, pretty lady," it was a voice she could faintly hear through the sounds of panic pounding in her ears. Strong hands took her by the shoulders and eased her out of the black, hairy void. Her heart beat with a ferocity that would not stop; a pain clawed at her chest and she thought she must be having a heart attack.

A face came into view. It was pockmarked and unshaven; a thin, unattractive mouth framed decayed teeth; a bulbous nose separated two bloodshot eyes that glared. They seemed to undress Brook as she stood shaking.

"Hey, lady," the voice came again, "don't get all shook. I'm yer friend." Brook swiped his hands away from her shoulders and, in a continuing move, she slapped the face so close to her.

"You filth!" she cried, "You unspeakable garbage." The mouth smiled, exposing more yellow teeth, and let out a husky but quiet laugh. "Now ain't you somethin', Miss Brook-hot-shit. I seen you looking at me." She swung again. Her hand was balled into a fist this time and she struck the obscene nose; blood spurted out onto the man's chest.

He put his hand up and dammed the flow as he said, "You got a funny way of showing you like me, you fancy bitch." Brook shoved at his chest. Her hand came in contact with the mat of sweat-wet hair. She cringed but kept pushing to get free of his trap.

She felt dirty, violated by his very presence in her room.

"What the hell are you doing in my room, Baldwin? You're not even supposed to be in the house. My Aunt will fire you for this."

The burly, slovenly man barked back, "You gotta be kiddin', bitch. I'm through workin' here, anyway."

The man was Baldwin Crane, a vagabond who professed to be a gardener. The magnolias had been in desperate need of trimming, so Willa had hired him. The estimated duration had been three days, but Crane had dallied with the tasks and stretched his employ to a week. Miss Finney had insisted he leave at the end of the week. "I'll not pay you for more than you have done, either," she had said.

He had been respectful to Miss Finney, even though she was harnessed to a wheelchair and quite defenseless. He had been brazen and rude to both Willa and Brook, but he had never been so bold as to come to their quarters.

Brook was frightened by his contempt. She lunged for the door and ran down the stairs. When she burst out onto the porch of the front entranceway, she was out of breath and near collapse.

From her wheelchair, Miss Finney begged, "My child, what on earth is the matter? You look as if you've seen a ghost."

Gasping for breath, Brook explained, "I wish I had. That pervert, Baldwin, just came after me in my room. I thought I would not escape."

Willa hissed in anger, "That pig! He came after me in the kitchen yesterday. I told him I'd slide a butcher knife into his stomach if he tried anything again."

Miss Finney cried, "I told you girls he should not have been allowed here more than three days. I've dealt with workers for decades. There are types who will step past proper boundaries if they are given half a chance."

The carriage driver had tied his rig and come up onto the porch. Miss Finney said to him, "Now, Clifford, you go up to the third floor and tell that reprobate that he is to get out of my home or I shall call the police." Then, softening her voice, she said, "You'll do that for me, won't you, Clifford?"

The huge, liveried driver smiled a toothy smile at Miss Finney and said he'd be just happy to do that. He moved his massive frame with ease into the house and headed up the staircase.

Miss Finney, in her best take-charge manner, ordered her nieces: "Well, don't just stand there. Clifford will take care of that unpleasantness. Now you get me into the carriage. I do not want to be late."

They wheeled her down the ramp. Until three years before, the old lady had been able to locomote her own wheelchair, but crippling rheumatoid arthritis had made her arms and hands worthless for anything more strenuous than turning a page, lifting a fork or pointing with a crooked finger. Getting her into the coach was not an easy task, despite the fact that she weighed only eighty-seven pounds. Willa and Brook slowly lifted her into the rear seat of the coach and, after propping her up with cushions, covered her with a warm quilt comforter that the driver had brought. By the time she was situated, the driver was back down and told them, "There was no sign of him, Ma'am. I looked around, but he was gone."

Having escaped the threat, Brook had been able to get her panic under control. Now anger was taking hold as she nearly shouted, "Well, I'll go find the bastard!" She made a move toward the mansion.

Willa grabbed at Brook. Miss Finney ordered: "Now you listen to me, young lady. We have an appointment and I intend to keep it. Clifford, please."

The driver offered Brook a hand up into the coach, but she balked. "No! Aunt Finney, that animal should be shown a lesson. He failed with me, he failed with Willa; maybe he will attack you."

Miss Finney could not fight back a laugh. "That is very kind, my child, but I think I am past that threat."

Brook had been so flustered by the incident that her suggestion had seemed reasonable. Now she saw the humor. She looked at Willa and the young women broke into laughter. Miss Finney nodded approval. She said, "Now, what that animal did to you was awful and he will be removed from my property. But such an animal is not worth disruption of our plans. We will take care of that problem when we return. Our city police appreciate my annual gifts to their associations; they will help us if we need it."

Clifford put the folded wheelchair on a rack at the back of the coach; Willa and Brook settled in their places.

As the two women adjusted themselves in their seats, Miss Finney chided Brook, "And, dear Brook, I do not approve of your language in front of the driver. Remember, we must maintain our position with hired help and tradespeople. The word 'bastard' is not becoming. 'Ingrate' would do very well."

Brook looked at the old lady with mixed feelings of warmth and contempt; her aunt clung to the standards of a defunct age. Brook had frequently, over the past ten years, had reason to feel animosity. On the whole, her aunt had been arrogant and overbearing. Brook was able to maintain calm by rationalizing that the old lady was motivated by familial love.

As always, Brook nodded her understanding. Willa, sensing the tension, patted Brook's knee and said, "I hope this does not disrupt your visit today, Auntie." The coach lurched as it began to pull away from the house. Miss Finney answered, "I am seldom disturbed by other people's misbehavior, Willa. I feel sorry for misguided souls."

Brook nodded, wondering if her aunt was referring to the misdeeds of the gardener or if she was rebuking Brook again. There was no more conversation in the coach as it went out through the ornate front entrance of the property. Willa broke the silence as she asked, "Auntie, does one ever tire of going through the Quarter?"

Miss Finney craned her neck, looking out both doors of the carriage before replying, "I do wish you could remember, Willa. You had enough French in Canada to be able to use it. The "French Quarter," as you are wont to call it, is, to us who have lived here, the Old Square: Vieux Carré, if you will. Please use that in conversation from now on. *Comprenez-vous?*"

Impatiently, Willa nodded and said, "I don't like to speak French, Auntie."

Miss Finney scrunched up her mouth, multiplying her wrinkles: "In French, *s'il vous plaît*. Please, for an old lady, Willa."

Willa showed anger, "*Cela ne me convient pas . . .*

I don't like it."

Miss Finney mocked a pout, "Enough of this. I will not press you again, Willa. I want to enjoy this outing. You worked hard to find someone for us."

Willa showed some remorse as she said, "I'm sorry, too, Auntie. I am tense, I am tired and, most of all, I am angry at that pig who tried to attack Brook. I'd just as soon kill an animal like that."

Miss Finney weakly raised a cautioning hand, "Now, we agreed we would handle that later. That person will get his just rewards."

The coach lurched as the driver yanked hard on his team to avoid hitting one of the tourist surreys. There was some customary back-and-forth from the drivers but it was in the Cajun patois and, despite the filthy language that was flying back and forth, the passengers were not offended.

They had been away from the mansion about five minutes and were moving along Chartres Street. The driver had strict, standing instructions to take his time whenever they were in the Quarter. He was never to take Miss Finney down Bourbon or Rampart streets; she hated to see her part of town defiled by tourists.

She did enjoy looking out at buildings that aroused fond memories: dinner parties in the Broussards; playful evenings in The Gem where the original "Mistic Crewe of Comus" came together to plan the first Mardi Gras; Sunday afternoon poetry readings in Audubon House on Dauphine Street; the Miltenberger House on Royal where, in 1911, when she was 14 years old, Miss Finney first felt a boy's lips on hers. So many memories of such nice times. But they were all in the past; the present held little hope. She was old, about as old as she felt she would be in her life.

Further along on Royal Street, with no orders from anyone, the driver pulled the coach to a halt in front of number 1140.

Willa leaned forward, pulled back the velvet curtain and looked out. With some impatience, she said, "This isn't the place." Then, louder: "Clifford! Not here!" Turning back toward her aunt, she said, "What an oaf! Really!"

Miss Finney shook her head and said, "He is not wrong. I always have Clifford stop here when we are abroad. It is the former home of the Lalaurie family, who were very close to us. The house is supposed to be haunted." Willa had not heard that before. She turned to Brook with a questioning look.

Miss Finney said, "Oh, don't look so surprised. Many of the old buildings in the Quarter have a history of being haunted. Our own mansion is supposed to have its share of mysteries. Some of the stories are linked to the Lalaurie House."

Brook smiled. Willa turned and looked back toward the house. Miss Finney spoke:

"The original horror in the Lalaurie House happened in the fire of 1788. Most of the old town burned; our original building was also lost. But on the Lalaurie grounds, back in their stable area, there were slaves who had been chained in their quarters. It was quite a tragic mess; two dozen poor souls burned to death while chained like animals. A year after the accident, Beauregard Lalaurie was lighting the fireplace in his bedroom quarters when the whole room burst into flames. It is said that as soon as he was dead from the fire, it extinguished itself. Quite frightening. Then his widow burned a hand so badly it had to be taken off; a child was burned while playing with a candle. The incidents were attributed to the ghosts of the slaves. A later generation, after one of their children nearly died when her hair burst into flames, had the old stables and slave quarters demolished. All traces of the former buildings were erased."

"Then stranger things began happening," Miss Finney

continued, "to people outside the Lalaurie family."

Brook and Willa split their attention between the building and Miss Finney. The old lady's eyes were slightly squinted, as if she were trying to focus back into her memory. She continued:

"There was one young—I understand pretty—thing who married into the family. On their wedding day, before leaving for St. Louis on one of the riverboats, they stopped to pay their respects to an infirm patriarch at the Lalaurie house. Unseen by anyone, and quite unexplainably, the pretty young bride fell down a flight of stairs and died from a broken neck. Everyone knew a slave had pushed her to her death." Miss Finney let that sink in, then added another: "And there was an Uncle Fred. I am supposed to have known him; I honestly do not remember. I am not positive he was a real uncle, but he was called 'uncle.' One day he left our place, headed for the Lalaurie house. Half the people there swore he arrived and left; the other half swore he never arrived. No matter; he never made it back to our home, and he was never seen nor heard from again. It was said the slaves had barbecued him for a meal, though some believed Uncle Fred had run off to Cuba with a Cajun girl of thirteen. Knowing the Finney family, the latter story is not incredible. So, girls, some of the family background is rather sordid."

Brook and Willa exchanged broad smiles; they obviously liked the story.

"Tell Clifford to continue on," the old lady ordered. The coach moved on through the Quarter and passed Jackson Square at an easy pace. Several minutes later the vehicle began to slow. The passengers heard the driver cajoling the horses as they turned down an alley that seemed much too narrow for the width of the carriage.

The driver knew what he was doing; he negotiated the tight alley entrance with professional ease. Once past the opening, the lane widened to leave several feet on each side. At the far end there was a garage area that was wide enough for turning the large coach around.

As the driver secured his team, Willa pointed out of the carriage and said, "Here we are, Auntie."

The alley was in disrepair. Brook could not contain her comment: "It sure does look bad, Willa."

Miss Finney, straining to lift her head so she could see outside, said, "Good Heavens, Willa, where have you brought us?"

Willa had anticipated the critical comments; opening the door of the coach and ignoring the chides, she said, "Clifford, please get madam's wheelchair." Clifford stood by his coach for an instant, scratched his head and asked, "You sure we is at the right place, Miss Will; Ma'am?"

Willa's reply was brisk: "Do as you are told, Clifford." Feigning obsequiousness, Clifford disappeared toward the rear of the carriage where the wheelchair was stowed.

Miss Finney was tense. "Willa, I think this is really a waste of time."

Willa replied, "Now, Auntie, he will just talk to you."

The aunt charged, "He will want money."

"That is nonsense, Auntie. He wants no money. You have nothing to lose."

"Hah!" the old lady scoffed, "I have nothing to gain, either. You said he extends life. Does he know I am eighty-five? He cannot make me young again and, at my age, that is all that matters."

Brook joined in: "Would you be happy just to think young again, Auntie?"

With a sad smile, Miss Finney reached feebly to pat Brook's hand. "There is nothing wrong with my thinking. How cruel to be this age and not be senile. To be fully aware of life but not a part of it." She paused, reflecting, then finished, "No, Brook, it is not enough just to think young." The driver snapped the wheelchair open and reached in to lift Miss Finney down from the coach.

Bordering the alley, sandwiched between the backs of two buildings, was a small courtyard. The place was in need of attention but held a charm that neglect could not ruin. The place seemed vacant; grass grew between the textured concrete slabs. Mud was caked in the blue and white tile fountain, which was dry. The traditional heavy iron fence and gate were badly rusted. The vines, which should have added color and life to the patio, hung dead, dry and brown.

As they unfastened the restraining straps across Miss Finney's lap and chest, she studied the setting. She asked Willa, "Are you sure, my dear? I don't mean to be contrary, but I can see why Clifford questioned the locale. It is quite unkempt and slatternly here."

Willa held her patience, "This is the place, Auntie."

Brook, not usually one to challenge Willa, did muster some spunk. "What kind of man is this? He must be without means."

Willa's irritation finally overcame her restraint. "Listen, Brook, you've been with Auntie for years and you've never really helped her. Unless you have some suggestions of your own, I recommend you keep your mouth shut." Brook reeled at the onslaught; Willa had never come down quite so hard.

Miss Finney jumped in to arrest the tension: "Okay, girls. Now this is just an experiment. We have entrusted Willa with the project and we must accept her guidance." Then, specifically for Willa, "I do appreciate your concern, child. I will not say more; I am in your hands."

Willa told the driver he could come back for them in an hour, but Clifford did not move. "Now, Miss Finney, Ma'am, if you want me to come in there with you, I'll sure do it, Ma'am." Miss Finney smiled and dismissed him with assurances that his concern was deeply appreciated but that Miss Willa was in charge. The coach pulled out of the alley as Willa took the large metal handle of the gate and gave it a twist. She moved the gate on ancient hinges that added their funereal chorus to the hollow sounds of their footsteps. The trio moved around the curve of the mountain and came to three steps at the entrance.

"Open it," Willa ordered Brook. As Brook stepped up and turned the knob, Willa lifted the wheelchair onto the threshold. Brook found that the door swung open with surprising ease. They were in a large, poorly lighted foyer. On one wall was a mirror, cracked and splotched with age. The other wall was filled with elaborate mailbox/intercom devices. Willa went to the wall and pushed a button in the grillwork of office six; there was no nameplate.

No voice came over the intercom, but a loud, harsh buzzer sounded, and a clicking noise came from the door to the first-floor hallway. The women entered and Willa closed the door behind them.

The hallway was small. Doors on either side were painted with names of firms that had gone bankrupt or prospered and found more suitable quarters. There was no sign of life. Ahead of them was another door, but it was different: It was part of a birdcage grillwork surrounding a tiny elevator. After a considerable struggle, they managed to get the wheelchair into the lift, but it was obvious that only one of the girls could squeeze in and ride to the third floor. There was a short, friendly argument: Brook felt Willa should go because she knew the person they were to meet. Willa felt Brook should go because Brook's traumatic experience with the gardener unsuited her for being left alone in a dark, strange place. Brook acquiesced.

The elevator was ancient. In a rare expression of humor, Miss Finney, her legs jammed against Brook's knees, said, "This could easily have been the very first elevator in Louisiana."

Brook was afraid to comment; she doubted there was

room to inhale enough breath to speak. She was beginning to feel mildly claustrophobic when the compartment rattled to a halt on the third floor. Hurrying as fast as she could, Brook pulled the expanding door open and eased her aunt's wheelchair out onto the landing.

The third floor looked worse than the first. Not only was the place in need of dusting, painting and carpentry, it also smelled as though it should be fumigated. The air was musky, dank and acrid; it attacked the nostrils and caught in the throat. Again, there were only two doors on the floor. One door showed the probable age of the last tenant; the peeling gold foil announced the place had been occupied by the New Orleans circulation office of *Collier's* magazine. There had been no recent occupants.

The other office showed its present denizen was one Mr. Carlos Ives, Clairvoyant Medium. The lettering on the opaque glass door had been done by an amateur; it had been a valiant effort, but the result did not look professional. In the lower right corner, where it said, "By Appointment Only," the effort seemed to be hurried and less valiant. From high above, fully another story up, a dirty skylight let a small rectangle of illumination drift down to expose motes of dust floating in the air. The whole scene, the whole mood of the place, the whole concept of the venture, finally unnerved Brook. Quickly she knelt down in front of her aunt and said, "I think we ought to leave here, Auntie. Really, this is all foolishness."

Miss Finney shook her head and gave a small smile as she said, "Now, Brook, just relax. There is nothing to all of this; we are pacifying Willa and we are having an outing, even if it is a little strange. Do not concern yourself, my dear."

Brook insisted, "It isn't just being kind to Willa, Auntie, there is something else I feel. It is . . . . "

The voice that cut her off shocked both Miss Finney and Brook: "I am pleased to meet you, ladies." They had not heard the door open nor the man approach them; suddenly he was just there. He said, "You must be Miss Alcorn Finney, and you," indicating Brook, who was frozen speechless, "you must be Brook." Both women were wide-eyed and silent. He added, "I am truly pleased to meet both of you. I hope we can find peace and joy together. I am Carlos Ives."

He was a small man, not a dwarf, but amazingly small: two inches under five feet, with normal proportions. Brook almost giggled, but was arrested by a look on Carlos Ives' face—a face full of malevolent power. She was not tempted to giggle again. Carlos Ives' face was confusing. One moment it was cherubic, glowing with innocence; the next moment it seemed demonic, radiating evil. Brook could not pinpoint the menace: the eyes were blue, not deep-set nor too close together; the nose was smallish, but not offensively so; the mouth was not too full or churlish. The face was framed with stylishly groomed blond hair, long enough to suggest a Prince Valiant look, but not so long as to be foppish. There was an ethereal quality to him. Brook felt some sort of power surging from him to her. Carlos Ives was a man to be respected.

He wore a white linen suit with vest. His shirt, tie and shoes were also white. Brook knew it was garish, but could not think badly of this man. He seemed to possess an irreproachability that forestalled criticism.

"Ladies, please come in. We will wait for Willa inside." He came forward and took charge of Miss Finney's wheelchair.

The outer office, the reception room of Ives' suite, was a jolting contrast to the rest of the building. The room had an opulence that made one forget the filth just outside the door. The furniture was modern and expensive. Chrome, glass and leather were blended in a futuristic mood that felt sterile, yet hospitable. The floor was parqueted, the walls papered with an art-deco pattern, the ceiling mirrored. High-tech lighting spotted accents in just the right places: on a Mhaer print, on an abstract bronze sculpture, on an arrangement of dried flowers in a free-form Stuben vase.

Ives pushed Miss Finney through the reception room without a pause. They went down a narrow hallway. They passed two doors. One opened into a small, neatly organized storeroom that held little more than a coffee-maker and an apartment-size refrigerator. The other door was cracked open and Brook glanced inside at a sparsely furnished executive office. At the end of the hallway a sliding door opened as they approached. Brook looked for some opening device but could not see anything that might have activated the door.

The room at the end of the hall was something the likes of which neither Miss Finney nor Brook had ever seen. The walls appeared to be painted black but were actually covered with a very dark brown suede. There were no windows. Two cut-glass pedestals supported a small, round, two-inch-thick slab of plate glass. Only the chairs seemed lacking in luxury, and those could easily have been costly; it was too dark to tell. The only light in the room had an invisible source and focused on the center of the table where sat a clear crystal globe ten inches in diameter: the traditional "gazing-ball" of gypsy fortune tellers.

Miss Finney spoke for the first time to Mister Ives. "Sir," she started, "I do fear there is some error here." Ives had moved around to face the old lady. He did not have to bend over to be at a comfortable height. Miss Finney continued, "I can see by the furnishings of your establishment that you cater to a clientele unlike myself. I do not, Sir, spend lavishly. He looked at her and smiled.

"Sir," Miss Finney seemed flustered. "I do not find the topic amusing."

Brook jumped in with, "I think we'd better go."

Ives glanced up at Brook, then back down to Miss Finney. He moved around the wheelchair to Brook. His eyes came at her with an unidentifiable searching; it was as if he were probing into her soul. He reached his hand up and touched Brook's cheek. What happened then was inexplicable. The touch was sensual, caring and longing. It was as if, in the same instant, she were being caressed by husband, father and son. She had never known a husband's love, she had never known who her father was, she had never borne a son; yet, with perfect clarity, she knew Ives touched her thus.

"Dear young lady," he said in a tone that anticipated tender acceptance, "Do not challenge me. Please trust me." In the space of a second a timeless intimacy enfolded them. Miss Finney penetrated the envelope. "Mister Ives, I think my niece is correct. We should go. Now!"

He came back to her and reached down to hold her wrinkled hands. She yanked them away. He said, "I feel hostility, Miss Finney."

She was impatient. "This is folly. I should not be here at all."

Ives shook his head, "It is not entirely folly." Her eyes challenged his confidence.

He continued, "You are here, most respected woman, because there is a glimmer of hope. I know . . . . " He indicated the crystal gazing ball. "I see such things."

"I am no fool, Mister Ives."

Ives lowered his voice so that Brook, standing at the back of the wheelchair, had to strain to hear and did not catch it all. "You are not ready to die, either. You would like to live forever, wouldn't you?"

Miss Finney bristled. "I told you, I am no fool. What do you want?"

"I want to help."

Sadness drooped on Miss Finney's face as she declared, "No one can help me." She paused, then added angrily, "And I will tell you this: I think you are a charlatan."

Ives gave her a bloodless smile and spoke through clenched teeth. "I may be many things in this life before I am through: charlatan, fraud, messenger."

Miss Finney's eyes locked on his. "Messenger?"

Ives nodded. "With a story to tell." He paused, glanced up at Brook who was gazing dreamily about her. Looking back into Miss Finney's eyes, he continued, "I will reveal something in order to gain your confidence, Miss Finney. Something that only you could possibly know. Something from your inner thoughts."

Again, Miss Finney bristled. "No one knows my thoughts!"

Ives seemed to move closer to Miss Finney's face as he said, "This morning, as you gazed from your window to the courtyard, you heard children playing outside your gate. Their voices and laughter burned into you like the fires of hell. 'Let me be young again,' you cried deep inside your soul, 'I will give anything.' Then a starling landed on a branch of the tree outside your window and you cursed your withered arm because you could not reach out to it."

Miss Finney paled. "You could not know that."

With a mild arrogance, "Couldn't I?"

The old woman grimaced as she twisted to look pleadingly at Brook. Brook jerked her head, as if to shake something off. "Do you want to leave, Auntie?"

The old woman's voice was weak with shock. "He is right, you know. I did hear children, and a bird did land on the branch."

Brook felt something clammy begin to pull at her insides. She whispered, "I don't like this, Auntie."

"Nor do I," the old lady said.

Ives reached his voice between them. "Now, ladies, do

36

not let this trivia interfere with our visit. Such idle mischief is irrelevant to our mission. He walked away from them toward the door. "Willa will be anxious to join us. You two just rest for a moment."

He left the room, closing the door quietly. The air in the room was frozen with fear. Brook started to speak, but her voice died in her throat. Miss Finney reached out a quivering hand, groping for security.

Brook came to the old lady and knelt down in front of her. "I'm scared," Brook whispered. Her aunt nodded, unable to voice words.

Brook looked toward the door, then back at Miss Finney. After a pensive moment, Brook blurted, "As soon as Willa comes in, we leave. I mean it, Aunt Finney, we have to get out of this place. It gives me the creeps. This Svengali that Willa found is evil!"

Willa's panic induced protective instincts in the old woman. Miss Finney struggled to shake off her malaise; she felt Brook's equilibrium dissolving in terror. She reached out and stroked Brook's hair as she said, "Now, we can be a little upset, but there is no reason to be overwrought. Try to calm yourself, my dear. This man cannot hurt us. His manner is part of his business. He is, I must admit, quite a showman."

Brook gave a sob of relief. She took several deep breaths and finally was able to say, "I'm sorry. I let myself get a little carried away."

Parentally, Miss Finney replied, "Not at all, Brook. This is a very silly thing we are doing. One should not play at the supernatural. I have always felt that, but when Willa came to me and said she thought a visit to Mister Ives would do me well, I agreed. Now, Brook, you must understand, it is a horrible thing to grow old. You begin to feel so peaked that you lose interest in life. Quite frankly, living itself loses all significance."

Brook was calming quickly to Miss Finney's voice. The invalid continued, "I must take all the fault on my own shoulders for dragging you and Willa here. For goodness sake, Mister Ives is simply a rogue trying to fleece people out of money. I've heard about his type since I was a girl. I should have known better than to put you to the bother of catering to an old woman. A silly old woman unable to cope with a universal problem."

Brook had recovered. "It is not a bother, Auntie. Willa and I want to help you. We know it is not easy for you. Getting older, I mean. We are trying to do what we can to make things better."

Miss Finney gave a broad smile and patted Brook's head again. The old lady spoke: "Lord knows why you put up with me, dear Brook. I have been quite a burden on you."

Brook was adamant: "Aunt Finney, that is the most horrid thing you have ever said to me. You saved my life! You got me out of that insane asylum; I'd be dead if it were not for you. You could never be a burden!"

"You are family, my dear," her aunt said, "I could not allow you to be incarcerated unjustly by those fools. Any person with a single strand of moral fiber would have done what you did. Killing that man was not an act of insanity; it was a service to mankind."

Brook had never discussed her disaster with Miss Finney; there had never been pressure to do so. She guessed Miss Finney had been given most of the information by the authorities who had arranged the transfer of custody. It did not matter; Brook was not ashamed of what she had done.

Miss Finney lowered her eyes. "I feel badly about all the trouble I am to you though, Brook. And I sometimes feel I should plan to do more for you."

Brook looked at her quizzically. "In my will," Miss Finney said. "I have not yet provided for you in my will."

Brook tried to cover her surprise. "Now, Auntie, there is nothing I would expect from you." That was not quite true; Brook had expected to be favored by her Aunt

Finney in the old lady's will. Learning she was not in the will was mildly annoying.

Miss Finney did not detect Brook's surprise. The old lady said, "I know I am not obligated, Brook; we are so distantly related that there is no legal or moral reason for me to bequeath anything upon you or Willa. It is just that you, Brook, have been so considerate over the past ten years. You have endured many things that a young girl should not have to endure. It seems something should be left to you to see you through. But I doubt I could do that now; I have set up everything in irrevocable trusts for the charities the family has supported over the years." Brook did not know quite how to handle all this. She could not understand why the matter had come up at this moment. She had simply assumed the old lady was going to leave her something: a few thousand dollars, perhaps, something to prevent her from being sent back to the state asylum. She had once, years ago, considered the possibility that Miss Finney would fail to provide for her. She really had no claim. But, by God, she had worked hard; she deserved some reward for her efforts. Life had been even harder lately, since Willa had arrived and imposed the rigors of running the mansion without household help. Brook wondered if Willa was aware that neither of them was in the will. They had never discussed the matter.

Miss Finney was talking again, " . . . and so we will just see what this horrid man has to offer. It might not be so bad once he begins."

Brook nodded blankly, her thoughts still on news of her precarious future. Mister Ives came back into the room in a flowing motion; it was as if he had not even opened the door. Willa was not with him.

Brook was immediately defensive: "Where is my cousin?"

Ives lifted an instructive hand and said, "Now don't get excited. Willa is out in the office. She would like to see you, Brook. And I would like to be alone with your aunt."

Brook started to protest but Miss Finney made a motion for her to do as she was told. "I will be all right here. You go see what Willa wants. Hurry, now."

Brook got up and looked first at her aunt, who seemed so helpless in her wheelchair, then at Mister Ives, who seemed so sinister. Suddenly he gave a broad grin and said, "Now, come on, Brook, don't be so serious. Life is not all that grim that we cannot find some fun now and then. Go see Willa. I think you will be happy with what she has to say."

Though he was smiling, though he was making light of the tension, though he could do no real harm to her, he still seemed sinister. Brook did not like what was happening.

As Brook entered the reception room, she was shocked. Standing in the middle of the room was Willa, beaming, glowing with apparent happiness. She looked like a teenage girl enraptured with her ideal. Brook's shock turned to anger; Willa had led them into a den of evil.

"Willa, you should be ashamed!"

Willa could not stand still; excitement emanated from her. Waving her hands in a frantic motion, Willa signalled Brook toward the front door. Without thinking, Brook obeyed the instruction, but she balked before pulling the door open. Willa and she were now standing close together. Willa whispered, "Don't talk now." And she motioned for Brook to proceed out the door.

Brook shook her head. "We have to get Auntie out of here. That man is demented and evil." Willa tried to check her hilarity, but could not suppress a choked giggle; she was doubled over with levity. Brook grew impatient. "Willa, what's come over you? That man is going to hurt her."

Willa was unimpressed. "Don't be silly, Brook. He is a

pussycat. He will do nothing but good for her. Outside . . . I've got to tell you something and they might hear us." Willa urged Brook to open the door.

Brook realized she would have to pacify Willa before she could reason with her. Reluctantly she opened the door and edged out.

The area was still dank and seemed more so. Willa, still buoyant and happily excited, mocked a grimace at the odor and indicated the elevator. Brook went along.

As the birdcage elevator car began its descent, Brook finally spoke, "Willa Hawk, I don't know what has taken hold of your senses, but you have gotten us into a lot of trouble. Aunt Finney is in danger. If she is not hurt, she will at least be insulted. Let's get her out of there!"

Willa smiled with a smugness that irritated Brook. Willa said, "Dear, foolish, simple Brook! What difference if she is upset? What difference will it mean to you and me?"

Brook offered, "She . . . she could . . . well . . . she could get upset."

"There, you see," Willa said with triumph, "there is nothing that you can think of that she could do to us. Could she throw us out of the mansion? Not likely. Who would take care of her? Could she hit us? No reason to even comment on that. Could she cut us out of her will? Well, we know about that, don't we?"

Brook's eyes widened. "How did you know? She only just told me."

Willa gave a laugh. "You are so innocent, Brook. I know a lot more than you think."

The elevator came to a stop with a slight bounce on the ground floor. With uncharacteristic haste, Willa yanked the elevator door open, grabbed Brook's arm and hurried through the foyer to the small courtyard in front of the building.

"Now," Willa began excitedly, "Let me tell you what is going on . . . ."

41

Brook raised her hand to interrupt. "Let me tell *you*, Willa! We are going to get Auntie and we are getting the hell out of this place!" Willa chuckled, then laughed loudly. She reached forward and embraced Brook, hugging her tightly. Brook fought for release, pried her arms loose, and backed away. Brook did not participate in physical demonstrations of emotion.

Willa ignored the rebuke, saying, "We have our chance, Brook. This may be the last chance we have."

Brook's urgency was mixed with anger now. "Willa! I don't know what 'chance' you are talking about, but I don't want any 'chance'. I am quite happy with my life. We must get back up there and get away from this place."

Willa's expression changed. She seemed to harden a bit, not so much that her exuberance was gone, but enough to make Brook pay attention. "Are you 'happy' that you have devoted ten years of your life to an old bitch who won't even provide for you in her will? Remember, Brook, it isn't as if she had grandchildren to think of. She has no one but you and me. After accepting your devoted service all these years, she has chosen to leave every damned penny to her foolish charities. Now, Brook, I know that must hurt."

Brook was somewhat appeased by Willa's pleading. "I just found out a few minutes ago. How did you know?"

Willa assumed a casual air and replied, "Oh, she told me a while back. I thought you were aware of her intentions."

Brook said, "I never really thought about her intentions; that was her business." Then, after a moment of reflection, Brook added, "To be quite honest, Willa, I did think there would be something, a token of gratitude. It has been ten years of my life."

Willa nodded as she reached out and drew Brook into the fold of her arm; Brook did not resist this time. Willa led Brook to a tile bench surrounding the fountain in the courtyard, and the women sat side by side.

Willa said, "You know, Brook, there is a good chance that when Auntie dies, you will have to go back to *that place,* again." Brook cringed. Willa tightened her arm around Brook's shoulder and went on. "The state would like to put you back there, Brook. With Auntie dead, they would have every right. I am a relative, but we would be thrown out of the mansion; I'd have to go to Canada, there would be no money, it would be ended." A glaze was settling over Brook's eyes; memories began to crowd in on her. Willa spoke, her voice hushed. "Remember how it was? Remember what happened with the others when you took your shower? Remember what they did to you and made you do to them? Remember the crazy guard who brought his brother in to be with you? Remember what they did to you in that room?"

Brook was crying, sobbing. A wrenching was shaking her whole body. Willa had touched Brook's deepest wound and reawakened her greatest fear: the fear of being forced to return to the asylum.

Brook let the tears flow and dropped her head onto Willa's shoulder.

Willa let the sobbing persist for a moment, then patted Brook's head, saying, "Take it easy, Brook. I will protect you. Just relax."

Soon Brook's emotion had run its course, and the sobbing stopped. The painful memories reminded her she must never let them take her back there. Willa was right, but . . . .

Brook looked at Willa, "How did you know, Willa? How did you know about what happened?"

Willa was ready. "Auntie told me." She made a gesture of finality.

"But she did not know, Willa."

Willa replied confidently, "Ah, but she did, dear Brook. You see, that was all in your asylum records. They insisted she read the entire file before they released you to

43

her custody."

Brook shook her head. "But not the part about the guard and his brother and what they did to me; that was not in the records. Nobody knew about that."

Willa nodded with a show of impatience. "Didn't they tell you? The guard was found out! He confessed all that he had been doing to female patients. He said you were his favorite. That's why they showed the report to Auntie: they thought you might also be some kind of sex maniac."

"But it was a lie," Brook protested through new tears.

Willa offered, "I know that, dear, and Auntie knows it was all a lie."

Finally, Brook's resistance collapsed. "Oh, Willa, what will I do? What will we do? I can't go back to that place."

Willa feigned righteousness. "And she has left you no money to live on. She has left me no money to take care of you. She simply, arrogantly, cut both of us out of her will. She did that, Brook, remember that."

Depression settled easily into Brook's mind. Hope for the future was slipping away from her.

The pair sat there several minutes. Now and then Brook would whimper or sob or sigh. She realized life had not been good to her. Her mother had been a loose woman, never married, frequently pregnant. Brook was the only child; the other pregnancies had been terminated by abortion. Lack of funds at the crucial time had permitted Brook to be born; the abortionist would not work on credit even for a steady customer. Brook's early life had been sordid; dozens of "uncles" dominated her memories. She had scraped through her youth unmolested in body, though her mind still reeled with the disgusting sounds of men having their way with her mother. Throughout her late teens, Brook had resisted her own natural desires and the amorous advances of boyfriends. She had chosen to "save herself" for her wedding night. Brook had held up her half of the bargain. Unfortunately, the man she had finally married had turned out to be evil personified.

She had killed her husband to end the horror, but the horror had continued in the state insane asylum. There she had been exposed to more sexual perversion and, if she had been sane at the time of her commitment to the institution, conditions there had rendered continued sanity impossible.

She looked at Willa, pleading: "I cannot go back to that place, Willa. I cannot!"

There was a stern look on Willa's face as she nodded agreement. Then, as if a switch were snapped, Willa's face beamed with happiness. "Now will you listen to me? Now will you let me help you have some kind of good life for a change?"

Brook, ready to hear anything hopeful, said, "What do you mean?" Excitement glowed in Willa's face. Her lips curved into a broad smile. "Will you listen to me? Will you let me tell you what I've been able to set up?"

Brook nodded silently, confusion on her face.

Willa said, "Okay, now listen. Carlos Ives," she indicated the small clairvoyant upstairs in the office, "Carlos is a con man. He has done some awful things and this is the worst. He is working on old women, trying to sell them on youth, or at least extended longevity. But it is great for us. He has figured out a way to get us some money."

Brook hesitated, then said, "Willa, I don't know if I like this. We can't steal from our own Aunt."

"Of course we can't steal: She is going to pay us . . . for services."

"I don't understand. This all sounds too silly."

"So you think that five thousand dollars is 'silly?' What about ten thousand dollars? Is that silly?" asked Willa sarcastically.

Brook said, "That is a lot of money, Willa."

Willa smiled. "Of course it is a lot of money; our aunt has a lot of money. Our con man/soothsayer up there can

45

get her to do the right thing with it."

"But how will he help us?" Brook was cautious.

"Okay, I'll tell you. But first, are you willing to go along? Do you want to have money that will make you independent?"

Brook answered both questions affirmitively. Willa began, "He has come up with a really good thing, Brook. Some of it you will find hard to believe. Some of it will make you laugh. But, no matter what you feel, you must commit to stay with it until the end. Do you promise?"

Willa had played her cards well. Foremost in Brook's thoughts was the threat of Miss Finney dying soon and the authorities coming to take her to the asylum. Willa had been able to trigger horrible memories in Brook's mind. A promise of cooperation in the pursuit of a secure life seemed to Brook a small price to pay for the reprieve.

"I promise."

Willa smiled, reached out and cupped Brook's face in her hands. "That is a promise you will never regret. Now listen."

Willa stood up and, as she spoke, she moved around the small patio, gesturing vigorously, flinging her head happily to accent a point. Brook listened with focussed attention.

"Carlos Ives has come up with a plan to make old people part with their assets. He has done years of research on this. He has traveled to Europe, India, Egypt and the Orient to research the scheme. It is not all just showmanship. Here is the premise: People want youth. Look at history, the efforts by nearly all cultures to extend life or to retain youth. I don't need to go into things like Ponce de Leon's Fountain of Youth or medieval magic concocted to achieve perpetual life; those things are not important. What is fascinating is that Ives has found one Zoroastrian sect that has developed a ritual involving an evil force named Angra Mainyu. Angra Mainyu is a sort of god who promises life in exchange for

46

murder."

Brook twisted her head and grimaced. She was not convinced.

Willa added quickly, "Oh, I know it sounds awful, but it is only the come-on. These religious people contend that through a certain ritual, you can gain for yourself someone else's remaining time. The ritual is simply: murder."

Brook jumped up. "Oh, no!"

Willa broke into a loud, joyful laugh. She went to Brook and grabbed her strongly, hugging her tightly as she said, "Don't be silly. It is all part of the con games Ives will tell Auntie she will benefit from such a ritual and, because she is crippled, he will tell her to have you and me do her handy work."

Brook pushed free of Willa's hug and nearly shouted. "I'm not killing anyone!"

Willa spoke quietly: "There is no need to kill, dear Brook. Believe me, there are those whom I would not mind killing. But this can be done simply by our arranging a phony killing. You see, what Ives found out was that there is a certain psychological effect on old people who think they have effected a murder. Just the thought of doing such an evil thing tends to make them feel younger. We let Auntie think she has killed someone and she begins to think she is younger. She pays us handsomely for our part in the thing. We can then take off and start a life, or we can sit around and wait for her to die. I'd just as soon take off, but if you think we should stay, I will. The only thing is: she will be pretty angry when the thrill wears off and she realizes that she is not getting any younger."

"But how could we get away with it? How could we stage such a thing? Would Auntie go along with the idea in the first place? She is a pretty moral woman."

Willa laughed again, "Hey, easy on the questions; I don't have all the answers. Ives will handle most of that with her. As for her going along, I just don't know. We will have to let Ives handle that. All I want is for you to know we can do something about our futures . . . if we want to. Will you cooperate? Can we hope for some kind of security in our future?"

Brook began thinking; there was a lot to think about. She did not want to seem to be groveling for money from her aunt, but surely money was going to be needed for survival. She did not want to become involved with disreputable people like Ives, but how was she going to get some money to put aside for the time when she would need it? There were so many questions. She would have to spend a great deal of time sorting things out in her own mind. But time was a luxury that Willa would not grant. She asked Brook, "Will you do it? We must get back in there. You cannot spend a lot of time. Either you agree or the deal is off."

Brook bit at her bottom lip, groping for an answer.

"Brook, you must decide. We must make the deal or not. If we don't, I am leaving today. I will not stay with that crabby old woman any longer unless you and I have something to look forward to. Decide, damn it!"

"I will," blurted out of Brook's mouth before she knew she was going to speak. A sudden, inexplicable peace descended over Brook; everything seemed right: the courtyard did not seem grubby, Willa seemed the only true friend she had in the world, the air seemed fresher and the sun felt warmer. Willa came and embraced Brook tightly. This time the demonstration did not offend. For the first time in her life, Brook put her arms around another woman and hugged with a feeling of affection.

The whole world was beginning to look right to Brook. Happiness would be a unique experience; she anticipated the future with pleasure.

Willa beamed, delighted to have achieved her goal. "Well," she said, "let's get up there and see what we are to do for the old bitch."

Smiling, they turned and walked toward the building.

Miss Finney knew she was in her wheelchair. But she felt free, as if she were flying, gliding, unencumbered. Suddenly she was moving horizontally; there was something sexual happening to her. She could not restrain the bursting inside of her. She willed her eyes open. She was still there, strapped into her wheelchair. The clairvoyant, Carlos Ives, sat across the table in deep meditation.

They had been alone for several minutes. Ives had spoken of pedestrian things while the quiet mood of the room sank into Miss Finney's consciousness. She relaxed.

Finally, before she could become impatient, Ives said, "We are going to approach a most serious juncture, Miss Finney. I know it will be some time before you can trust me, but I need to talk freely. I will say what is truth to me and if you have difficulty with that, then we will try to reason together. Quite unexpectedly, I was visited last night by a frightening revelation."

There was a skeptical look on her face.

He said, "You must concentrate on your inner soul, Miss Finney. That is the only way you can help me open the channel of communication between the earthly world and the world of spirits. The spirits want to come to us."

Weakly, Miss Finney chided, "That's silly."

Ives' mood and manner changed violently. He opened his eyes, stood up and said, "I have transgressed, dear lady. I am contrite. I will trouble you no further. We shall end now . . . ."

Miss Finney raised a crippled hand. Her shrill voice shouted, "NO!" and then, trying to restore decorum, she added, more quietly, "Let us continue. I will not interrupt."

As he lowered himself back into his seat, Ives spoke in a hushed, confidential tone. "This is important, Miss Finney. As I said, we are approaching an important juncture. I can only go forward with your total cooperation."

Miss Finney, attempting a calm voice, said, "Mister Ives, please be patient with me. I have never subjected myself to . . . well to any . . . I mean, to any . . . . "

"Outside force," Ives offered. She nodded. He said, "It is natural to resist, because what we are dealing with is the unknown. For many years I have traveled, seeking truth. Miss Finney, my journey was fraught with danger; my constant companion was doubt; my nourishment was hope; my goal was this moment."

She raised an eyebrow. He explained, "My goal was the moment when I could say to a fellow human: 'I know!'" He let the drama of the statement sink in. She broke the silence: "I am truly sorry, Mister Ives; I am embarrassed at myself. I have come to you of my own free will and I am not being held prisoner. You must forgive an inconsiderate old lady. I fear age has made me insensitive."

Ives corrected her: "I feel age has made you honest, Miss Finney. You admit your doubt. I only beg you to try and accept what I have learned is the truth. You might even try to accept my honesty on a provisional basis. You cannot hurt yourself by saying I speak the truth and allowing yourself the proviso of saying: 'He is a fool!'"

She smiled, feeling a bit guilty.

"Here is where we are, Miss Finney," Ives began his dissertation again. "I have been granted certain powers that I am to share with a few people in this world. You are one of the few."

Miss Finney was in a quandary; she had come to this man for help, yet now that she was here, she did not feel he could be of any help. She said, "I don't really know where this is getting us, Mister Ives. I appreciate you offering to share your powers with me, but I don't know if I am worthy."

"Worthy?" Ives challenged. "Do you question worth when I have told you a power greater than both of us has

decided? You do not determine such a thing, Miss
Finney. You decide only whether or not you *want* to
become a party to the offering. It can mean eternal life.
Is that something that appeals to you?"

She replied, "Appeals? Yes, of course. Any person
would seek eternal life. I merely question that such a
thing is possible."

Ives nodded his understanding. "A reasonable doubt. I
can only beg you to trust me. You must trust someone,
Miss Finney. If you are to have the blessings of youth, you
must seek help outside yourself. If you cannot come to me
completely, you cannot reach your hopes and desires.
Look at it logically, Miss Finney: If you could do it by
yourself, it would already have been accomplished. I am
telling you I can give you what you desire. But it is vital
that you put yourself in my hands. All of what you want is
possible. Trust me." The old lady let her head sag down
onto her chest. She did not know what to do. She really
did not believe in such shenanigans. In fact, she knew
such things were fraud. But she desperately longed to feel
young again, to be rid of the pain of her illness, to forget
the sight of her emaciated muscles, atrophied from lack
of use. She knew this man sitting in his theatrical setting
was a cheat, but she had to turn to someone. Ives was
right: she could not do it on her own. She began to cry.

It was a weak cry, really a mild sobbing, accompanied
by a few tears that spilled out of her eyes and coursed
down the crags and wrinkles of her face. Ives reacted
immediately. He moved quickly out of his chair and was
at her side in an instant. His voice was gentle, tender.
"Dear lady, please." He touched her hands, her shoulder,
her face. She wept more bitterly. He whispered, "There,
there, now. Cry if you must. I am here to help."

She whimpered, then cried pitifully, "I am so sad. I do
not want to die! Oh, please help me."

Ives reached out and embraced her, holding her tightly
as the sadness spilled from her. Shortly she began to get

herself back under control. Ives continued to hold her. Suddenly, as if she had just become aware of his body holding her, she pushed him away; no one was to touch her this way. "Please," she said in a hushed but urgent voice. "Please do not touch me."

Ives eased back. He showed no remorse; his face glowed with warm understanding. "I hope you feel better for that." She nodded. He said, "I think we had better stop this meeting. I was wrong to accept you; I should not have accepted on faith what your niece, Willa, told me. This was all a mistake. *My* mistake."

Miss Finney was daubing at her tears with an embroidered hankerchief. Her motions were ineffectual; the muscles would not respond properly to her commands. She said, "I am sorry, Mister Ives; I should trust you. Look: I cannot even wipe shameful tears from my wrinkled face. And, Mister Ives, thank you for your tenderness. No one has hugged me like that since I was a child. I appreciate it."

Ives stood in front of her, looking concerned, "I hope I was not too forward; my actions were motivated by compassion."

"I take no offense," Miss Finney replied. "It was an appropriate gesture for the situation." She smiled and added, "I rather liked it, as a matter of fact." Then, attempting jocularity, she said, "We old gals do not get much affection."

Ives gave her a broad smile and returned to his chair across the table. He said, "I think we had better terminate this venture though, Miss Finney. I don't think I can do anything for you. I am sure you understand."

Miss Finney's voice fell to a nearly inaudible level. She said, "I really am sorry, Mister Ives. I am truly sorry."

He nodded. "I believe you, Miss Finney, but there is nothing I can do. I do not mean to be arbitrary, but we are getting nowhere. For us to accomplish anything, I must have your complete trust or, at the very least, your willingness to *consider* trusting me. There are too many obstacles in our path. I cannot go on."

She looked at him. Her eyes hardened as she accused, "You want me to offer you money, is that it?" He shook his head. More bitterly, she said, "There is something you want; you do not do all this for nothing."

He smiled and gestured resignation. "That is just what mean, my dear woman. You seem determined to put obstructions in our path. Why don't you simply trust me? Let me help you; let me show you the way to a life of youth, happiness, and, I must add here, other things you thought would never be yours again."

She looked at him as she questioned, "You sound more mysterious than ever. What did that mean?"

Ives began, for the first time, to show impatience: "I will not push you, but we must have complete trust."

She pleaded, "But how, sir, can I so completely trust someone whom I have just met? That asks too much, do you not agree? I would trust you if I knew you or if you offered some credentials. But you offer nothing other than a minor exercise in logic."

As if it were final, Ives shrugged his shoulders and said, "That is to be it, then."

She was torn with the emotion of all that had happened to her since she had entered this room. Normally, Miss Finney had much of her own way; she surrounded herself with an insulation that guaranteed she would be catered to. This man was challenging her, making her uncomfortable, accusing her of being obstreperous. Yet, for all of that, she did not want to leave; she wanted to go on with the venture, though she had no idea what it involved. Somewhere in her mind, she did have confidence that Ives would do something for her. Even if that something was nothing more than making her feel better, it should not be discounted.

She thrust back her shoulders, raised her head, and said, "I will try, really try, to place my entire trust in you,

Mister Ives. What am I to do?"

He studied her for a moment before he spoke: "I hope you are being completely honest with yourself, Miss Finney. I am going to ask you to do some things which are, or will seem to be, absolutely contradictory to your character. I will demand some things which will seem impossible for you to comprehend, but you will have to respond to my every command. Diuturnity, the extension of life, does not come cheaply. I am not speaking in financial terms; I mean something more lasting than money. You have been chosen and you must accept." He leaned forward so that the glow from the crystal ball made his eyes look like huge black sockets in his face. He added, "You will have to commit your very soul if you are to accept the gift of life on earth. There can be no turning back."

For the first time since meeting Ives, Miss Finney did not act as if he were performing some kind of charlatan's act; she had a strange feeling this man, this small person, was there for a definite reason and she must yield to his will. She had never done such a thing in her life. She decided to yield.

Quietly but with conviction, she said to him, "I trust you, Mister Ives. I accept your will."

He made no gesture towards her. He simply nodded, placed his hands firmly on the sides of the crystal ball and told her, "Now you must concentrate with me, dear lady. Reach your hand out and place it on the globe of truth. We will both seek our instructions. The spirits will tell us."

Miss Finney did not find it easy to touch the crystal ball; it was nearly out of her reach. As soon as her fingers made contact, things began happening. The room went colder, so cold that she wished she had brought a warmer wrap. There was a ringing, which she felt rather than heard, and the lighting in the room changed perceptibly, yet she could not have said in what respect it changed.

One of Ives' hands came to hers and he covered it, yet there was still no warmth.

"Oh, spirits of the night . . . oh, messenger of the morning, hear me." Ives paused. Miss Finney felt her eyes begin to feel tired. She let the lids drop. Ives continued, "Hear me, spirits of the night, you spirits who dwell within the realm of this good woman. Now spirits, through me, plan a journey for Miss Alcorn Finney, a proper journey through which I will send her on as you command."

Miss Finney forced her eyes open. Something was going wrong; something was happening that she did not like at all. Her hand began to tremble and Ives sensed the movement. He took hold of her hand and kept a firm grip. In more than sixty years, no man had held any part of her body, yet she accepted it. But there were other things: she felt lightheaded, there was a chill in the room but she felt feverish. She wanted to speak, but she could see Ives was concentrating. An alien voice within her own mind told her that talking to Ives would do no good, he could not hear her. She wanted to fight her feelings; she was accepting what was going on, she was becoming a part of what Ives was doing. She wanted to fight, but she wanted to join. She wanted to give herself to this. She knew it was vital for her to yield completely and she felt herself saying: "I trust you . . . I trust you . . . I trust you." She could not stop the words from hissing out between her clamped teeth. Then she felt confidence wash down over her body like warm water. She knew she was committed; she knew she had accepted this man as her guide. She looked at him with admiration as he took up his supplication again:

"Oh spirit of the night . . . come to us. Hear that we are ready to accept your guidance. This subject . . . Miss Alcorn Finney . . . wants very much to serve you and she awaits instructions for her journey. Visit me once again. In the presence of this woman, reveal the miracle of everlasting life that can be hers. She is a chosen one, as you have said . . . enter into us . . . speak to us."

Nothing happened.

Miss Finney wanted to help Ives, she wanted to cry to him that she was helping. She needed to reach out to him and let him know they were together now and she trusted him without reservation. She pleaded for something to happen, for him to be rewarded for the effort he was making on her behalf.

He spoke again, his voice raised. He sounded a pleading, a begging, a commanding: "Oh Lord of Light, Son of the Morning, hear my petition on behalf of thy servant, Alcorn Finney. She comes to you in need, she sees the right of wrong, she is bound now to serve the one who is Master of the Earth. Oh spirit, come to us. Hear that we are ready to accept your guidance. Enter into us. Speak to us . . . ."

Miss Finney nearly screamed in fright: Ives' face was changing, contorting, twisting in seeming agony. His teeth were bared as his lips stretched tight across his mouth; spittle slipped onto his chin; his eyes glowed with a green fire. The eyes seemed to hate. She wanted to jump up and run from the room, but she was frozen and could not even release her hand from his grip.

He spoke again. At least, his lips moved. The voice that emerged was not his. "You must take a life and add to yours. Take a life and add to yours." The voice was the embodiment of evil; its sound had a smell, its words hit like punches. The voice went on: "Every soul you send to me will mean a gift of years for you. Your life will be forever; your life will be eternity!" The voice was an obscenity, a vulgarity that splashed filth on listening ears. But suddenly Miss Finney realized she had heard a truth, a promise, a commitment.

Ives' head had fallen down onto the globe. His hand slipped free of hers. He seemed to have passed out.

Miss Finney screamed.

Brook and Willa had come into the reception room just thirty seconds before they heard their aunt's scream shatter the silence of Carlos Ives' offices.

When they had first come in, they had been full of excitement and curiosity as to how Ives would handle their Aunt Finney and what the details of his scheme would be.

As she closed the door, Willa whispered, "I hope the old bag really falls for it. Don't you want to fool her, Brook?"

Brook held back a mischievous laugh and raised a finger to her lips to "shush" Willa. "I will, but I'm scared."

Willa hissed, "The old bitch has used you for years and still you worry. Well, don't! She is not worth it. We will get her money and get the hell out of this stinking city."

Then came the scream. The two girls ran down the hall and plunged into Ives' room. The mystic was sprawled across the table holding the globe. He was obviously unconscious. Their aunt was rigid in her wheelchair, her eyes locked open, her mouth still blowing out the shrill scream.

Brook dove to her aunt's side and grabbed at the old lady's hand, which were sticking out in front of her, rigid as claws.

As soon as Brook touched her aunt, she cried to Willa: "She is cold as ice. It's like she's dead."

Willa was standing, taking in the whole scene. She merely nodded to Brook, who yelled back: "Dammit, Willa, do something! I think she might be dead or having a stroke."

Willa walked over and leaned down to her aunt. Her face moved slowly closer. Her eyes kept driving into Miss Finney's. Willa said, "Auntie, it is going to be all right. Do not panic. Things are going to be all right." Willa reached up and stroked her aunt's face. The old lady's eyes blinked. Brook burst into tears.

Ives began to stir. He came to slowly but did not seem disoriented or disturbed. He was merely returning. Brook spun at him: "What have you done to my aunt? I'll have you in jail for this."

Ives ignored Brook and leaned sideways to look at Miss Finney. The old lady had finally breathed. She pumped air into her lungs; her chest heaved in recovery. Her eyes met Ives' and the two looked at each other for a long moment before he asked: "Do you still trust me?"

She nodded weakly.

Brook was getting angry. "Well, I am not in any mood for trust, Mister Ives. I think you are a dangerous man."

Ives pushed himself up and stood, sucking in several gulps of air before he said to Willa, "Get your friend out of here. I must talk to your aunt for one minute. Then you will take her home."

Oblivious to Brook's protests, Willa shoved her into the hallway and pulled the door closed behind them. Outside, confronting Willa, Brook was furious: "He is a madman, Willa. We cannot go on with our plan."

Willa, annoyed, but also a little amused, scolded Brook: "You silly oaf, don't you know a con game when you see it? That Ives is a hell of a lot more than I thought. I'm really impressed with him. He is putting on quite a show."

Inside, as soon as the girls were out of the room, Ives moved from his chair to Miss Finney. He placed himself at her knees, within her line of vision, so that she did not have to labor at keeping her head up. He asked again, "Do you trust me?"

She said, "Oh, yes. There is no doubt."

He asked, "You heard the voices?"

She was weak, but she began, "Y . . . yes. I'm . . . I'm not sure what it . . . what it means, though."

"What don't you understand?"

She shook her head as if to clear mental cobwebs. "I do not know what the voice meant by: 'Take a life.'"

Ives nodded, paused and said, "The spirit, the voice that was speaking to you through me, was asking for a life. The life of another. And, in return, that life is given to you."

She chewed at her lower lip, trying to comprehend. "Given? Given to me? How?"

Ives showed some confusion for the first time. He spoke with reservation. "I do not know 'how.' Such things are not for me to know. I am merely a messenger telling you what you must do if you choose to live. If you decide to live, perhaps . . . forever."

She was trying to understand, but it was all too much for her. "Forever? How do I take a life? What do I do? How can I live forever?"

He moved his face close to hers, reached up his hands and caressed her cheeks as he said, "To put it bluntly, Miss Finney, you must *end* the life of some other person."

She gasped as Ives continued: "You must end someone's life so that the remainder of that life will be passed on to you. That is what the message meant."

Her eyes grew wide with terror. "But I could not do that. To kill another human being . . . not if it meant living. . . ." She could not finish.

Ives flushed with anger. He grabbed roughly at the old lady's shoulders; his fingernails dug into her flaccid skin.

She sobbed, "You're hurting me."

He ignored her. "Do not tell me you 'could not do that.' I am commanding you to do what you must. There is no choice now; you made your commitment and you must adhere to the instructions. You will take a life and what is left of that life will be given to you."

He shook her. Her weak neck muscles could not stop her head from bobbing. He charged, "You will do what is ordered!"

Weakly, almost unintelligibly through her sobs, she cried, "I do not want to die."

His eyes glowed with a demonic radiance as he whispered, "You will not die! You will gain everlasting life. All you must do is follow orders without question. Take a life."

Now she was crying. Her voice cracked. "But . . . how? I am an old woman." She lifted up her hands, crooked as talons but barely able to flex. "Look at my hands," she whined, "How could I kill anyone?"

He let go of her shoulders and trembled with rage. "Get others to do your bidding! Those nieces of yours, get them to kill for you. Do something! I do not care how! Just do it!"

As if magically, he took a deep breath and was suddenly pacific, bending close to Miss Finney's face, tenderly reaching up to wipe the tears away as he said, "Now get yourself under control, my dear lady. You just calm yourself and let tranquility come into your body. Things are going to be good in your life. If you do as ordered, you will not die. You will do as you have been ordered; there is no choice now. You came to me with a heavy burden. You go home free of problems." He reached out and embraced her and she felt warm.

Still convulsing from her crying, she said, "Oh . . . thank you. I will do what you ask. I do not know how, but I will. God help me."

Ives stared hypnotically into her eyes. "It is not God who wished to help you."

He straightened up and moved to the door. As he opened it, he spoke to Willa and Brook: "Your aunt and I have had a most taxing encounter. She has much to think about. I ask you not to disturb her thoughts."

Willa moved to push the wheelchair. Brook ran forward and arranged the quilt over the old lady's lap. As the chair began moving out the door, Brook began to speak to Ives. The man raised a finger to his lips and, looking to make sure Miss Finney could not see, he gave a big wink to Brook. Then he nodded as if to say, "Hurry, she is all set up."

Brook gave a broad smile and ran after Willa.

3

Miss Finney sat in her wheelchair by her bedroom window, right where she had been left three hours earlier when they had come back from Carlos Ives' office.

They had ridden home in silence; only Clifford had attempted discussion: he was concerned about Miss Finney's health. She had looked awful when he had returned with the carriage. The driver had fussed and fumed, but Miss Finney had insisted she was perfectly well and had not been abused. With those assurances, Clifford had driven them home to the mansion in short order. The old lady had been taken right to her rooms.

There she sat, thinking.

For some reason which she could not grasp, she felt compelled to obey Ives. In the first place, she had never been the type of woman who easily submitted to orders. In the second place, and more importantly, he had told her she was to kill someone. She would never have believed herself capable of such a thing; now she knew she was.

The mechanics of the act posed more of a problem for her than the act itself. Of course, Brook and Willa would have to help. Miss Finney had just decided to put her proposition to them, and to offer them a sum which would make involvement worthwhile.

Money was a tool she knew how to use. For half a century she had managed her own finances. She knew both Willa and Brook were virtually penniless. Both girls were now aware they were due no gift or inheritance. They would be agreeable to almost any task, assuming the rewards were large enough. To Miss Finney, money was unimportant compared with the possibility of living longer. If she was to believe Ives, then she would see a long life. She would consider no assistants other than her two nieces; if they refused, she would have to take some other action.

Miss Finney was amazed at herself. She was sitting in the quiet beauty of her home contemplating terminating another human being's life. Startling! She really did not know what to think of herself. She had come from a reasonable background: she had been raised to be a good Methodist and to believe in law and order. So where did she find the gall to consider such a thing? It was not as if she were a prison executioner with a legal . . . if not moral . . . rationale for taking the life of a convict sentenced to death. It was not as if she were nobly delving into the morality of euthanasia. If a loved one of hers were in the final agony, she could possibly justify a temporary disregard for the sanctity of human life.

But neither of these hypotheses fit her situation. She was acting on the suggestions . . . orders . . . of a virtual stranger. She was giving consideration to snuffing out a life for no better reason than that she had gone to a fortune teller and he had told her to.

Who was this person, this Carlos Ives?

In her day, he would have been termed a twerp. A small, insignificant man.

Until he grabbed hold of your eyes with his eyes.

The most vivid recollection Miss Finney had was Carlos Ives' green eyes penetrating her very soul. There had been the dilemma of his touch: first icy, then warm. And there had been that one major contact when he had embraced her: it had been gentle, nearly paternal, and yet there had been a sexual quality to it. Something about Ives bothered her more than the physical contact: He seemed to project power.

The power that had come from Ives had penetrated to her soul, and the result had been profound. She had trusted this small man so much that she felt she could stand and walk. At moments she had felt she might jump and run just to show the extent of her belief in him. The mood that had captured her consciousness reminded her of descriptions she had heard of religious encounters— being born again. But Ives offered more than rebirth; he offered her eternal life. Rebirth is extraneous to one who has life eternal.

She halted her thoughts with an abruptness that hurt as they slammed to a stop. "Is that what I really want?" she thought. Out loud, she said, "I wonder if that is what any of us really wants?" Then, mulling over these thoughts, she began to challenge her own dreams.

"Why do I want eternal life?" she began. "I don't know why I would want that pain. My mind is alert, but what can I do with it except remember the past? I have outlived what few friends I had in my lifetime. I no longer try to find new friends because those I cultivated when I was turning sixty died off and left me alone. Besides, I seem—even to myself—to be a crusty old dowager. Is it that I am aloof and above all others, or is it that I am trying to fulfill the stereotype? Probably a bit of each. But there is little left to an old woman. I am not about to become old mutton playing the young lamb. Brook and Willa provide companionship, but not friendship. The age difference is simply too much to span. I cannot expect them to think like octagenarians; they cannot expect me to think like a young woman. Lord knows I have tried. I have attempted humor; the best I could come up with was: 'I'm getting to the age where a lifetime subscription does not seem like a good business deal.' They laughed, of course. They even laughed the second time I told it. It is sad when an old woman knows she is being tolerated and humored.

"But what are the options? Only one: death."

"I do not fear death; I dread dying. Death offers no threat, only mystery. Death will be the end of all things. The light will go out and that will be all, or perhaps it will be a move into something else, an afterlife. Dying is the horror. Suppose there is pain; it could be unimaginably painful. Who knows? None of us have experienced that and lived to tell it. Oh, there are the life-after-life people who say they have experienced death, but suppose they only experienced the initial throes of death. There could be more. A nightmare of pain so bad that none could come back from it. We all know how bad a toothache is; we all know the pain of a broken bone; those have definable parameters. Death might be more. Death might be such an agony that the human mind cannot conceive of it.

"So, it is better to live than to die?

"Who am I kidding?" Miss Finney chided herself, "We all want to live. I don't give a damn if all the people I ever knew are gone; I'll get along without them. I can't deny wanting to live. But youth would be nice."

"Mister Ives did not tell me what application would be made of the years. Would they simply be added on, and would my body decay until I was a hundred-year-old physical wreck? Or would the years be subtracted from my present age? That would be the best. I can see myself young again, free of aching joints and crippled hands. Oh, to have legs which would carry me, legs on which I could dance again!"

She gave a broad, beaming grin. "Wouldn't that be nice? To go to a dance again. How long has it been? Let's see." She paused and calculated, then continued, "Sixty-four years. My God! Sixty-four years since I have danced with a man."

She folded a cloth of obscurity over those thoughts; she would not travel back to that time in her life. The memory of her love was kept well cached. None would hear of that time in her life. Yet, the thoughts pushed toward the surface again. She did not like the turn her thoughts were taking; she was adamant about reflecting on her one love.

She wanted to be away from the window, to be distracted. The memories were battling their way into her thoughts. She chewed at her bottom lip and pounded her hand weakly on her lap. She could not grip the rubber tires and push herself away from the window.

She called out for one of the girls to come, but she knew they were down in the kitchen and could not hear. They were not due to come up for another hour. Miss Finney wanted to change things now. This was all wrong; that man had started things in her mind that she could not stop.

Why had she gone to him? Why was she considering his foolishness? Why was she wasting the little time she had left in her life?

Because . . . because she wanted to avoid dying.

"Oh, damn," she hissed. She had never in her life cursed in front of anyone. But she knew the words, and frequently . . . especially over the past few years . . . she was wont to use them in the privacy of her own room when she realized that her life was slipping away, inexorably slipping away.

That was why she wasted time on Carlos Ives: her time was limited, frighteningly limited. She had to trust in something.

But killing? . . . murder? Why did he need such a profound action?

What right did she have to even consider taking another's life in order to extend her own?

She had no right. It would be obscene to rationalize such a thing.

Ives' words came to her: "You could live . . . forever . . . forever . . . forever."

She cried out: "Oh, I want that! I want that!"

She knew she would have to yield to the demands of this man, Ives. She knew she would have to find some way to get the girls to help, to find some victim, to do what she had been ordered to do. Within her she felt there were to be no more questions; Ives had ordered and what he ordered was right. It was the law.

That was not as hard for her to accept as she thought it might be. Submission to Ives' will was less of a burden than she had anticipated. As a matter of fact, she thought, it was kind of nice having it all set up for her. There was no question of morality, no challenge to ethics. Ives had stated the conditions quite simply and his will was to be done. For a time she had felt she had options. That she could, in the tranquil privacy of her rooms, consider the alternatives and then make a deliberate decision. But, as she delved deeper and deeper into her own thoughts, she realized she had made a total commitment during her visit to Ives' offices. She had taken on the obligation of doing what he ordered. And, with the acknowledgement of that acceptance, she found it less difficult to address the problem: How to do it?

In the huge kitchen, Brook and Willa were busy with preparations for the household evening meal.

"Hey," Willa said, "I just thought: Should we make a plate for Baldwin?" The statement, for all its innocence, plunged into the peace of the room like a vengeful dagger.

"Damn," Brook exploded, "I forgot all about that rotten bastard. I swear, I forgot. I'll kill that. . . ."

Willa stopped the tirade by raising her hand and interjecting, "Whoa there, gal. I was only kidding. I'm sure the oaf has taken his leave. We would have seen him by now. So don't get in a tizzy over nothing."

Brook's voice exploded: "Nothing! Nothing? You call having that scum touch my body nothing? I'll be damned." She moved, nearly lunged, across the kitchen toward the telephone that was hanging by the pantry entrance.

Willa asked, "What are you doing?"

Acidly, Brook said, "Calling the police. That filth should be in jail."

In movements that were quicker than Brook could see, Willa crossed the room and grabbed Brook's hand as it reached for the phone. "Don't," Willa ordered. "Don't be a fool."

Brook's eyes asked, "Why not?"

Willa, calmly now, said, "Look, he is probably gone. Besides, we sure don't want a bunch of police around here if we are going to be working with Ives. The less attention the better. We are going to have one tough time pulling it off, anyway. Don't make it harder, Brook." Then, tenderly: "Please."

Brook was tense, but she yielded. "All right. But if he comes near me, I'm screaming for the police."

Willa smiled, then laughed. "I'll scream with you. I hate that animal."

Willa reached up and stroked Brook's cheek. "Okay?"

Brook nodded, "Okay."

Willa went to the massive range where she had been busy frying small crepes. Miss Finney loved crepes at her evening meal. Brook was at the large worktable in the middle of the room, tossing a salad.

"How is this all going to work out, Willa?" Brook asked.

Willa, flipping a crepe with dexterous skill, said, "We will have to see. I don't really know. I didn't have time to talk to Ives and I'm afraid to use the phone."

"That's silly," Brook chided, "There is no way she can hear." Willa, still busy at the range, replied, "That's true, but have you ever heard of telephone lines getting mixed up, crossed?"

Brook laughed, "You're kidding."

Willa did not smile. "Kidding, hell. There have been

lots of times when a person has accidentally cut into another line. It has happened to everyone."

"Not me," Brook said.

Willa shrugged her shoulders, "Big deal. There is a lot that has not happened to you. That's why I want to get you out of this mausoleum."

There was quiet for a few minutes. Brook finished the salad and was preparing a tea trolley to move dishes and food into the dining room. Willa had finished her artistry with the crepes and was simmering the orange sauce in a skillet. "You'd better get the old gal downstairs," she said.

Brook stopped putting the silverware on the tray. After a moment of reflection she said, "You know, Willa, I really do have a bad feeling towards Aunt Finney."

Willa did not look up, but asked, "Why now, after all these years?"

Brook explained, "I think it has just sunk in that she was willing to die and leave us absolutely nothing to get along on."

Willa nodded.

Brook was taking plates out of the cabinet as she continued, "You know, there is a better than even chance that the authorities would have slammed me back into that damned insane asylum? Just because she decided we did not deserve anything."

Willa stopped what she was doing, "We deserve a lot, Brook. We sure deserve a hell of a lot more than we will be getting even if this deal with Ives goes through. I've put up with too much from that old hag. Changing her clothes, wiping her mouth of dribble, sitting and listening to all that junk she has to say. I don't know how you put up with it as long as you did."

Brook put down a plate and walked over to Willa. "I'm telling you, Willa, if this doesn't work with Ives, I'm leaving."

Willa smiled sarcastically. "Just like that. Leaving and simply telling the authorities you are now mentally healthy. That there is no need for them to worry about you. You have about as much chance of getting away with that as you have of flying to the moon. They would have every cop in Louisiana looking for you as soon as the old lady could get somebody to dial a phone for her."

They both laughed. They took perverse pleasure in Miss Finney's complete dependence. They knew she would offer to reward them for helping her.

Brook stopped laughing and said, with a serious tone, "You know, Willa, we could wait for her to die. It won't be too long now. She is really frail. We are her kin and we could go to court and claim a piece of the estate."

Willa turned back to her orange sauce and began stirring. "If I know anything about Auntie—and I know her type—she has covered that with her damned lawyers. All she has to do is leave five or ten dollars to each of us and the rest of the money can go to whomever she stipulates. She covers herself with a token gift. I think it would give her pleasure."

Brook's face twisted in confusion, "I'm starting to really hate her. I don't know why. Maybe we will get our share without anything bad happening. That is, if she believes Ives."

Willa's face was grim as she said, "She'll fall for it. She's up there now thinking about life eternal. We're just going to kill off people, as many as we can, at . . . let's say, five thousand dollars a head. That should add up pretty quickly."

Brook corrected Willa: "You mean we will pretend to kill them, Willa. I think you made a goof."

Willa gave a big smile. "Pretend, of course. We'll shoot 'em with blanks, hand 'em a few bucks and send them on their way. Then we'll pocket the profit."

Brook was not so sure. She asked, "Do you really think she'll go for it?"

Willa replied, "Since we are in no position to kill her and inherit her fortune, then there is no choice. She has to go for it. Look, you've looked after her for ten years and all she gave you was room and board. And you, fool, felt it was your duty to be nice to the old lady. But I'll tell you this: I am not hanging around for ten years. I'm already sick and tired of pushing her around in that contraption of hers. We have to get some cash so we can move out."

The two women stood there looking at each other. Willa turned off the flame under the sauce and Brook spoke, "We'll do it, I'm sure."

Willa carried the skillet to the work area and said, "It really isn't fair, me coming in for a few weeks and getting out of here with a lot of cash. You're good to share it with me."

"Don't be silly," Brook replied. "Why shouldn't I share? It is all your idea, isn't it? You found Ives. Without you, I would have been out of here without a dime. At least this way, I may have a few thousand dollars to start with. And I won't have to worry about those police and doctors putting me back in that nut-house."

Willa asked, "Is being here with her better than being back there . . . in that . . . place?"

Brook nearly cried. "Hell, Willa, you don't know. Besides, when I first came here, she was kind. She was the only family I had in the whole world."

Willa, not looking up from what she was doing said, "What about the man you killed? What about his family?"

The question plowed into Brook's chest and bumped the air out of her; she could not speak for a moment. Willa had no right to chastise her.

Willa broke the silence: "It makes no difference to me, Brook. Actually, I have very little use for men at all. I'd just as soon kill the whole bunch of them off. But then we'd have no one to foster more women, would we? No, I think you did right in killing that pig. You slit his throat, didn't you?"

Brook cried, "Stop! Willa, please. Don't! I didn't mean to kill him. . . ."

Willa reached out and took Brook into her arms, "There now. Don't be upset. I'm sorry."

Willa patted Brook's hair and mumbled sounds, like a mother calming a frightened baby. Brook started to cry. Willa let her cry. "I want you to remember the bad things of the past so you will work for a good future," she told Brook. Brook cried back, "I will work, Willa. Please don't keep reminding me." Willa nodded, gave Brook a tight hug and went back to making the sauce. It took several minutes for Brook to get herself under control. They finished the food preparations and went into the dining room.

In the darkness outside the kitchen, the gardener eased back against the wall, hoping they could not see him as they went into the other room.

The vagabond and would-be Lothario had been peeping on them for a few minutes. He could hear nothing; he wished they had opened a window.

Their actions had provoked prurient thoughts in his mind. For some reason he ignored the possibility that they might have homosexual inclinations. All he could see was two women needing affection so badly that they were hugging each other. His mind was depraved enough to think he could solve their problem. He breathed deeply.

His limited brain did not allow him to regret scaring Brook earlier. He had stood there in the doorway watching her put on her bra, then her slip, and finally her blouse and skirt. It had been so exciting that he'd had to go to her, to caress her, to have her completely. She had rebuked him but, to his warped mind, this was merely a provocation on her part. Really she was eager to have sex with him, he thought.

He started to work his way through the bushes so he

could watch them in the dining room, but something caught his eye and he froze. Willa was coming back into the kitchen.

She went to a cabinet and opened a drawer. He could not tell what she was doing. Finally, she brought out a small ladle. From her movements, he could tell that she had called to Brook in the other room, probably to tell her she had found the ladle. She started to go into the dining room and he made a move to follow, but she stopped.

He stopped.

She put the ladle down on a counter top and hiked up her skirt.

Hot damn! He had seen Willa do that before. The elastic of her pantyhose did not hold well over her slim hips. She was standing with her back to him and all he could see were her buttocks. Her hands worked quickly, pulling the waist up where it should be. Just as she was lowering her skirt, she turned and he could see the flatness of her stomach. He would enjoy a bit more flesh; he was used to chunky women. But Willa might be a gratifying partner in the sack. With her clothing back in place, she grabbed the ladle and went through the door to the dining room.

Baldwin reached down and felt at the front of his trousers; Willa's display had aroused him. He stood there rubbing the bulge in his pants, resenting Willa and even Brook for not going out in the yard and making the tensions flow out of him. He felt anger toward them and thought he would be justified in storming in and taking both of those bitches.

He was also a coward. He knew he would do nothing of the sort. He decided to go to the dining room and see what peeping he could do there. If nothing seemed worthwhile, he could go back to his room in the stable area and use one of his pornographic books to help him forget Willa and Brook. He eased up to the bay window of the dining room and held his breath as he raised himself up to look inside.

Holy Shit! Willa was alone in the dining room and she had raised two of the windows up a couple of inches. Blood began pounding in his temples. He was fearful that the noise of his pulse could be heard a hundred feet away. This was one big temptation. She was alone, she really needed a good screw. He was a man . . . more than enough . . . to take care of her problems. All he would have to do would be to raise the window and climb over the sill. He could be inside in seconds; she would welcome him. She'd be down on the floor faster than he could drop his shorts. He'd plunge into her, she'd love it and she'd be grateful for the rest of her life. He studied her body. Except for the slim hips she looked great. She had an ample bosom, nice legs and . . . he knew from a few minutes ago . . . a well-rounded rump.

She was busy setting the places and distributing the food. When she went to the far side of the table and bent over to fill a water glass, the top of her blouse fell forward and he could see the outline of her bra and the cleavage between her breasts. That was too much. His hand moved from his trousers to the window. He would move slowly; he did not want to foul up this chance. He needed a woman. His thumbs found a grip on the bottom of the window and he began, ever so slowly, to lift.

It was as if someone had dumped a whole tankfull of ice water on his head: voices came from the hallway. Brook was bringing Miss Finney into the dining room. He cursed out loud, but it was hushed enough so that they did not hear him. With his pulse pounding in his temples, he could not hear what they were saying. He only knew he had been thwarted again. This couldn't go on much longer. He was going to have one of these women . . . even if it had to be the old lady. He hovered in the darkness, listening. Miss Finney was voicing polite compliments about the dinner preparation until she spotted the crepes Suzette. With real sincerity, she thanked Brook and Willa for their special effort.

Brook said, "It was Willa, Auntie. She did them and made your orange sauce just right."

"How nice," Miss Finney said as she was wheeled into place at the head of the table.

They ate their salad and made small talk until Miss Finney brought up Ives. She said, "That is an interesting man you found for us, Willa. How on earth did you know to take me to him? He seems quite sincere and honest.'

Willa answered, "I did not really know he was good, Auntie." She stopped eating to talk and butter her Melba toast. She continued, "One of the women at the coffee shop gave me his name, I telephoned him and made the appointment. I really cannot take any credit. You have to thank Brook, too. She was the one who gave me the most encouragement." Then, after a pause and a bite of toast, Willa added, "Quite surely, you didn't offer much encouragement, Auntie. I thought you'd never agree to go. Are you sorry you did?"

Miss Finney shook her head, "Most definitely not! You must know it was quite an event for me."

The conversation died while they ate a serving of poached salmon, dressed in Brook's homemade mayonnaise and garnished with cold asparagus tips.

Coffee came from an automatic drip appliance Willa had bought and kept on the sideboard in the dining room. The crepes were through and the second cups of coffee poured when Miss Finney asked: "My dears, do you believe in the supernatural?"

Such a question asked prior to that day would have been met with complete confusion. Such matters had never been discussed by Miss Finney. But, considering Carlos Ives' arrival in their lives, both nieces gave some serious thought to an answer.

Brook replied first, lying: "I do, Auntie."

Miss Finney asked, "And what do you believe, Brook?"

"I believe there are spirits all around us."

"Interesting."

"Yes," Brook acknowledged. "Unfortunately, we have no communication with them. If we did, they could help us."

Miss Finney nodded her head. "Now, that is a most profound observation on your part, Brook. I had no idea you were so attuned to such matters."

Brook nodded. "Oh, yes. I think there are really spirit forces that can do amazing things."

Willa kicked Brook's foot under the table. It was too much of a good thing.

Miss Finney looked at Willa and asked, "And you?"

"There is no question about the spirits," Willa said, "but I have never spoken to any. I don't know anyone who has."

The old lady asked, "And if you did speak to one, and if the spirit did tell you to do something, would you do it?"

Willa took charge. She did not want Brook overdoing it. "It would depend on what the instructions were."

Miss Finney challenged, "If you had communications with a spirit and that spirit was truly interested in you, would you listen to it?" Willa nodded. "Well, suppose the spirit told you to do something, something that might even be in conflict with your own good judgement, would you do it?"

"No!" Willa said and concentrated on fixing another cup of coffee. Brook had sucked in a deep breath. She feared Willa was going to blow the whole deal for them.

It was nearly two full minutes before Miss Finney said, "Suppose I told you that I had had communications with a spirit who had given me specific instructions. Would you think your old auntie was mad? Would you laugh at her?"

During the lull, Brook had decided she would not jeopardize the plan; she would let Willa do the talking.

Willa answered, "First, dear Auntie, no one could ever think of you as mad. Second, it would not matter whether we laughed or not. If you believe in a spirit, that is your business. No person has the right to interfere in another's life in such matters."

Aunt Finney sipped her coffee, spilling a few drops on the napkin Brook had tucked at her chin. Embarrassed, the old lady dabbed the dribble and spoke: "Did you see what just happened? Do you see how helpless I am? Don't answer; the questions are rhetorical." She gazed at the two younger women and said, "A spirit did speak to me. Today. At Carlos Ives' office." Brook and Willa feigned surprise, hoping they were acting well. It did not matter; Miss Finney was not paying attention. Willa asked her to tell about the spirit contact. "It was quite strange," Miss Finney said. "It was not as if I was contacting a particular spirit; it was no one I knew. Yet, the feeling was that I had known the spirit forever. It was not a relative, at least not one I could identify. But, more importantly, the spirit was a force, a power, rather than an individual. I felt complete power emanating from somewhere." She stopped. Both girls waited. Miss Finney said nothing.

Brook could not stand the suspense. "What did the spirit say, Auntie?" Willa gave an angered glance at Brook; she had wanted the old lady to proceed by herself.

Miss Finney smiled at Brook. "Yes, thank you, Brook. My mind was wandering." Miss Finney cleared her throat and continued: "The spirit spoke in audible words— through Mister Ives' mouth, of course—and he told me a wonderful thing was possible!"

To prevent another lapse, Willa asked, "What was possible?"

A glaze came over Miss Finney's eyes as she replied, "The spirit told me I could have eternal life."

Willa said quickly, "And you believe that?"

Miss Finney nodded. "There is no reason to doubt."

A radiant smile flooded onto Willa's face. Now that the

old lady was convinced, the rest would be a piece of cake. Willa prodded, "What upsets you, Auntie?"

"Oh, dear child," the old lady was pulling herself into the conversation again, "that is a lovely promise, but there are some things that can be and some that can never be. I am afraid eternal life will be denied me."

"Why?" asked Willa.

The old lady was acting nervous. "Because . . . because the voice told me I would have to do an impossible thing. . . ."

Willa spoke again: "Nothing is impossible, Auntie. . . ."

"This is impossible," the aunt said. "What I was told was evil, fiendish. I cannot tell you."

Brook, not looking at Willa, joined in, "Tell us, dear Auntie. That's what we are here for. Nothing you could say would be so fiendish that it would hurt us."

The old lady was working herself into a state of tension. "I am really ashamed to talk about this. It is too evil."

Willa replied, "Tell us, Auntie, please. We want to help."

"Yes," said Brook.

The old lady took a deep breath. "You are sweet girls."

Brook demanded, "Tell us."

The old lady paused, "They said I could live forever if . . . ."

Willa was getting impatient. "What, dammit?!"

In times past in the Finney mansion, such a vulgar outburst would have aroused the wrath of the mistress of the household. But things had changed. The old lady ignored Willa's outburst and moved laboriously ahead, saying, "I really don't think I can even say the words to you young ladies."

Brook replied with patience in her voice, "Tell us, Auntie."

Willa urged, "Yes, please. We want to help."

Quietly, Miss Finney said, "They said I could have

eternal life . . . if. . . ."

Both girls demanded, "If *what?*"

" . . . If I took someone's life."

Brook's shock was not all theatrical. She gasped, "Take a person's life?"

Impatiently, Willa ordered: "Shut up, Brook. She said what she said!" Then, Willa said softly to her aunt, "Do you have faith in the voice? Do you believe it?"

Pitifully, the old lady's voice wavered as she affirmed, "Oh, yes, Willa. I do have trust in the spirit. Mister Ives has proven it to me."

Willa asked, "Then what will you do?"

Miss Finney replied, "What can I do? Nothing. Look at me." She lifted her arms up, barely achieving chest height. Her cramped hands looked like talons on a dead hawk. She cried in anguish: "What can I do?! I am weak . . . sick . . . crippled. I can do nothing!" She nearly gagged on a deep gasp of air. "I must die!"

Willa had anticipated her aunt's despair and rose placidly. Brook moved out of compassion. They were at Miss Finney's side as she burst into tears. Willa offered: "We will help you." At the same time, Brook was saying, "Please don't cry, Auntie. We'll help."

The old woman's head fell onto her chest; her thinning white hair fell out of its bun; her left arm began a spasmodic convulsion.

Brook was scared; Willa was stolid. They stroked Miss Finney and urged her to calm down.

"I . . . I . . . am lost . . . I will die." The crying increased.

Outside the window of the dining room, the gardener could not figure out what was happening. He could not hear; he could only watch. Some indistinct sounds reached him. He heard the old lady cry out, but he could not discern the words. He was enjoying the torture of looking at the girls, though. Willa was leaning over the wheelchair; a button on her blouse had come undone and he could see the full outline of her breast through the cleavage. Brook had nearly stumbled in her urgency to get to her aunt. She was in a half-sitting position in front of the old lady, her legs positioned so that he could see her thighs and even a glint of white panty. It was becoming too much for him. His trousers were bulging, pounding with urgency; his breath was coming in gasps. He convinced himself that both of the girls were aware he was there. He was sure they wanted him, that they needed him as much as he needed them. Boldly, not able to contain his irrational passion, he moved from the dining room window toward the back porch. He would go into the house and wait in the pantry. One of them would sense he was there and one would come to him . . . offering him a . . . he would . . . . Thoughts became a tumbling jumble of erotic flashes in his perverted mind. He slipped into the house.

Miss Finney's crying could not be heard, she had lowered it to a mewl; Brook and Willa coddled her. Whimpering, the old lady personified self-pity as she repeated, "I will die . . . I will die."

With a strong voice, Willa cut into the whining: "Maybe there is some other thing you can do, Auntie. I will call Mister Ives."

The aunt shook her head, "The spirit was clear . . . I must take a life."

"But how could you?" Brook pleaded, "How could anyone?"

Miss Finney recovered some composure. "Exactly, dear Brook. That is the point: How could anyone kill someone?"

Willa challenged them both: "If it meant living forever, some people would not care."

"I would not care, if I could do it." The old lady shocked Brook with her candor.

"Auntie," Brook pleaded, "you can't mean that."

Miss Finney stiffened. The crying was done. "I am afraid that I could, Brook. If I could do it physically. Think of it, Brook: to live forever, to never experience dying. Oh, yes, dear girl, I would do it. But I cannot do it; I am sick and lame. I could not kill a fly, let alone another human."

Coldly, pointedly, Willa asked, "If you could do it, Auntie, who would you kill?"

The room was silent. None of them seemed to even breathe.

After a moment, the old lady replied, "I don't really know. I had not thought about that aspect because I am incapable of the physical act."

Willa responded, "Well, you'd better think about that. Living forever is something that seems worthwhile."

Miss Finney nodded eagerly. "Yes! How many people in the world have been offered such a gift?"

Brook said, "Not many . . . none?"

Willa said, "Many, maybe. How are we to know?"

Miss Finney said, "It would be worthwhile, Willa. I know that sounds evil of me; it sounds like the ultimate selfishness. But I am being honest. It would be worthwhile."

Willa said, "We could help."

The statement settled like a blanket of silence. The three women looked questioningly at each other.

Miss Finney settled on Brook because the girl seemed to be the most pensive: "Brook, would you help?"

"I . . . well. . . ." Brook stuttered, "I . . . don't know . . . I. . . ."

Willa, emphatically: "She will, Auntie."

Brook agreed meekly: "I will, Auntie."

Miss Finney shook her head, "I could not ask you. That is too much to ask of anyone."

Willa asked, "What did Ives say?"

With some assurance, because she had been leading up to this moment, Miss Finney said, "Mister Ives said that it would be quite understandable for me to enlist some assistance. He said it must be someone who could be trusted. He even suggested you girls, but I rebuked him. That would be too much to ask; you have done so much for me already."

Willa stated: "I will do it."

Brook, with a visual prodding from Willa, said, "I'll do it, too."

Miss Finney said, "You girls surprise me. Why will you help?"

Willa was ready. "For money, Auntie. For money."

The mood in the room changed. Miss Finney tightened up, narrowing her eyes in contemplation and punctuating her thoughts with: "Ah-ha . . . ah-ha . . . ah-ha." She studied each girl. She said, "So we have a mercenary motive: it is not all for the love of dear old Auntie."

Brook looked away, embarrassed. Willa stared coldly back into the eyes of her aunt. Willa said, "You would be getting more than anything money could buy, Auntie. You have chosen not to bestow anything on us in your will. Besides, there is a chance your will might never be executed; you can live for all time. Brook and I would be the same as everyone else: helplessly mortal. But you would go on and on. We would help you if you gave us money so that we could enjoy our little remaining time here on earth."

The old lady had a mean look on her face. She looked insidious and formidable despite her physical weakness. As she mulled over Willa's argument, the expression on her face eased, then became soft. She looked at Brook. "Brook, will you help?"

Distressed, Brook flitted her eyes from Willa to her aunt and back. Miss Finney demanded with absolute authority, "Look at me! I asked you a question: Will you help . . . for money?"

Barely audibly, Brook said, "I'll help."

Arrogantly, the old lady demanded: "Say your answer,

Brook, so that I can hear it: Will you help me kill someone for money?"

Mustering strength, Brook said, "I will."

There was a pause, then Miss Finney said, "You both will help in this effort?"

Willa was brutal: "Look, old lady, you have our answer. You pay us; we'll do what you say."

With discomfort, Miss Finney looked at Willa and said, "Your attitude seems quite modified, Willa. Just minutes ago you were full of dear aunties and solicitious smiles. Now you are crassly mercantile. What has changed you?"

Boldly, Willa said, "We want money, you have money. That is all there is to it. You get to go on living for as long as you keep killing people. Brook and I get to have some cash, get out of this dump and do some living. For a while, anyway. I'm sick and tired of you treating us like slaves. Now we are equals, dear Auntie; you need us."

Miss Finney showed no anger. She smiled and said, "I appreciate your candor, Willa." Then she turned her attention to Brook. "And you, Brook. Does Willa speak for you?"

Brook nodded meekly.

"Well, now," the old lady said with some satisfaction in her voice, "it seems we have a bargain." The girls nodded together. Miss Finney said, "We must now strike a price." Willa smiled. The old lady said, "A price that is commensurate with the service. I am sure we can arrive at an equitable figure."

Willa glared. "I don't happen to know about 'commensurate' or 'equitable,' Auntie dear, but I do know you'll pay us well."

Miss Finney nodded with a smile. "And that is just what I intend to do, dear Willa."

She turned to Brook and said, "Brook, dear, do go get us some sherry. We will have a drink to commemorate our bargain. Then we will negotiate a price."

Willa stood and said, "We don't need any drinks, old lady. This is business now."

Miss Finney nodded agreement, then argued, "We do not have to get testy, Willa. I agree we are in a business situation, but there is no reason for us to comport ourselves as common tradespeople. Let us keep some social decorum." The old lady gave a wave-of-the-hand gesture for Brook to get the sherry.

Brook went to the sideboard and took out a Waterford decanter. Willa, her voice brittle, said, "Brook, if we must have a drink, let's use some of the good stuff. Right, Auntie?" The old lady shrugged her shoulders. Willa ordered. "Go get that bottle of Napoleon in the pantry . . . the thirty-year-old stuff."

Miss Finney said, "That seems appropriate. Please get it, Brook."

In the pantry, Baldwin had been able to hear only muffled sounds. He had crept to the kitchen door, but he had felt too vulnerable there and had returned to the shadows of the pantry. He worked out a plan, a scheme for conquest. He would wait for the meal to be over. He knew the normal routine. One of the girls would take the old lady into the sitting room at the front of the mansion where they would listen to the radio and play checkers or dominos. The other girl—they took turns—would clear the table and clean up the kitchen. Baldwin fantasized that the one who came to clean up would start on her work, then he would present himself to her, probably without clothes, so they would waste no time. He had a vision of her smiling, running into his arms and kissing him full on the mouth. She would anxiously strip off all her clothes, eagerly climb onto the worktable and beg him to have his way with her. If it did not go that way, he would simply knock her out and rape her, as she deserved. Either way was fine with him. He waited.

Brook was at the dining room door when Willa said,

"Hold it, Brook. Don't go yet."

Brook stopped and Miss Finney asked, "What is it, Willa? Do you renege on our deal?"

With contempt, Willa replied, "I have no plan of reneging. I think we'd better set a price right now, though. Then the deal will be set."

Miss Finney said, "While we both seem to be gaining from this . . . association, dear Willa, I am afraid it is really a seller's market and you are the sellers. How much?" The question flew out like a dart. Miss Finney wanted the matter settled.

Brazenly, Willa said, "Five thousand."

Miss Finney did not react. Willa added, "Each." Miss Finney still did not react. Willa was silent. Brook took the pause as a bad sign and started to say something, but Willa commanded her to be silent.

Miss Finney said, "Five thousand apiece. Isn't that rather high?"

Willa said, "A small price for eternity."

The old lady nodded and looked angry. "Since when, dear Willa, has five thousand dollars become a 'small price' for the likes of you? I doubt you have ever had that much in total assets in your whole life."

Willa was also getting angry. "Don't you worry about me; just come up with the money."

Brook inquired meekly, "You do have it, don't you, Auntie?"

For an instant, there was no sound, then the old lady gave a nearly childlike giggle. "Yes, Brook, I have the money."

Willa burst into laughter. "Well, I'll be damned." The tension broke. Brook smiled, not knowing her innocence had averted an ugly scene. Through her relaxed bubbling, Willa said to Brook, "Go get the brandy."

She gagged. Vomit surged up into the back of her mouth. She fought to swallow it.

A vile hand was clamped over her mouth. It smelled of sweat, urine and dirt. It forced her mouth open and a filthy, salty taste mixed with the bile churning in her throat. The other hand had explored her chest for a moment, tearing a buttonhole, scratching a breast, bruising a nipple. It had been there for a year-long instant, then it snaked clear and dove to her skirt. The fingers groped at her skirt and slip; then they fumbled inside her panties. All the time she had been fighting, kicking, twisting. With each move, the hold on her became tighter; the will of the attacker became more intense.

She could hear his voice pleading in her ear: "Hey, take it easy. It's me. You wanted me."

Brook was as furious with herself as she was with Baldwin; she should have called the police. She had forgotten him in the whirlwind of events. Now, because she had been careless, she was being molested. His fingers were probing into her body. She tried to bite the hand blocking her mouth, but she could not get her teeth into the palm. She kept trying. Suddenly, the hand was out of her pants and grabbing a fistful of hair at the back of her head. In a quick move, the hand over her mouth flew down and yanked at her left wrist; her arm was twisted painfully behind her before she could scream.

"You yell and I'll break your arm," Baldwin said. She was fighting, not to keep from yelling, but to keep from passing out from the pain in her arm. The last thing she wanted was to be unconscious with his filth around her.

Slowly, with an iron grip, Baldwin moved Brook's face close, closer to his. She could smell some putrid odor from either decayed food in his stomach or poison seeping from abscessed teeth. Their mouths came in contact and Brook was ready to let the vomit fly up out of her throat. But it would not come, not even when he forced his tongue in between her lips, then her teeth. It was a violation of the grossest form to her; he had soiled her and she wanted to hurt him, to injure him. Her hand searched around the pantry shelf.

It was a difficult search; she had only one hand free and she was also trying to get her mouth free from the slime that was trying to conquer her. She touched cans: soups, vegetables. None would work as a weapon.

Something was going on. She could not tell what he was doing, but he had lessened the pressure on her arm. He still held onto her wrist. He was moving her hand. She touched his body and felt as if her fingers would turn to ice. He was trying to force her to fondle him. She flung her free hand around, praying she could grab something to use as a club.

Her body was convulsed with horror; he had jammed her hand inside his undershorts. She was losing control, it was getting away from her. Blackness dodged around her peripheral vision and she felt her head beginning to slip backwards. The last thing she remembered was Baldwin's slobber on her face and a series of animal-like grunts coming from his mouth as he thought she was surrendering to him.

When she awoke, for the first couple of moments she could not open her eyes. There was something wet and sticky on her face; it lay on her eyes, inside her nose, across her mouth. With gentle fingers she touched around. The liquid was drying on her. It was also on the front of her blouse. For a moment, every despicable thought she had ever had blinked through her mind. Hate blossomed in her, then a lump of despair settled in her throat. She resigned herself to the obscenity of the attack and decided she must either fall back into the protective oblivion of unconsciousness or face reality. She forced her eyelids to break through the blinding stickiness. Willa was leaning over her. Miss Finney was in the doorway to the pantry.

"Poor child!" cried Miss Finney.

"That bastard!" exclaimed Willa. This time, the old lady did not scold her for the profanity.

Brook lay on the floor of the pantry, looking up at her aunt and cousin. She wanted to cry.

She moved her hands to her blouse. It had been ripped open. Her bra was twisted out of place and there was pain in her left breast. Her skirt was in place, but she sensed that she was not wearing panties. She moaned.

Willa knelt close to her. "Don't worry; he didn't get at you. The sticky stuff is brandy. I came out to see what was keeping you and he was hunched over you ripping at your panties. I grabbed the bottle and belted him. The bottle broke; he didn't. He just passed out. He is locked in the laundry room."

Panic still gripped Brook as she pleaded, "He didn't . . . . "

Miss Finney said reassuringly, "Willa did a perfect job of saving you, my dear. That scoundrel is the essence of filth."

Brook shook off the fear that had paralyzed her. She pulled herself up and adjusted her blouse. She said, "This time I'll call the police. We've got him now."

Willa reached out and put an arm around Brook's shoulder. The gesture was as much an arresting device as it was a comfort. Willa said, "I think we'd better wait a few minutes. We have something to talk about."

Brook tried to shake off Willa's grip. "We can talk while we wait for the police. I want that man in jail. Now!" She realized she was still trying to shake free of Willa and she was failing.

"Willa, let me go," Brook demanded.

Willa tightened her grip as she said, "We will talk."

Brook looked at Willa, then at their aunt. A sudden realization began to creep into her. "No!" she thought, "That's not right!"

Their aunt Finney spoke. "Brook, try and be calm. I think we have arrived at one solution for a couple of problems."

Brook heard herself saying adamantly: "NO!"

The old lady seemed not to hear as she went on: "Your cousin and I have decided that this person, Baldwin, is a disreputable and ignominious being. I have decided he is not worthy. He will be the first person we use to satisfy Mister Ives' requirement."

"But we can't . . . . " Brook was cut off by Willa, who said, "We can't wait to keep our part of the bargain." Then, turning to Brook, she said, "You go to the sink and clean off that brandy. Get cleaned and get your clothes in order. I will take Auntie into the parlor. We will all talk there." Brook was speechless. Willa, with a playful swat at Brook's bottom, said, "Go on now. Hurry and get cleaned. Oh, one thing . . . he ripped up your panties. I threw them in the trash. Hurry now."

Willa wheeled Miss Finney out of the kitchen.

Baldwin regained consciousness quickly.

It was black in the laundry room; only the smells of bleach, powdered soaps and fabric softeners saturated the air; the excessive cleanliness was overpowering.

The man reached up to explore the searing pain at the back of his head. There was a noticeable lump, a gash in the skin, and stickiness matted in his hair. His fingers moved, following the stickiness. It was on his neck, on his shoulder, on his chest. It was warm and sticky and . . . *"Shit! It's blood!"*

He moaned and started whimpering. He stumbled, trying to get to his feet. He banged against the dryer and the door popped open. Light. The convenience light of the clothes dryer came on. It was not much, but it was better than blackness.

Urgently, he stroked the stickiness on his head. His hand darted back down into the glow of the light: there was no blood. He tried again, then again. Still no blood.

Tentatively, he touched the goo on his fingers to his tongue. A grimace twisted his lips. "Son of a bitch . . . it's booze."

His mind fumbled with the events leading to his awakening in the dark room. It took several tries to get it all organized, but it finally came clearly into focus. The main consideration was that he had not consummated the act with the girl. That galled him. If he was going to get his head knocked in at least he could have gotten satisfaction with the girl, he thought. In spite of the pain in his head, he still resolved to have his way with her. As payment, punishment, reward, physical necessity.

He found a light switch, flicked it on, then studied where he was. He had never seen the washing room. There was a washer and dryer, an ironing board and a mangle. Shelves were stacked with linens and piles of clothing to be pressed.

He looked at the door. It was in character with the rest of the mansion: big, strong, secure.

He decided he'd wait and see what was going on.

Brook sat at the kitchen worktable, her head cradled in her hands.

She had heard the noise from the laundry room of Baldwin bumping into the dryer. The clatter had accosted her, a chilling reminder of a hellish experience. She had thought to run from the room. But she knew the door was massive, the lock was sound. Baldwin was safely incarcerated.

The thought that he was merely a few feet away made her angry. That man had tried to infect her with his filth and might have succeeded had it not been for Willa's quick, effective actions. Brook had never thought of herself as a vindictive person. Even when she had been committed for killing her husband—an act which most felt was justified—she had not harbored ill feelings. She had held no grudges.

Now she felt differently.

Baldwin had defiled her and, though it would be a new experience for her, she was determined to have him penalized. She even started towards the telephone to call the police; Willa was not there to stop her this time. She could call the police. They would come and that slime would be punished.

But Willa had said no. What else had Willa said? That Baldwin could be the first victim for Aunt Finney's charade. That would be nonsense; this man was guilty of a heinous crime. He should not take part in a game, a farce; he should be thrown into jail.

Brook's head snapped up from her hands. She shook it to fight back the thought that was trying to formulate itself in her mind. It kept coming. She jumped out of the chair and ran to the sink. She turned on the cold water and splashed her face, then her hair. She splashed again. The thought kept coming. Roughly she yanked at the soft Irish linen dishcloth and frantically dried herself. She rubbed vehemently, so that it hurt.

It did not work. The thought was there. Baldwin is to be killed!

"Oh, no," she said aloud. She was scared and angry. Her aunt and cousin had used her. They were going to kill that man in there. Brook hated him; she had good reason for wanting to see him hurt. But DEAD! NO!

Breath came with difficulty. She was gasping as fear moved into her chest and squeezed her heart.

She battled the blizzard of thoughts that swirled in her head; she must think clearly. She could call the police but, if her aunt were angry enough, she would not back up Brook's story. Willa would be upset after all the trouble she had gone to, and she might not back up the story, either. The police frequently took a skeptical view of rape accusations, anyway. It could mean being sent back to the asylum!

But she could not let a man be murdered.

A hand came around and touched her neck.

The scream was not loud, considering Brook's state of mind. It was not audible in the front parlor of the mansion where Aunt Finney sat.

Willa hushed Brook by offering soothing words and drawing her into her arms. "Easy, dear Brook. Take it easy." Brook could feel tears spill out uncontrolled. She let her head be cradled on Willa's chest.

"Oh, Willa. It is so . . . . " Sobbing interrupted her. "It is ssoooo . . . horrid."

Quietly, comfortingly, Willa cooed, "Now . . . now. It is going to be all right." Willa hugged Brook tighter and Brook felt a comfort that she had not known since childhood. She felt secure.

Willa eased her hold, then backed off as she said, "Are you going to be okay now?"

Brook savored the security and did not want to break the spell by talking. She nodded.

"Are you sure?"

Brook said, "I'm sure. Thank you, Willa."

Willa reached out and put her warm palm against Brook's wet cheek, "Don't thank me. We need each other." Brook nodded agreement. With a noticeable change of mood, Willa spoke: "You are all cleaned up?"

Brook forced a smile. "I was a mess."

"Nonsense." Willa moved away, halfway to the laundry room door. "We must do something about this rodent."

Brook stood as she said, "I want to call the police."

Willa nodded understanding, then said, "Aunt Finney wants to kill him."

The expression on Brook's face evidenced distress. Willa broke into a laugh. "Isn't it great?" Willa was acting like a teenager excited about her first date. "It all fell right into place for us."

Despair showed in Brook's eyes. "We cannot kill him, Willa."

Willa flitted back to Brook and grabbed her shoulders, sheer joy radiating from her face. "We don't kill him, you silly egg. We pretend, just as we agreed. Aunt Finney will be none the wiser."

Brook was confused. "But how?"

"It's easy." Willa left Brook and went to a drawer under one of the kitchen counters. "Ives set the whole thing up with me earlier." Willa took out a large shopping bag and pulled a small revolver out of the bag.

Brook was tense; Willa handled the gun like a criminal. "Hey," Willa chided, approaching Brook, "take it easy. This is no big deal. It is only loaded with blanks. Look." She tried to hand the gun to Brook, but Brook refused to take it.

Brook was aghast, "How would I know what a blank or a bullet looked like? I have never been around guns."

Willa explained, "Well, it is loaded with blanks. They make a big bang and some smoke, but that is all. A gun needs a bullet to kill. We will use these blanks and shoot at Baldwin, he will play dead and dear Auntie will give us five thousand dollars each."

Brook said, "It sounds too simple."

Willa agreed, "It sounds too simple. Right. But we are going to do it just about that simply. All we have to do is get that toad," she gestured toward the laundry room door, "to go along with us and it will be easy. Just that easy."

Brook had been through a lot, so Willa was not too impatient as Brook unboggled the confusion swirling in her mind.

"Will he do it?" Brook now indicated the laundry room door.

Willa shrugged and said, "That's up to you."

Brook's eyes widened. "I will not talk to that animal."

Willa continued her casual air. "Well, it is up to you. Do you want the five thousand dollars, or not?"

"No!"

Willa gave another shrug. "That's up to you."

They stood there, looking at each other. Brook had no idea what Willa expected of her; no one could expect her to even look at Baldwin, not after what he had tried to do to her.

"No!"

Willa stared.

Brook was deeply hurt that Willa would expect her to have dealings with a man who had coerced her.

"No!"

Willa's eyes did not blink. There was no movement except a slight chest expansion as she breathed. Brook's chin began to quiver. She sucked her lower lip between her teeth to stop the movement.

"I will not do it!"

"What?" Willa demanded, her voice low but firm.

Brook was flustered. "Whatever it is you want, I won't do it."

"Listen, dear girl." Willa took a step closer. "You just listen to me. I know what you have been through. That piece of garbage in that room should be castrated. But we need him. Our dear aunt, bless her soul, came up with the idea that Baldwin should be the first killed so that she can gain life. Now, we know it is all a bunch of bullshit; we know that Ives is playing a con game on her. We know the old lady is probably going to croak from the excitement. But we have struck a deal and we are going through with it."

"But . . . . " Brook's protest was cut off by Willa.

"But. . . . Crap! Now you get this straight. I know you are not thinking right, so I am thinking for both of us. If we are ever to get out of this place, we have to pull this off. Now, Ives has set it all up; the only thing we have to do is take part in the play-acting."

"But with him . . . ?"

"But with . . . anybody." Willa sensed she was making headway and pressed on: "Now listen, Brook, it will not

93

be all that bad. All we have to do is talk him into being the first fake victim and we will be at the beginning of a winning streak. There is a whole world out there waiting for us. Hell, we've both earned some good times. With the money from her we can get down to having fun."

Brook had been captured. Willa continued, "All it will take is getting that pig in there to go along with the game. Tell him we'll pay him."

When Brook asked, "How much?" Willa knew the plan was set.

"You tell him we'll give him a hundred dollars. Now, that will accomplish two things: One, he will help us get the money out of Aunt Finney and two, with that cash in his pocket, he will gladly get out of our lives. Two problems solved for the price of one."

Brook's skin crawled. "I really don't want to talk to him, Willa."

Willa nodded. "Sure, I understand that. But I've got to be in the parlor with Auntie when you come in. I'll have the gun."

The mention of the gun worried Brook again. "Nothing can go wrong, can it, Willa?"

Willa scolded, "You quit doubting me, you silly girl. You do your part; I will do mine. And tomorrow, we will each have five thousand dollars." It had taken time for Willa to ease Brook back into the plan, but it had worked. Brook gave a big smile of comradeship; the conspiracy was proceeding as planned.

Brook spoke: "I hope I can talk him into it."

Willa issued a dirty laugh. "Dear Brook, the way that outgrowth of a cesspool has been attacking your body, he'll do anything you ask him to. Since you are throwing in money along with everything else, he would probably do cartwheels for us."

Brook bristled. "What do you mean, 'everything else'? I'm only giving him money. Nothing else!"

Willa reached up and patted Brook's cheek as she said,

"Now, dear, you do what you must. Just get him into the living room. Quickly. Aunt Finney is itching to kill someone."

Brook wanted to challenge Willa again, but her cousin was out the door to the front parlor before any more could be said. Brook did not feel an urgent need to get the plan rolling; she dreaded opening the door.

She spent several minutes getting her thoughts in order. She would be able to handle the gardener; surely he would be afraid of the police.

When she finally did open the door, he was sitting on top of the washing machine, glaring.

"Don't move," Brook ordered as he made to jump down. "You make one move and I'll lock you in again." He did not speak. "You know, the New Orleans police can do a pretty nasty job on rapists. Do you want them to take you away?"

No answer.

"Now you listen to me, Baldwin. I can have you put in jail and they'll throw away the key. Do you know that?" No answer.

"My aunt is a very influential woman." Brook's voice was beginning to be flecked with fear; she was not bullying Baldwin the way she wanted to. She wondered why he did not react.

Baldwin was gauging two things: What she was getting at, and how he could make it out the door. He knew there was something afoot; if she were going to call the police, they'd be there already. She wanted something. As for getting out the door, he would not rely on it; it was too far and she could slam it shut too easily. He listened. Brook knew she was beginning to show a lack of confidence. She realized she had better quit bluffing and make Willa's offer.

She made the mistake of scolding first: "You have done a very bad thing, Baldwin. I am furious, my aunt is angry and we have nothing but contempt for you." With that speech, Baldwin sensed he was not in any major trouble. He was confident the cops were out of the picture. Good.

Bumbling her start a couple of times, Brook was finally able to say, " . . . Uh . . . well . . . you see, my cousin, Willa, has a favor to ask of you."

Baldwin finally spoke: "Huh?" He was flabbergasted they were even talking to him. Now they wanted a favor. Maybe things would be okay.

Brook plunged right in: "Would you pretend to die for a hundred dollars?"

Baldwin felt heady, like the time he had given blood three times in one day to get money for a whore and a bottle of muscatel. He thought he might fall off the washing machine. He grunted another, "Huh?"

Brook repeated: "Would you play dead for a hundred dollars?"

A confidence engulfed him. "Play dead?" Brook nodded.

Baldwin chuckled. "Do I have to roll over and bark first?" Brook remained stoical.

Baldwin was gleeful. "You're serious!"

Brook replied, "I am serious, Mister Baldwin."

He wanted to slide down off the washing machine, but she still looked tense. He asked, "Why should I pretend to die?"

Brook began to show what he had been hoping for: fear. She explained, "My cousin, Willa, asks that you pretend to die, because my aunt was told by a clairvoyant that she would inherit the remainder of a person's life if . . . if she killed that person."

She had not noticed Baldwin easing down off the washing machine. He said, "She's batty."

Brook, groping her way, took that tack: "She is quite 'batty,' Mister Baldwin. But we feel it is necessary and effortless to appease her. Why not play the game? She will be happy in her fantasy . . . and you will have one hundred dollars."

He mulled over the proposal for a few seconds while he edged from the front of the washing machine to the front of the dryer. The open dryer door acted as a gate; he could not advance further without being obvious. Finally, he asked, "What do we have to do?"

Brook felt tension easing in her; he was willing to go along with the ruse. She said, "My cousin has a gun loaded with blanks. We will go into the parlor at the front of the house. My aunt will think you are being brought there to be killed. We will tell her that you think you are going to do some handyman chore, that we have tricked you. She will shoot you, you will dramatically fall to the floor. We will wheel her out of the room and you can go on about your business."

Baldwin laughed. "For a hundred bucks, you can shoot me with blanks all night."

Brook tensed as she asked, "Then, it's a deal?"

Baldwin nodded. "It's a deal!"

Boldly now, Baldwin walked the length of the laundry room and came to the door. For a moment he felt Brook was thinking about slamming the door shut. He was right, but she fought back the urge; she wanted to follow through and not make Willa angry. Besides, there was ten thousand dollars involved.

Baldwin moved past Brook. She was repulsed as the odor from his body and mouth wafted to her; she struggled with an urge to flee, to run away from this obscene human.

He stopped and turned. His hand reached out, not for Brook, but for the edge of the door. Brook was trapped. She could not suppress a squeaky groan, but she was proud she did not scream the way her mind had told her to.

He was close, too close. That smell.

It was worse as he opened his mouth to speak. "Okay, broad, we got a deal. Now, what's in it for you?"

Brook clamped down on her voice, fighting to keep the

tone from rising. She said quietly, but with obvious tension, "What do you mean?"

A smirk curled the corner of Baldwin's mouth as he said, "You've got your hands on a nutty old woman with a few million bucks. Now you ain't in this for nothing. What's your deal?"

He edged closer. She controlled herself.

With some indignation in her voice, she said, "I have no deal. Now back off or there will be no deal for you, either." She was proud of her strength.

"Shit," he said, "that's fine with me. You kill the deal, I'll just walk in there and tell her the trick you are trying to pull!"

Brook pushed up her chin, feigning contempt. "She would not believe you."

Baldwin argued, "She might! I've decided I want a better deal."

Brook paused. She wondered where she had gone wrong. She feared angering Willa.

"How much do you want?" she asked.

"Five hundred."

"Five hundred?"

"Five hundred dollars," Baldwin confirmed, then added, "and. . . ."

Resentment surged up. Brook's voice wavered. "And . . . *what?*"

He brought his face close to hers.

She could not handle that; it was too much. She struggled to get past him. "No! Let me go! Let me. . . ."

He put a finger over her lips. The smell of sweat and urine now mingled with the smell of the brandy still sticking to him. Brook's stomach decided it must be purged immediately. She gagged.

Baldwin took his offending fingers away. Quietly, with the confidence of a man who knows he stands a good chance of winning, he said, "Look, pretty thing, I'll go along with your deal. Now you listen to my deal. If you don't, I'll go in there and tell the old dame you're making a fool of her. You don't want that, do you?"

Brook wanted to run, to smash his face, to knee him in the groin. She stood glaring at him.

"Will you listen?" he asked.

"What is it?" said Brook in a brittle voice.

He leaned close and brought his lips a half inch from her ear. His pungent odor was strong, the stubble of his beard brushed her cheek, his lower body pressed against her stomach. He spoke in a barely audible whisper and went on at great length, vicariously experiencing the vulgar things he described. Brook parried the filthy words as blows to her mind. They slipped past her with only a glancing impact. She blocked them so well that she was never able to recall them.

But it had been evil and he had enjoyed doing it to her.

"You promise?" he begged.

She nodded. "I promise. Just as soon as we take care of my aunt."

A leer spread over his face as he asked, "Do you think your cousin would go for it, too? We could have a three-some tonight."

Steeling herself, Brook said, "Maybe. I'll ask her."

He moved his hand up and cupped one of her breasts. "You're a lot better stuff when you ain't fighting."

Lightly but firmly, she moved his hand and stated, "After. We will do that sort of thing after. Now we should go in."

"No," he ordered, putting his hand back.

"Now listen!" Brook was beginning to lose the battle against her anger.

He brought his mouth close to hers and said, "Just one, to get me in the mood to die."

Her "No!" was cut off as his mouth covered hers. She felt the most vile thing in the world was happening to her. His tongue darted in and out of her mouth. She could taste the pus coming from the abscesses in his decaying

99

teeth.

She wanted to die. But hope calmed that desire and hope let her stand there for the lifetime of an instant that it took for him to steal a kiss.

As he stopped and withdrew his mouth from hers, she was desperate to spit. But such a thing would probably just move him to more obscenity.

He grinned. "You like that, huh?"

She refused to give him that. She said, "Maybe I'll like it later."

He chortled as he said, "You want to try something else? The old dame can wait."

"No," she urged, "later. That will be nicer."

He pouted and said, "Well, okay. Let's go get me dead."

He laughed and stepped back to let her lead the way.

The front parlor in the Finney mansion was like all the other rooms: large. But, eons before in the family line, one predecessor had acquired an extraordinary collection of Sheraton furniture, and the parlor was furnished with groupings and single pieces of magnificence. There was a warmth and comfort that would seem impossible in a room the size of a tennis court. The parlor was intimate.

Miss Finney's favorite part of the room was the west side, where there was a sculptured marble fireplace. A pair of divans bracketed an inlaid table. Her wheelchair, strangely, did not seem out of place pulled up to the table. Aunt Finney wore a long skirt and a high, ruffled blouse. The fireplace, now functioning with a cast iron gas log, flickered out complimentary, soft lighting that gave a sepia glow to the people sitting, waiting.

Briskly, Miss Finney demanded, "Willa, what is keeping them?" Willa merely shook her head. The old lady shriveled up her mouth and hissed, "You answer me, young lady. I want to know what is taking so long. I want to get on with this."

With some disdain, Willa lolled her head back and looked up at the pattern of dancing fire shadows on the ceiling. She quipped, "Maybe they're finalizing the deal."

Angrily, Miss Finney demanded, "What does that mean?"

Willa exploded. "Maybe he's screwing her!"

"Willa!"

"Well, maybe he is." Willa was rapidly pulling her anger under control, "Maybe Brook had to let him screw her."

The old lady's voice cracked. "I could not let her do such a thing for me."

Willa laughed. "Maybe she's like a lot of others: maybe she's asking for it."

Aunt Finney retorted, "I'll not have such talk in my house, Willa. You stop that drivel right now."

Willa did not reply.

For the umpteenth time, Willa lifted the petit point cushion aside. There lay the .38 caliber revolver she would use.

Abstractedly, Willa said, "You're right. I wish they'd hurry."

With a "Hurumph" and an "Exactly," Miss Finney agreed.

The gun was cold to the touch. She had held it, handled it, for quite a while; it never seemed to get warm.

Willa looked at her watch. Two things registered: it had been a long day and Brook was taking too long. She decided to give Brook another five minutes and then go out to the kitchen. She hoped she would not come upon Baldwin struggling to couple with Brook again. The sight had been ludicrous.

A small, frightened voice said, "Please let it work."

Willa looked at her aunt. The old lady's eyes were closed, as if in prayer.

Willa shattered the quiet: "Are you praying, Auntie?"

"No." Miss Finney sounded tired. "No."

Willa pried, "Do you have faith in that Ives person, Auntie?"

"Humm," Miss Finney was pensive. "I must have faith in him, Willa, dear. There is not much time left for me. There is not much left that I can have faith in."

Vaguely, Willa said, "I guess you're right."

With a little more vigor, the aunt said, "I know I'm right about one thing: faith. I had faith in the doctors, but all they can tell me is what is killing me. They can handle the diagnosis and prognosis with amazing precision. But, in spite of their exorbitant fees, they can offer no cure. Not one of them comes out and says age is the killer; they all isolate a particular ill and say, 'Sorry, old gal, it is going to get you.' What kind of a profession is that?"

"I know," Willa offered.

Seeming not to hear, Miss Finney continued, "And I had faith in the Almighty at one time. All my life I was taught the promise of the Christian faith: salvation, peace, love, joy in heaven. Religion borders on criminal fraud: they don't know. I trusted them and practiced the rules of love. All it did was get me hurt. This hurt bores through faith and burns to the middle of a heart."

Willa pulled herself erect. She had never heard her aunt talk like this. She had never heard Brook say their aunt talked of such things.

Willa asked, "Why are you saying these things?"

With some sadness, the old lady said, "You see, dear, if this does not work, there cannot be much more time for me. The doctors have a long list of various illnesses which are invading my body. Each infirmity is potentially fatal. They compete to affect my early demise."

Willa shook her head in seeming pity.

Compulsively, the old lady cried, "I . . . am . . . dying." Each word had a special, sad emphasis.

Willa left the divan and moved to her aunt. In a tender gesture, she touched the wrinkled face and said, "Now you must not think that way."

A tear splashed onto the sad old face.

Willa took a finger and wiped the tear away. In a whisper she said, "Auntie, you have placed your faith in Carlos Ives. You are right this time."

The vacant gaze and mechanical nod indicated the old lady had little faith or hope.

Willa snapped her eyes down to her watch. Where was Brook?

Miss Finney's voice was weak as she said, "This is all so foolish, Willa. I know there is nothing to what Ives has promised. But I am doing it. If it works, would that not really be something? But it will fail. All else has failed."

Willa was suddenly intense: "Now, listen, Auntie." She took both the old lady's hands into hers and pressed them. "You listen to me. Brook will be here in a minute. You must be strong; you must believe. Remember, you have made a pact with Ives. There is no turning back; there is no giving up. You prayed with Ives, you called on the spirits to help. They are going to help. You must do what you agreed to do. You must find the strength."

Forcing her crooked back into a more erect position, the old lady smiled weakly and said, "I will do my part, Willa. I have promised and I will do it. You have done your part and I promise to do . . . . "

The old lady cut herself off. Her eyes left Willa and darted to the doorway.

Willa quickly turned and saw Brook standing beside Baldwin.

Willa sidled to the divan and casually replaced the petit point cushion.

In his crass, throaty voice, Baldwin asked, "Well, what's going on in here this evening?"

Even the man's clothing seemed to violate the serenity of the room; his person was the ultimate insult.

Miss Finney forced a passable smile. "Well, good evening, Mister Baldwin," she offered in a courteous manner, "Will you please join us?"

Brook led Baldwin into the room, saying, "Mister Baldwin has agreed to fix the cellar door, Aunt Finney. I thought we might offer him a glass of port before he begins."

"Please take a seat, Mister Baldwin." She indicated a straight-back chair several feet away from her; she may have to play a part, but she would not let her furniture be soiled. "I am quite concerned about your behavior, Mister Baldwin."

Comically, he hung his head and said, "Gee, I'm awful sorry, Ma'am. I must have gotten crazy. It won't happen again."

With an aloofness that seemed too easy, Miss Finney said, "Your work in the gardens has been satisfactory. I have agreed to let you remain with us for another three days. Will you be able to accommodate us, Mister Baldwin?"

He displayed his decayed teeth again through his ugly smile. "You bet-cha, Ma'am. I ain't got nothin' to do. I'd like to work on that fountain, too. I bet I can git it workin'."

Willa wished her aunt would not play the game so well. Baldwin was not drinking the port that had been poured for him. Willa interjected, "Do have your drink, Mister Baldwin."

He nodded and picked up the crystal port glass. She urged him, "Please hurry, Mister Baldwin."

He gulped the port.

He held onto the glass as he openly studied Willa's body. He licked his lips.

Miss Finney did not try to hide her contempt. "Now, young man. I think you came here to fix a door. Please be at it."

With arrogance, Baldwin raised a warning hand. "Hey, take it easy. If I'm gonna be around a few days, you oughta be nicer to me. Besides, if you're real nice, I'll get some good humor back into these two gals of yours."

Willa's face hardened as she shot a stony glare at the gardener. She ordered, "You get to your work, Mister Baldwin." Then, to Brook: "Will you show him the door, please? It's the one to the basement."

"Baldwin, follow me." Brook was beginning to show some fear in anticipation of the pending performance; she hoped Baldwin would pull it off well. Willa would then have to use her strong personality to get him off the property. They might even have to raise his share, but they could surely buy him off. Willa could; Brook was positive.

Baldwin stood and weaved slightly as he said, "Hey now, old lad. . . ." He cut himself off. "I mean, Ma'am. I'm really sorry about what happened earlier. Your niece and I have talked it out and we got all that junk straight. I ain't gonna cause you no more trouble."

Miss Finney nodded and said, "I am quite positive of that."

He went on as if she had not spoken: "And you gotta know I'm really glad for the work yer givin' me, Ma'am. I'm really gonna do a bang-up job for you out in them gardens. You wait an' see."

She gave a flippant wave of her hand, dismissing him. He did not understand the gesture.

He said, "I ain't really bad, Ma'am. I just got a little carried away with your niece and . . . . "

Her voice nearly screeched. Miss Finney ordered, "You get out of my sight."

Willa panicked; she was sure the whole scheme would fall to pieces. She ran to the man and took hold of his arm, trying to steer him toward the door. Brook stood watching, not knowing what to do.

Willa steered Baldwin well for a few steps, then he reached behind her and slid his hand onto her bottom.

In a move that was not seen by Miss Finney or Brook, Willa whipped a hand down, grabbed Baldwin's wrist and removed his trespassing hand from her bottom. She said, "Take it easy, buster. You don't have rights to this body."

He leered again and said, "We'll see about that."

"This way," Brook urged. Willa returned to her aunt.

Going down the hallway, Brook scolded, "What were you trying to do in there? You can't stay on working for my aunt. You are supposed to be dead. At least you will be when she shoots you."

Oafishly, Baldwin said, "Yeah, I didn't think about that. I guess she's kinda dumb, too. She hires me, then she shoots me. This is all kinda nuts, if you ask me."

As they reached the basement door, Brook said, "We did not ask you. Just you play your part and do it well."

Coyly, he said, "I'll try."

She ordered, "You will do it, or no money."

Baldwin retorted peevishly, "Aw, you broads is all the same. You got no sense of humor." He took a screwdriver out of his hip pocket and opened the door. He began to look at the hinges, as if to find what was making the door stick.

"How's this?" he asked as he fiddled with each one of the big hinges.

"Just great," Brook said as she eased away from him.

He knelt, peered at the brass screws, and toyed with them, acting as if he were going to tighten them.

Brook had moved ten feet down the hall when Willa arrived, pushing Miss Finney.

The three women stood watching the fool play out his part of the drama.

He stood and smiled, trying to let them all know he was wise to their act, and that he was going along. He said, "This door's got some screws loose."

He had turned to speak to them. They waited until he turned back to inspect the top hinge.

When he was artificially engrossed in his chore, Willa reached down into a pocket of her skirt and pulled out

106

the revolver. With a deft motion, she placed the gun in Miss Finney's lap. The weight of the weapon was too much for the old lady to lift. She cried, "But . . . I cannot do it . . . You must do it . . . Willa . . . You said you would."

Willa commanded, "You must do it. You must!"

Miss Finney cried in dread, "I cannot do it. It is too heavy."

Baldwin had tried his best to act as if he could not hear, but it was too much. He was on the brink of uproarious laughter. He lowered the screwdriver and turned to look at the trio.

At that instant, Willa demanded, "Auntie, you must be a part of it. I'll help you."

Baldwin said with mock alarm, "Hey, what's goin' on here?"

Emphatically, Willa shouted, "I'll help!"

They could see Miss Finney straining. Her eyes flickered, her jaw fought against the shaking; she put so much effort into lifting the gun that her whole body vibrated with a convulsive energy.

The gun rose to chest level. Willa leaned down and lent her hand as a support. Baldwin, playing the fool, feigned a horrified look, whining, "Oh, please, don't shoot me. I'm too young to. . . ."

The sound of the blast muffled the rest of the sentence. The bullet exploded into his throat. A second shot caught him in the chest. Blood splattered in back of him before the momentum of the slug threw him through the doorway to the basement.

The women stood there, listening to the echo of the bullets and the pounding as Baldwin tumbled down the steep stairs.

At first, Brook thought the man had done an incredible job of acting, but within seconds she saw the blood. This had not gone as planned. Dozens of thoughts jammed her mind. All that emerged was a slurred stream:

"Ooh-noo . . . ooh-noo. . . ."

Miss Finney had watched Baldwin with no wish to miss any detail of the event. She had taken part; this had been her killing. She wrenched her head toward Willa and gruffly enjoined, "Take me to my room, quickly. NOW! *Quickly! Take me!*"

Leaving Brook to stand dazed, Willa spun around and wheeled the old lady toward the elevator to take her to her room. Brook did not move until she had heard the movements upstairs that meant her aunt was in her room. Then, with slow, deliberate steps, Brook went to the door. It was splattered with thick, red blood that ran down the enamel of the door. She reached up and touched the liquid. Her fingers slid down the door. As in a trance, she looked down the stairwell: The steps were bloody. At the bottom, tangled like tossed covers of an unmade bed, Baldwin was trying to do something with his one free hand. The movement was feeble.

One foot followed the other. She descended gingerly, holding the bannister tightly, imagining her shoe might slip in a puddle of blood. She was not afraid of falling. Her fear was of getting blood on her. That seemed to be a vulgarity beyond imagination. At the bottom of the stairs, she had to twist and leap gymnastically to reach the basement floor without nudging the form of the man.

It had all gone wrong; blanks could not do this. Maybe he had cut himself in the fall. There was too much blood. How much blood is there in a human?

The blood oozed on the concrete and formed rivulets that flowed toward Brook's shoes. She stepped back. A sound gurgled out of the opening that had been his mouth; the skin had been torn away when the bullet ripped at his neck. She leaned toward him. She could not step closer because the rivulets of blood had become a single snake which slithered toward her. The sounds were unintelligible.

Why won't the blood stop?

Nobody could have that much blood.

It keeps coming. Maybe there are more holes.

She found a route around the red snake and moved close enough to squat down and lean over him.

Eyes opened in what had been his face. It was so badly skinned and scraped from the fall down the stairs that it was no longer a face.

She could see it now: it was only one eye. The other eye was nestled in the crook of his nose.

She wondered if he could see out of the eye which slithered on the face. It was still attached.

The noise gurgled up again.

Firmly, with authority, she told Baldwin, "Speak up if you want me to listen. Don't talk gibberish. She remembered that someone from her past, her mother, or a nurse, or someone had told her never to speak gibberish. The enjoinder apparently had impressed her. She hoped it would be effective on Baldwin; she really wanted him to collect himself.

More blood, this time from the mouth, accompanied the sound: " . . . Itssss."

"What?" she demanded.

"It . . . ssss . . . It's just. . . ."

"Dammit! Baldwin! Talk!"

"It . . . sss . . . It'ss . . . just a game. We . . . just playin' a game . . . . "

There was a noise—a death rattle—that followed the last word, then a red foam gushed up and flowed across the face. Brook spoke aloud to herself: "He is dead . . . he is dead." It was a rather mild statement, she felt.

When Willa came hurrying down the stairs, Brook abandoned her mildness: "He's dead! You killed him! YOU! KILLED! HIM!"

She began to pummel Willa's head and shoulders.

Willa grabbed Brook by the shoulders, gave a hard shake, then a quick slap on the face. Brook was calmed immediately.

In an icy voice, Willa said, "He is dead, Brook. *We* killed him."

Brook shook her head, trying to affect innocence. Willa glared. "We are in this now. *We* have killed him."

Brook cried, "But it was supposed to be with blanks."

Willa, unruffled, replied, "I had to do it that way. We could never have trusted him. You want to be rich, don't you?"

Brook did not reply. Willa shouted, "Don't you?"

Meekly, Brook replied, "I want that, yes. But not like this. We just murdered a man, Willa. Doesn't that mean anything to you?"

Willa looked down at the corpse on the basement floor. Only contempt showed on her face. She replied, "He was less than nothing, Brook. He will not be missed . . . by anyone." She paused, then looked up at Brook and continued: "I hated him for touching you. The things he did to you, the things he wanted to do to you!"

Brook shook her head as she said, "Not this way. He was filthy, but he did not deserve this; no human being deserves this."

Arrogantly, Willa charged, "He was not a human being; he was filth, garbage, the feces of society. The world is well rid of him."

"We killed him," came absently from Brook.

"Right," agreed Willa. "Don't forget that, either. But don't worry. I will protect you."

Brook was angry. Her nostrils flared and her eyes narrowed as she said, "I don't need you to protect me, Willa. You did that once and look what happened." She pointed at the tangled heap that was Baldwin.

Willa nodded with patience and said, "You will need me to protect you . . . you'll see. Before it's all over . . . you'll see."

Willa's veiled threat stabbed at Brook's mind. "Before it's over?"

Willa nodded.

4

Miss Finney sat in her wheelchair. The day had been taxing.

There had been emotional turmoil: decisions to be made, morals to be compromised, the exhilaration of hope combatting the depression of despair. She sat there, drained. When the event had finally happened, some urge, some wisdom from without had spawned need for privacy. Once in the room, Willa had wanted to help undress the old lady as usual and make conversation. Miss Finney would have none of it. She demanded solitude.

"I'll come back in a few minutes," Willa had offered.

Miss Finney had been emphatic and final: "Leave me. I will see you in the morning." Then, with no consideration or courtesy, she had shouted at Willa: "Get out! NOW!"

The old lady did not know how long ago that was. She did not care. She sat in the darkness, thinking.

At first there was a dissonance to her thoughts. They created a kaleidoscope of images from all times in her life. She could not control their order or their nature; it was as if her mind set off on a helter-skelter journey, defying all discipline.

She resisted, trying to control the reveries, but she failed and finally gave up. Vignettes drifted in and out of her mind uninvited and unwelcome. Then the memory that was stored deepest in her mind emerged. She had not wanted the recollection to surface, but before she could fight it back, it was there. She was swept up in the currents of the past:

No person will ever enter this part of my mind; none shall ever hear what I can only say to myself. I will not share this, because one cannot share loss, and my loss has been the greatest ever suffered. My sadness is mine alone. The beauty of what is gone will be locked in the inviolate sanctuary of my mind.

It was in the winter of 1925 when I finally was able to stop, reflect and organize what had happened. This is set down as it was arranged in my mind then, at my home in Montreaux on Lake Geneva. The home is gone now; I sold it when I decided to spend the remainder of my life in my parent's home—ancestral, if you will—in New Orleans.

This testament will survive for all time; it will exist the day after forever. I will tell none; none will dare ask.

I prohibit any person from intruding in this, which is set down in the ultimate privacy of my mind:

It began during the devastation of the First World War. I was a young girl, twenty years old, living as an expatriate in France. Exiled is a melodramatic term; expatriated is more civil. My status was simply that I did not wish to live with my family in Louisiana. They did not really want me around. They were eager to support my whims; I lived well in Paris.

The war had been stumbling along since 1914. It did not seem that 1917 was to be a year of major consequence. Men would be killed, money would be squandered, small patches of worthless soil would be reddened with the priceless blood of young men from all nations. There was a growing hope that the United States would come into the war; their manpower and resources would tip the scales. Of course, the French and the British would be forced to resent the Americans for coming in; we tend to hate those whom we are forced to accept as saviors. There was hope they would come in and hope they would stay out. There was no way to tell what they would do.

Some Americans came over, desperate to fight, but it was not that easy. Both the British and the French were afraid to aggravate the delicate political situation that existed back in the United States. President Wilson had asked Congress to allow him to arm the U.S. merchant vessels on the high seas. The Germans were using submarines to sink American ships, and American sailors were dying. They needed protection as nonparticipants in the war. The United States Senate, yielding to a strong isolationist faction, had voted against arming the ships.

So it was a tricky situation, and many of the young men who wanted to fight were forced to drift around Paris, yearning for a way to show their mettle against the dreaded Huns.

I met John toward the end of 1916. We would fall in love, but our love would end in tragedy.

Our encounter happened with the swiftness of a pleasing thought. It began with a spontaneous tête-a-tête in a coffee shop on the Champs-Elysées in the afternoon. Then we walked through the streets of Paris hand in hand. Finally we rode through the city and through the night, ending up at dawn in a tiny garden by Sacré-Coeur on the hill at Montmarté.

In my twenty years I had remained a virgin. I surrendered to John that dawn, probably on sanctified soil. There was no clear reason why I offered my purity to him after years of resisting dozens of other suitors. Maybe it was because he demanded submission less than the others; maybe it was because he was eager to get into the war and would be exposed to death. Maybe it was because I needed him more than I had ever needed any man. There is no real explanation, and there need be no excuses. We loved and found the appropriate rewards. We experienced the sexual joys of new love for three days. We left my apartment only to buy food; we would not spare the time to sit in a restaurant. Impatience and lust made us practically uncontrollable with each other. In the three days, we ruined four meals, burning the food to cinders or letting it sit on the plates as we made love on the floor of the kitchen.

We felt that sex was a miracle created especially for us. Surely, others may have found satisfaction in sex, but *we* had discovered the secrets of the ultimate human contact. We would keep those fantastic secrets between us. None could share; no others were emotionally equipped for the riotus fornication bestowed upon us.

We were one. We were one until the fourth day when John, not really wanting to go, not really insisting we go, suggested he might check his mail and see if his friends were about.

He never got to look for his friends. That casual excursion ripped John away from me before the end of the day. A letter from home was the culprit.

His mother had died. He would have to return, because his father was gravely ill due to the loss.

My own parents had offered me little in the way of love. When I saw John's face as he read the letter, I knew fate had denied me a special gift. My own parents were not worthy of such emotion. John's background made me understand how he could love so deeply: love was his way of life. He had taught me to find and release the love that had been locked deep within me.

But, as I had loved, I also lost. I left him that night at the railway station, where he caught the night boat-train to LeHavre. From there he would sail for the United States.

I had always been blessed with adequate financial resources, so it was natural for me to suggest that I, too, go on the night train and sail for the United States. Why not? I had no reason not to. My life, my love, was about to step onto a train and pluck from me the joy of love and companionship that I had just found. To John, though, the loss of his mother was a spiritual event. He could not think of our romance while grieving for his mother and fearing for his father's life. My love for John taught me unselfishness. I had to let him go.

I lasted only thirty-six hours in my apartment; John's absence turned it into a tomb, a crypt that housed too many memories. I moved to a new, less spacious apartment near the Ile de la Cité. I cloistered myself and waited. The waiting became a way of life for me, a permanent way of life, because I heard nothing from my love in the United States.

Unbeknownst to me, my diabolical landlord was insulted by my leaving and destroyed John's letters instead of forwarding them to me.

I had stopped writing after receiving no reply. I felt used and dirtied by the man who had professed to love me.

Finally, when my former landlord took ill, one of his employees forwarded a letter to me. The news it contained made my heart explode with happiness. John was in the army and coming to France with other Americans to fight against the Germans. But the postmark was weeks old, too old for me to send a reply with my new address. I went to my old apartment to beg the landlord to tell John where I was. But the man had died and his apartment house stood vacant.

I posted notes to John on the door to my former apartment. Three times I went back to check. Each time the note had been removed. It seemed insurmountable forces thwarted my efforts to rejoin my love.

Agonizing over my plight, finally I resigned myself to sitting out war and waiting until John went back to the United States; I would be there, waiting for him. But . . . I thought the unthinkable. Suppose he were killed? I had to find him. I needed urgently to find my love.

Initially, I tried to buy my way to him, but I met with no success. The task I had set out to accomplish was a formidable one: to find John among the ranks of the Americans. Four million, seven hundred thousand men participated in the awesome war effort. My job seemed impossible.

With the help of some close friends at the U.S. Embassy, I was enlisted as a nurse in the Army. I was given an adequate, but much too rapid, course in nursing by the Sisters of Healing at the Ursuline Hospital outside Paris. They seemed to be offended by my goal, but pressure was brought to bear on my behalf through the offices of the Ursuline Convent in the French Quarter of New Orleans. My parents had made sizeable contributions to the convent in years past. Their donations finally reaped dividends.

By early 1918, I was functioning as a nurse in the U.S. Army, doing my best to help with the war effort, but letting nothing get in the way of my search.

There was a force deep within me that urged, demanded that I get to John. There was an accompanying gnawing at my thought processes, a warning for me to hurry, an ominous and misty presentiment of impending danger.

After several months of sandwiching my search between nursing duties, I found out which unit John served in. After that, it was simple to locate the unit. In what seemed to me to be a reasonable request, I asked to be transferred to that area. I do not like to recall my introduction to military bureaucracy and the bungling of a simple, valid request. Three weeks of red tape tried my patience to its limit; I requested leave to go to the area on my own. It was vital that I go soon.

Huge battles were being waged. It was determined that my talents were needed due to " . . . major conflicts which are about to take place." My request was dismissed with a shrug. I left my nursing unit that night without permission.

It was late the next morning when I arrived at a hospital processing area near John's division. In uniform, I was able to drift around and glean information regarding transportation to the front. I approached a supply officer talking to a nurse. They were standing beside an ambulance van that had been converted to a supply vehicle.

I introduced myself and said, "I was told you were going up to the Marne River. Do you need any help?"

The man, who seemed much too young to be an officer, replied, "We sure do need help. I'm Royce. This is Nurse Pointeer. Where are you assigned?"

The thought of lying occurred to me; it would be so easy. With all the shooting going on, people were not asking to see printed orders. I told Lieutenant Royce that I had left my unit and why I had left.

I added, "I was on my way to a dressing station at Belleau Wood . . . when I heard about the Third Division." The Third was John's division.

Nurse Pointeer said, "They were at Château Thierry. They caught hell."

I nodded and told her, "That is where I am going. I must get to the Third."

Royce cut me off. "I understand. It's your business. We'll take you with us." Then he said to the nurse, "Okay, secure the back of this buggy and let's get moving."

They had such spirit, such eagerness. I had my own spirit and eagerness, but my reasons were different ones.

We moved out over a flat piece of dirt that was supposed to be a road. It ran through a devastated pile of rubble that had been a town. Ahead of us were tall, billowing clouds of black smoke and we could hear the thunder of General Pershing's artillery above the roar of the truck. Along the road, coming toward us, were lines of straggling soldiers with reddened bandages. Later, going in our direction, were lines of straggling soldiers without reddened bandages.

As we rode, I talked about John and our love. I told the two strangers my story. They listened patiently.

Lieutenant Royce asked, "You think he's by the Marne?"

They were skeptical as I told them, "I know he is there. I feel it . . . I feel drawn to him, as if . . . as if he were calling me. Once I thought I heard. . . ."

The nurse, Pointeer, asked, "Suppose he has been. . . ."

The lieutenant gave her a sharp look. She changed the end of her sentence: " . . . suppose he's been wounded?"

I thought before answering. Then I said, "That is why I am here, I guess . . . Don't you think so?"

Royce tried to cheer me up. "We'll be there soon. Don't tell anyone you're supposed to be at Belleau Wood." He offered a smile to lessen the shock of: "They shoot deserters, you know."

We came to a huge area that had been set up as a forward aid station. The activity was furious. Wounded were being brought in faster than they could be taken care of, and rows of men were lined up on pallets in the mud. I left my new friends to their chores and went looking at the faces of the boys lying there, hoping to be saved. John was not among that bunch of wounded. I hurried around, asking questions to find out what the situation was. It did not look good.

There was word of a broad German advance along the whole front. There was rumor of a retreat. I hastened my search. It did no good. I came back to Lieutenant Royce and Nurse Pointeer. They had unloaded their supplies and were getting ready to give assistance in one of the tents being used as a first aid dressing station. The noise of the enemy artillery was getting louder.

As I walked up, Royce asked, "See him?"

I shook my head. "No!" He gave me a brotherly pat on

the shoulder and said, "That could be good, you know. If he is not here, then he might not be wounded."

I would have liked to accept his moral support, but I had heard, "Not all the wounded were brought back from the front. They were forced to leave some."

I looked up toward the shelling. It was getting late, both in time of day and in time before the enemy attack advanced. I said, "I want to go to the front. I must!"

Royce asked, "How do you know he's been hurt? Has someone told you?"

I said, "No one has told me. I know."

The young lieutenant was laboring with a problem. I was making his life more difficult than it had to be. I felt I was imposing. Finally, he asked me, "Can you drive?"

I told him I could.

As if he were taking a plunge into an icy stream in the middle of winter, he said, "Take the truck. Get back here as soon as you can. I could get into a lot of trouble over this!"

Bursting with excitement, I leaned to him and planted a kiss solidly on his cheek. He blushed deeply, and I realized he did not appreciate affection, even platonic affection.

"Thanks," I said and climbed into the truck. With a minimum of difficulty, I was on the road toward the front and the trenches.

I do not know what battlefields are like today; I do not want to know. I do know the battlefields of World War I could match Dante's vision of his inferno. Organic life was absent. Organic life is absent in cities, where plastic plants fight to survive a carbon monoxide atmosphere, but in France, it was different: Man had intentionally set out to defile the land. He was perfecting his skills at the Somme and the Aisne and Belleau Wood. The grass had been trampled to death. Whatever blades had attempted a comeback had succumbed to mustard gas. Ten-foot-wide pock marks showed where artillery shells had burst.

Six-foot-wide slits showed where men had dug trenches to protect them against the shells. The war had raged so long that trees destroyed in the early phase had begun rotting. Barbed wire lay rusting.

And the smell. A stench. Every vile putrification ever known was there: Water trapped in the shell holes, human waste in the shallow latrines, flesh decaying on bodies.

I was looking for John in that Hades. I was not flitting about, randomly moving from point to point. I had direction. Some compelling guide was leading me with purpose. I do not know what the force was. I have never experienced such a feeling since.

I had left the truck somewhat protected by an escarpment near the site where John's unit had been fighting. The area was abandoned. No sounds were to be heard other than the loud pounding of the German guns reaching out their fingers of death.

I did not need help; I knew where I was going. I do not know why I knew.

Night was falling. It was difficult to see the steps leading down into the trenches, but, with increasing frequency, German shells burst and supplied flashes of light.

I was at the bottom of the stairs, standing in the trenches. Planks had been laid to keep feet out of water; all they did was let the feet stand in water on planks. The walls were mostly mud infrequently supported with burlap bags. Ladders stood ready to be used by innocent youths ordered "over-the-top" . . . to death.

I moved along the darkness of the trench, holding my hand to my nose and mouth, trying to filter out the putrid odors. It was no use.

The sector of trenches had been totally abandoned in anticipation of the German attack. I thought for a moment what it would be like to be caught there when the Germans poured out in their advance. Would dozens of the filthy Huns ravage me? No! John was there, I knew that. He would protect me.

I came to an opening in the trench. The opening was dug into the bank, and a canvas rag served as a door.

I pushed my way inside.

This is the one moment of my story that I wish I could share with others. Not many, just a few deserving others.

But who would believe me?

There was a golden glow in the room that had been the company command post of John's group. The glow could have come from the old-fashioned kerosene lanterns, but they were not lighted. The glow could have come from the low wattage electric lights that hung from several beams, but there was no electricity.

The dank, eerie place glowed, I contend, from the love between John and me.

He was there, standing at the opposite end of the room, as I knew he would be. My premonition had been correct.

"I love you," I called and took the first step before running to his arms.

"I've been waiting," he said. "I love you."

He was in uniform. His clothing was amazingly clean. My own white uniform was spotted and stained, and I had only been traveling. John had been fighting a war in the trenches.

I had faltered after my first step. The run had never started. I had, for some reason, stopped myself.

I moved to take another step, but John raised one hand and admonished me: "Wait! There is no time for us now."

Confused, hurt, I cried, "I don't understand. Are you . . . are you hurt?"

There was an ethereal glow about him. He radiated love for me. He was beautiful. He answered, "I'm not hurt any more, my love. I had been shot and they thought I was dead. But I am all right now. Look at us, my darling, we are saving the world."

I wanted to fly to him, but something held me back. I pleaded, "I do not want to save the world, my love. I want to be with you. Let me see you."

Again, with finality, he ordered, "No! We will be together . . . someday. I will find you. You must wait for me."

I told him, "I can wait. But I don't understand."

His voice was strange. His tone changed as he told me, "I have many things to do . . . now. I must repay what is . . . due."

I begged, "Come with me, John. I have a truck. We will be safe."

His lips moved and he was saying something, but there was a deafening explosion as a German shell landed near the command post.

"John! *Please!*" I screamed.

Dirt and wood fragments began falling from the crude rafters. The concussion of the shell had thrust me away from the door to a side wall. Not toward my love. The look on his face was as loving as any person has ever shown another. There was a smile, the same smile that, in times past, had come to his face after we had climaxed and we were resting. I needed to kiss that face.

Ignoring his protest, I lunged away from the wall and cast myself at my love. Another German shell exploded, this time right over the command post. No ears had ever heard a louder noise. The ground shook as if it were some liquid mass of jelly. I could see the inadequate ceiling of the room begin to collapse. Dirt poured down; beams snapped and fell in front of me. Before the blackness came, I saw his face. It was a spectacle of brilliance. It was love.

It was two days before I came to. When I did, I was far from the front, cocooned in the pristine comfort of a hospital bed. Nurse Pointeer was standing to one side, Lieutenant Royce at the other.

"John?" I spoke my first words. The effort made my

head hurt. I reached up and felt bandages.

Nurse Pointeer cautioned, "Take it easy. You've had a serious injury."

"John, where is John?"

Royce said, "We found no one but you."

I argued, "But he was there. We talked. He must still be there. We must go back . . . ."

Royce shook his head. "There was only you. Really. We got you out just before the German advance. We were lucky to make it."

I explained, "We talked. He was there . . . . "

Nurse Pointeer countered, "Perhaps he got out and went looking for help. He may show up . . . at any time . . . . "

She was not convincing. Royce was investing some effort in trying to comfort me. I realized John had been lost. I sought comfort in the blackness of unconsciousness.

Rehabilitation of a head injury can be instantly successful or prolonged. Mine was instant, but the medical authorities insisted my recovery was to be gradual. I did not care. I let them play at their profession. I wanted nothing to do with the world. I was passive in accepting what they ordered until they ordered me back to the United States. Winning that battle was tantamount to conquering any injury. I won and I was well. I would not leave Europe until I found John. I knew he was still alive.

The war ended and my goal became more manageable. I searched. It was not long before I was known as the young lady searching for a dead man. But I knew he was not dead. It was up to me to find him. Months passed into years; desire became obsession. I visited every hospital that had been near the fighting areas. I went into Germany and financed extensive research of the available prisoner of war records. Nothing showed that he had been treated in a French hospital. Nothing showed that the Germans had ever taken John captive.

My parents died. I did not care. The influenza epidemic took their lives and left me an orphan. The only real effect the event had on me was that I was a wealthy orphan. I began using large sums in my search, but nothing was successful.

After exhausting every possibility in Europe, I went to the United States and tried to find John's father.

That was when my findings began to make sanity a difficult thing to hold onto.

John's father had died, predictably, shortly after John's mother had died. Searching for friends and relatives was not easy; there had not been many of either.

But when I did find something, it was so devastating I nearly lost control of my mind. I credit my faith in John's love with my continued sanity. What I learned was too much!

An aunt told me John had been lost when a German submarine sank the ship on which he was coming home to his mother's funeral. Impossible! I had written to him; he had written to me. The woman took offense at my challenge and was frightened at my claim.

I left the aunt. There was no use trying further, She claimed John had been lost on a ship. I knew she was wrong. John had served in the army after the death of his parents.

A substantial retainer to a prestigious New York law firm launched my effort to get a look at John's military records. The senior partner of the firm took a personal interest in my case and finally called me into his office six weeks after starting.

He had disturbing news. Through political influence and application of funds, he had gained access to John's records. It had not been easy; such records are privileged. John had served; he had gone to France. He had been in the Third Division at the Marne. But, with the confusion of retreat and subsequent counterattack that had led ultimately to victory, there had been a foul-up and tracking him had ended at that point.

No one could soothe my indignation. "What do you mean, "ended at that point"?"

The lawyer, a kindly soul, was as flustered as I was. He said, "From the time John went to the front, there is nothing else." He closed the folder and tried to be paternal and wise: "I know it is hard to accept, but you must remember that we had nearly five million men in the service during that war. It is impossible to handle five million of *anything* without misplacing some. In a war, we happen to be dealing with people's lives."

He did not come across as paternal or wise to me; my anger exploded.

It was too bad that old man had to bear the brunt of my frustration. To be told the man I loved had been *lost* or *misplaced* was too much to handle.

The lawyer in his wisdom let me rage on. My anger was spent in a few minutes. He tried to placate me: "Every war has its unknown soldiers; there is a tomb for them in Arlington National Cemetery. Each nation has a similar shrine. Men are not only killed in war; many are lost. It is a sad fact of war, Miss Finney. I am sorry to tell you this is all we could find."

I settled my account with the law firm and added a bonus to compensate for my tirade. I went back to Europe. Active searching finally gave way to passive hoping. In a few years, the pain had subsided. In a few decades, the memory demanded less of my time. My account never diminished through the years. It grew. My thoughts would find another gem from the moments I had had with John. I would take that gem, polish it to perfection, and set it in the proper place among the other jewels that were my recollections of the only man I had ever loved.

After several hours—or was it minutes—the maelstrom

of her memories subsided and she sat in limbo. She wondered what, if anything, was going to happen to her. At some time during the night, she remembered vocalizing some thoughts. It was the only time she had spoken: "I did it . . . I did what you asked me to do . . . the remainder of his life is mine . . . you promised . . . you promised. . . ."

She did not know whom she had addressed. She supposed she was hoping, wishing that the words would traverse space and fall on Mister Ives' ears. She felt he knew. How could he know?

She had, through the day, performed well. She had handled the God-fearing trepidation that had attacked her. She had subdued the attack of morals. None around her had sensed that the very suggestion of murder had been repugnant to her. She had kept her reaction veiled.

But Ives knew. She and Ives were kindred spirits, and she liked that. He did not care if she had great moral compunctions, as long as she submitted to his standards. That was all that mattered. All along he had been aware that Miss Finney had moral reservations about killing. All along he had known she would do his bidding.

With the act done, she found she liked it; she liked the sensation of murder. It occurred to her that murder might just be a universally satisfying evil. Of course, doing it to a nonentity like Baldwin had some modifying effect; he had deserved death.

Who can say that, other than God? God! The word came hard to her mind. She had been taught as a child that God was with her. In silent anger she questioned: "Where were you when my hands became twisted and useless?" There was no reply. "Where were you when my legs lost the muscles to hold me up?" There was no reply. "Where were you when my lungs gasped with unbearable pain?" There was no reply.

But Ives had replied. He had offered her something

that no religion, no God, no prophet could offer. Ives had offered life.

She sat, drained, wondering if she should nap or sit and wait. She could not nap. There was a dim glow, the light of dawn. It seeped into the room and she was shocked: She had sat awake the whole night. Nothing had happened. Why not? Why should it? Ives had not promised anything would happen if she killed. All he had said was that she would be granted more years of life. She had no way to prove Ives right or wrong. How would she know when she was supposed to die? How would she know she had lived past that time?

She must trust Ives. She trusted Ives as she had never trusted God. Ives. Trust Carlos Ives. Trust anyone but God.

The light crept into the room; she could start to see things now. She looked down at her cramped hands. They were twisted and gnarled. Ugly. Her legs were ugly, too. But she could not see them. They were covered with the shawl. Her face was uglier than anything. She had stopped looking into mirrors years before. The wrinkles had become so foul that she could not stand the sight. When she washed her face, her fingers touched the hideous flaps of skin and she was disgusted. But she had to look at her hands. They were always there in front of her. There were wrinkles in her hands, too. And brown splotches called liver spots. They looked like symptoms of leprosy. Her veins mounded up, pressing, trying to get out of the skin. The veins were a sickening blue. Her fingernails were cracked and ridged and jagged where they had broken. The knuckles were knobbed, swollen and twisted. She had to look at her hands; they were all she could see.

A beam of light came in through the window and landed on her pained hands. There was warmth. Of course there was warmth; the sun is warm. No, this was different. The warmth came from within. It was not heat from the sun. Dizziness invaded her head. She felt as if she would pass out. She fought to retain consciousness.

It happened slowly. Long minutes, possibly hours, passed.

But it was happening. It was in the joints first. The swelling began to diminish. Barely perceptibly at first, then with dramatic swiftness, the swelling lessened and, as it did, the pain began to subside. She was concentrating so intently on that phenomenon that she did not notice the skin begin to tighten, a few of the wrinkles begin to disappear. She began to believe what was happening and to shake with excited confusion. It was happening! Look at my hands. They are changing. "Oh, thank God!" The hands kept changing. The pain was passing. She could move her fingers. Shortly there was a change in her arm muscles; she could raise her arms with no pain of arthritis. "Oh, thank God!" There continued to be a heat inside her hands and arms. They were coming out of pain as a butterfly comes of its chrysalis. What joy she was experiencing! For some reason, for some unexplainable, beautiful reason, she was ascending from a valley of pain to a plateau of peace.

"Oh, thank God!" She stopped herself. Why thank God? Why thank anyone? She had done it herself. She had killed. That was the promise. "Kill and gain life!" Thank God, indeed. Thank no one. She had done it alone. She had shown the ability to do what was necessary. She had done it and . . . and LOOK!

She raised her arms high, her fingers straight, soft and lovely. Look, damn you. . . Look, all of you! I am well! She savored the moment and studied her hands. They had not become the caressable hands of a young woman, but they were not the ugly, claw-like appendages of a crippled old woman, either.

She experimented. She reached up and touched the buttons of her blouse. For the first time in six years, she was able to undo a button. Excited, her mind clamoring for things to try, she dropped her hands and took hold of the rims of the wheelchair. She folded her fingers carefully, tightened her grip and pushed. The wheelchair moved.

She could move herself! Eight years! Eight dependent years since she had been able to locomote herself. She spun the chair around. She rolled herself to the window and looked out. It was not yet full dawn. She was anxious to see the sun full in the sky. She wanted to see a bird land on the sill. "I can touch him today. Land, bird, and I will touch you with loving hands." She urged her rapture to fly out the window and find Carlos Ives; she wanted him to know of her exhilaration. Somehow he knew. She was sure that he knew.

Then came the inevitable. She cried, dropped her face down into her hands and cried.

5

The loud *th-waang* was followed by a deep *th-thump* as the arrow sank into the target made of a cotton bale.

Brook's tone was accusatory. "How . . . how can you do that?" The shivering in her body caused a tremble in her voice. She had not stopped shivering since Baldwin had been killed the night before.

Willa did not let the tone of Brook's voice get to her. She took out another arrow and placed it in the bow. She spoke as she went through the mechanics of aiming the arrow: "You must learn to handle adversity, dear Brook." She paused as she took a breath, pulled back on the bowstring and let fly. *Th-waang Th-thump.* She continued: "Some things just happen. There is nothing that can be done. What is past is . . . . " She dropped the speech and busied herself with another arrow.

The night before, with Baldwin lying dead on the basement floor, Brook had wished desperately that she could faint. But she had not fainted.

She could not even hope for the bliss of sleep; her mind pounded with an agony of guilt, her body shivered in continuous shock. The pounding and shivering were still there the next day.

During the night, Brook had stayed in her room, wrestling with all that had happened.

She had refused to help Willa dispose of the remains. The mere thought of touching Baldwin's corpse brought Brook to the verge of nausea. Willa had handled the job by herself. Baldwin was buried in the gardens where he had worked the night before.

Willa had insisted Brook come to the gardens. She had wanted Brook to know which section of the property must not be disturbed, at least until the body was decomposed enough to prevent identification.

Nausea had caught up with Brook and she had spent hours being sick. Willa had still insisted.

They had come into the garden on the west side of the house, the one with a dozen or more small plots of dirt that were in blossom at various times of the year. Willa had chosen the plot that had just bloomed and been reworked for new planting in a few weeks when the fertilizer had been assimilated.

They stood there, looking down at the freshly turned soil, and Willa said, "For the first time in his life, that pig is going to do something useful: He'll fertilize the plants."

"That is disgusting," Brook spit out. "You are the coldest person I have ever known." With a throaty laugh, Willa reached out and draped an arm over Brook's shoulder, pulling her close. For an instant, Brook appreciated the contact. It was a piece of security and physical warmth. Brook wondered if she could ever be warm again. She was wearing a sweater and light jacket, but she still could not stop shaking.

"You are silly," Willa chided. "Don't let that get to you."

Brook pulled away and challenged, "You act as if this were an everyday occurrence."

"Wrong," Willa came back. "I've never killed anyone. This is the first time."

Willa paused. Brook knew it was a purposeful pause, to give her time to dwell on the fact that she had killed a person before. Willa let few opportunities pass to remind her of that tragedy.

Willa repeated, "*My* first time. But I will not let it destroy me." Brook glared. Willa continued: "Baldwin was like an animal that must be destroyed. There is nothing more to it than that. We eliminated a blight on the human race and we used him to get ourselves some money." Willa paused and gave that some thought, then said, "I hope it will get us some money. Auntie might not give us the cash if she doesn't feel like it. We should have gotten the checks before we did the job."

Brook said, "I don't care about the money!"

Willa said angrily, "Who do you think you are? Just who in the hell do you think you are? We went through a lot for that, Miss Brook-Big-Shot. You sure better start thinking about that money. Without that money you get shipped back up to the state nut house. You want that?"

"No!" came automatically from Brook.

Willa stepped closer and raised her voice. "You want to go back up there and let those guards get their hands on you? You want that one to make you strip, then stick his gun inside you while you . . . ."

"STOP!" Brook burst into tears. "Please, stop."

Willa reached out to comfort Brook. She spoke softly: "I had to do that, Brook. You are acting like a fool. We must get the money. That is why we went through that mess. Listen, I was the one who had to drag his body out into the garden. I had to dig the hole, put him in and cover him up. His blood spilled out of his mouth onto my leg. His urine escaped onto my hands as I pulled him into the hole. Now, I did that. You hid in your room!"

Brook cried, "I'm sorry." She was truly sorry. Whenever Brook was reminded that the next phase of her life could easily be a return to the state institution, she was quick to feel sorry.

They had gone from Brook's room to the garden. Willa had brought along Brook's archery set in case they were to meet anyone coming onto the property.

The plot, the place where Baldwin was buried, was near the sliver of grass that had always been used for archery.

Th-waang Th-thump: Willa sent another arrow spearing into the cotton bale.

"Let's go," Brook pleaded.

"Why?" Willa asked, "We don't have anything to do until old Auntie decides to give us a call. She was nasty as hell last night: 'Don't bother me!' Big deal. She is some pain in the butt."

"Should I go up there?" Brook gestured towards the upstairs bedroom of their aunt.

"Nuts to her," Willa said as she loaded the bow again. "She owes us money and she can go jump in the lake until we get paid."

Brook sat on a bench. She did not want to walk on any dirt in the yard. Baldwin might be below. She said to Willa, "You are really a cold person, you know that?"

Willa said, "I like to think of myself as 'cool.'"

Th-waang Th-thump.

"No," Brook argued. "I really think you are cruel, too."

Willa shrugged.

Brook continued: "You have accepted the hospitality of Aunt Finney, yet you are willing to stand here and deride her."

Willa whipped around and shouted, "I killed for that old bitch! Don't lecture me!"

Defensively, Brook replied, "Well . . . I killed, too."

Willa grinned. After a moment, she said, "We are in this together, Brook. I'm only on edge because I'm afraid that Aunt Finney will still be sick as can be, and that she will not give us the money."

Brook nodded understanding. "That was a chance we had to take."

Willa shook her head, "We should have asked for the checks before."

"She wouldn't have given them."

"Probably not."

"We could have tried."

133

"We should have done it."

Willa looked up toward Miss Finney's bedroom and shrugged. "I'll bet we screwed up. She won't give us a damned thing."

Brook said, "But Ives claimed just the idea would make her feel better."

"Psychosomatic cure, is what Ives called it," Willa said. "He said religious sects he studied had records of total recovery from major illnesses. Shit! I hope she feels better."

Brook turned and looked up towards her aunt's quarters again and whispered, "Me, too. Please feel better, Auntie."

Two more arrows flew before Brook spoke again: "Willa . . . suppose someone comes looking for him?" She pointed to the garden plot.

Flippantly, Willa replied, "Now, who would come looking for him?" She gave a laugh.

Then there was a man's voice.

"Hey."

That was all, just a male voice saying: "Hey."

Willa looked at Brook. Brook wanted to run. Both women froze.

"I heard you talking," said the voice. "I'd like to say hello."

By now they could tell the direction of the sound. "At least," Brook thought, "it is not coming from Baldwin's plot."

A head came up over the wall.

Both Willa and Brook were more than startled; they were scared for an instant.

Then a pleasant face rose into view and a friendly voice said, "Hey. I'm your new neighbor."

The women waited several moments while their blood pressure returned to a manageable level.

The man, Raymond, looked at the two women and seemed satisfied just to stand and gawk.

Willa spoke. She seemed to have less hostility in her voice than Brook would have imagined: "You have a funny way of greeting new neighbors. Do you always climb walls to say hello?"

He laughed and said, "Actually, I haven't climbed the wall. I'm standing on a garden table. I've just moved in and, when I heard you talking, I figured we should get acquainted."

Brook was the one showing hostility: "You were listening to us?"

"Yeah," the man beamed, "I was wondering who you were looking for. You lose your dog or cat?"

Glances flew back and forth between Willa and Brook. Neither wanted to answer, but both knew one of them must. They spoke at the same time.

Willa said, "No," and Brook said, "Yes." Willa said it was a friend; Brook said it was their cat.

The man silenced them with a wave of his hand. "Losing a friend or a pet is a bad thing. Let's drop it. I don't really care. I just wanted to say hi. My name is Raymond Oxford Brown the Third."

Neither woman spoke.

Looking at Willa, he mocked, "And you are . . . don't tell me . . . you are Robin Hood with your trusty bow and arrow."

Willa smiled a tepid smile. She gave the impression that she was mildly charmed.

Brook surprised herself by saying, "We are not friendly people, Mister Brown. We stay to ourselves. We expect the same from others."

Willa scolded, "Brook!"

Increasing the sharpness in her voice, Brook said in Willa's direction, "We can do very well without prying neighbors." Then, turning back to the man, she ordered, "Kindly hop down from your perch, Mister Brown. You are violating our privacy."

The man waved surrender as he said, "Now that we

have gotten off to such a good start . . . maybe I'll be around later to borrow a cup of sugar!"

With a nastiness she had never used before, Brook said, "You will not be welcome, I promise you that!"

With unhappy resignation, Raymond moved to get out of sight as he said, "Well, good morning, anyway. You are named Brook. I'm sorry if I intruded, Brook." In Willa's direction he asked, "And you are . . . ?"

"Willa," she said, "Willa Hawk. I'm pleased to meet you. Please forgive my . . . ."

He disappeared from view.

Brook stormed over to Willa. Their personality roles had changed abruptly. Brook did not understand, but she continued: "Don't be nice to him, Willa. He'll start coming around and he'll ruin everything."

Willa quipped, "Don't be silly, Brook. He seems to be a very nice young man. The first I've seen in years."

Brook was furious. "How can you say that? You hate men! You have just seen him for a few seconds. What is going on?"

Willa said, "He just seemed like a nice guy."

Brook grabbed at her own hair and yelled, "Am I going crazy? What is going on?"

Willa came close and stroked Brook. "Now, calm down. We don't have anything to fear from that man. He seems like a nice person. It might be good for you to know a nice person for a change, Brook. I might arrange it."

Brook shook her head in total confusion. "We can't let him come around here. My God! We just killed a man. We have to make plans. We have to get our money . . . we have . . . we. . . ."

Willa slapped Brook. "Stop!"

Brook broke down and began a hard, wrenching cry. The hysteria that had gripped Brook lasted nearly ten minutes. In that time, Willa kept a protective arm around Brook's shoulders and walked her through the acre and a half of property surrounding the mansion.

Tensions eased and they were concluding their walk when there came a call from the kitchen: "Brook! Willa!"

The two women looked at each other. It was their aunt calling, but not from her bedroom. She was in the kitchen! They ran as fast as they could.

She sat in her wheelchair, right in the middle of the kitchen. There was a beaming grin on her face which neither girl had ever seen before.

"How did you . . . ?" It came from both of them at the same time.

They stopped and waited. The old lady had an expression of pride and accomplishment.

She was dressed in a different outfit. It was apparent she had dressed herself. Her presence in the kitchen showed she could wheel her own chair and operate the elevator.

"I feel very good," Miss Finney said.

Brook asked, as if unsure she was seeing reality, "How did you . . . ?"

The old lady said, "I do not really know, Brook. Something happened during the night. I guess it had to do with Ives and his promise. I guess killing that pig, Baldwin, gave me some life."

Brook did not hear the words. Her own thoughts had been jamming all other sounds. Brook stated, "Your clothing. You changed."

Miss Finney nodded. "That was quite a chore. But I managed. I think you will find somewhat of a mess in the bathroom. I scattered my other things and did not bother to pick them up. I hope you will understand. Bathing myself for the first time in years was quite a joy."

Willa, her voice even, said, "Don't worry about that, Auntie. We will take care of that. We are both dumbfounded that you have recovered."

"No more so than I, my dears. Now, let us have some breakfast coffee in the dining room in five minutes. We have some things to discuss. I will be waiting there."

The pair stood with jaws slack, watching Aunt Finney as she moved her own wheelchair. At the door, the old lady stopped and chided them: "Hurry, now. We have things . . . good things . . . to do. Hurry."

Like robots, Willa went to set up the coffee tray and Brook began preparing the coffeemaker. They were almost finished when Willa finally asked, "Are you surprised?"

Brook stood dazed and answered, "You bet I am. I can't believe it."

Willa said. "It sure is dramatic, but it is not surprising."

Brook said with disbelief, "How can you say that?"

"It's easy. You are looking at the results of a classical psychosomatic rejuvenation."

Brook queried, "You mean she's cured?"

"Nope," Willa said as she arranged the silverware on the trolly. "That would be possible only if her illnesses had been psychosomatic. Aunt Finney had crippling rheumatoid arthritis, which was diagnosed by medical experts. That cannot simply go away."

"Then, what?"

"Well," Willa walked to where Brook was standing so she could speak more softly, "our dear aunt got herself so hyped up on this mumbo jumbo from Carlos Ives that she convinced herself there is a cure. She thinks Baldwin's death has subtracted years from her age. Now, Ives never told her anything like that would happen. He just promised a longer life. But she worked the whole thing up in her mind and convinced herself that she is getting better."

"I don't believe that." Brook was brittle.

Willa smirked. "What do you believe? Ives set a spell and our aunt is growing younger?"

Brook was upset. "Don't make fun. This is serious."

Willa agreed. "You bet it is serious. We've got to get our money and get the hell out of here."

"Why?"

"Why?" Willa laughed. "I'll tell you why: She could die!"

Fear slapped onto Brook's face. She could not speak.

Willa continued, "Aunt Finney is a very sick old woman. She is not able to move her arms. Now, she gets something into that nutty head of hers and begins to think she can grow younger. That is not what Ives told her. She is making all that up in her head. Can you imagine what it is doing to her body?"

Brook demanded, "What do you mean?"

"Can you imagine what hormones are flowing, what glands are pumping, what organs are being taxed to their limit? That old gal has put herself on a chemical high that makes it possible for her to do anything. For a while. Then: *Crash!* She's got to come down. When she does, she will probably be dead."

"Oh, no! We can't let that happen."

Willa retorted, "It is not up to us. It has already happened. The only thing we can do is get our money and get the hell out of here."

"We can't leave her," Brook complained.

Willa said with sarcasm, "We don't have to worry about that, dear Brook. Nature will do it for us. She is as good as dead. It won't take long."

The two stood looking at each other, the import of the situation sinking in on each.

Brook grabbed at the coffee pot and headed out of the kitchen. Over her shoulder she said to Willa, "I don't believe you."

Willa gave a light laugh and went to get the coffee trolly.

In the dining room, Miss Finney greeted them with a cheer that had not come from the old lady in several decades. There was a radiance emanating from Miss Finney. Brook could not refrain from letting out a cry.

Miss Finney scolded her. "Now, dear child, do not be

139

silly. I would rather you found some real happiness in my situation. This is the greatest thing that has ever happened. Do you realize that what you girls have done has given me a new lease on life? I have hope! I can face living, I have hope for the future."

With a childlike manner she instructed, "Now, first the coffee. We must all get ourselves settled. This is a momentous event."

Brook poured, Willa passed the cups, they all settled down.

Miss Finney withdrew slips of paper from a skirt pocket and waved them playfully in the air. She announced, "I have . . . for you . . . your rewards."

The two girls acted embarrassed. The old lady leaned forward and handed a check to each.

Brook could not look at hers. Willa did look and said, "There is some mistake, Auntie."

"Oh?"

Now Brook looked at her own check and agreed with Willa: "Oh, yes, Auntie, a great mistake."

Willa said, "The checks are for ten thousand. We agreed on five thousand. We must give these back to you."

Miss Finney waved a cautioning hand. "Not at all, my dears. You are justly rewarded for a valiant effort. Such payment is so small, so insignificant compared with what you have given me."

Brook struggled to hide the guilt she felt. If what Willa said was correct, they were really cheating the old lady.

"I feel awful," Brook admitted.

Willa sensed what might follow. "Brook feels awful that we must ask you for the money at all, dear Auntie. It is just that we must provide for our own futures."

Miss Finney grinned broadly. "I agree completely. I am quite anxious to see that each of you has a fine future. I doubled my contributions to you because I want to ensure that we get moving rapidly. There is no time to lose."

Brook was not sure she had heard the words correctly. She looked at Willa and found no comfort there; Willa was looking quite complacently at Aunt Finney.

"I don't understand," Brook said.

"Simple, my dear." The old lady spoke evenly and calmly. "We will be about our duties. We must plan. We must execute. We will do what must be done. We must continue."

Brook tipped over her cup of coffee as she jumped up, shouting, "Oh, no! No more!"

Willa ordered Brook to sit. "Be quiet. Listen to Auntie."

Brook was shaking. "No! No more!"

Aunt Finney was intense. "Do not press your luck, Brook. Remember, you owe me something. And yet, I am willing to give you more money . . . a lot of money . . . *Tonight! Do . . . you . . . hear . . . me? Tonight!*"

Brook ran from the room. They heard her running up the stairs.

Miss Finney looked at Willa and ordered, "Go to her. Make her see sense. We must move tonight. The supply of souls is inexhaustible. They are out there . . . waiting. Go to her!"

Willa rose easily and, as she moved to leave, she replied, "Of course, Aunt Finney. The supply is inexhaustible."

As an afterthought, the old lady stopped Willa with a gesture and asked, "Did I hear you talking with someone out in the yard?"

Willa nodded, smiled and replied, "He is our new neighbor. He bought the de Montespan property. His name is Raymond."

The old lady frowned. "I do not like that."

Willa was still smiling. "I think he is nice. You should meet him."

Violently, Miss Finney said, "No! We can have no strangers around here. Not at this time. I will not have it.

Stay away from him."

"That might be difficult," Willa argued. "He seems to be a friendly type."

Coldly, her aunt hissed, "We need no friends. Go and get Brook under control. We must have another victim . . . tonight!"

Brook stood in the dank hallway and was scared.

A thing as big as a small dog skittered across the floor near her feet. She knew it was a rat.

The malignant odor was still there, just as it had been when she had first brought her aunt to the offices of Carlos Ives. But this time he had told her to wait in the hall, giving her a feeble excuse. She was furious with all of them: her Aunt Finney, Mister Ives, and, most of all, Willa.

Willa had come up and forced her way into Brook's bedroom. Brook had wanted and needed to be alone. The murder of Baldwin had been hard on her, but she felt she could recover. Murder *should* be hard on a person. What confused her was that she was not running out of the house, escaping, getting away from this madness.

Madness! That was it: the whole thing was mad. Especially, Brook thought, especially Willa. Willa had taken the whole incident casually. Baldwin had been a scum, but he had not deserved to die. Brook could think of no valid reason for anyone to die. And with Baldwin, Brook had been the most abused, the most offended. Yet, as hard as she tried to understand, she could not excuse murder.

Willa had forced her way into the room and begun to cajole Brook.

"Please, you have to help, Aunt Finney needs our help."

Brook's voice rose to nearly a scream: "Are you crazy?

We cannot kill!"

Nastily, Willa reminded Brook, "*I* have never been in an institution." She let that comment cut into Brook for a moment before saying, "We do not have to kill. I have it worked out."

"I will not listen," Brook declared and flung herself onto her bed.

Willa came over and sat down, talking softly. "It has been difficult for you, Brook. But this can be the end of it all. Look, the old lady thinks she is being affected by Ives' mystical ritual and she thinks she is going to get better. She has promised us more money."

Brook cried, "I don't care about the money."

Willa argued, "Money will buy freedom. For both of us."

Brook had heard the arguments. She had been tricked and would not go along with any of the foolishness again. The battle between the two women went on for nearly twenty minutes before Willa, seething with rage, stormed out of Brook's room.

Within an hour, Brook had been summoned by Miss Finney.

Frigid in her tone, Miss Finney ordered, "Brook, you must drive me to Carlos Ives' office. Right now."

Willa did not drive and the old lady refused to use taxicabs. She was willing to use a hired coach from the Quarter, but Clifford was engaged elsewhere. Brook was to drive, and that was all there was to it. Brook obeyed the commands; that was what she did best. She did not like battling anyone and would rather follow orders. Willa waited in the car. Miss Finney wheeled herself into Ives' suite.

Brook stood in the dirty, fetid gloom of the hallway outside the offices.

They had left her alone for ten or twelve minutes. She was frightened and pensive.

In her isolation, she had made a decision: The check

would go back to her aunt and Brook would leave the mansion.

It was a brave decision for a woman with no money and no right to leave. The problems would be ironed out as they arose. She had to leave.

And leave Willa!

Willa presented a dilemma for Brook: friendship balanced against fear.

Willa's offer of friendship was welcome. Brook had had no friend from her own age group since childhood. Willa professed concern, demonstrated affection and offered assistance. A friend.

But fear tipped the scales the other way. There was sexual fear because Willa frequently—too frequently—would touch or hug or make some kind of contact. It was not an overriding fear; Brook thought she might be hypersensitive to such actions. Willa was probably simply, innocently affectionate.

The overriding fear was of Willa's abiding coldness. She could evaluate situations with a logic that transcended all emotion. Brook did not like unemotional decisions; they were lacking the human quality.

Stripping away emotions was what Willa did best, and it alarmed Brook.

Willa's attitude was apparently that there was no reason to do what their Aunt Finney asked; they could stage a killing, they could act out a farce and collect another five or ten thousand dollars. That simple compromise would give the two women substantial financial resources for the future. No matter what happened to their aunt, they could control their own lives.

What had happened with Baldwin had been a fluke: the bullets had chambered accidentally, there had been no intention really to kill. Brook knew that was a lie, but she was willing to believe it so she would not have to face the truth: Willa had diabolically planned to kill Baldwin. It would be best to leave.

Another rat skittered down the hall, and Brook felt an urge to run into Ives' offices. Her stomach churned with anxiety. There was too much going on. The hand that touched her was freezing cold. The chill went through her clothing and iced her skin.

"Come," was the command. Ives' hand clamped onto Brook's shoulder and steered her into the office.

She was relieved to be away from the dark hall and the rats, but she was afraid of being under Ives' control. He still personified evil to Brook.

He hustled her through the reception room, which was empty. Partway down the hall, he angled her through a doorway and into a sparsely furnished office.

He was short, much shorter than Brook, but he moved her with strong hands.

The door slammed and he spun her around to face him.

She resisted the urge to smile at his size. Resistance was made easier by the demonic look in his eyes. Ives was furious.

His voice squeaked: "What the hell do you mean? Who the hell are you to screw up? What am I going to do about you?"

He did not, was not, demanding answers. He was letting off steam.

The release did not soothe his anger. "You stupid bitch. I've got an old lady in there that thinks she is going to become the medical wonder of the twentieth century and you are playing Mary Poppins. Who the hell do you think you are?"

Brook could not answer. She had never received such an oral lashing.

Ives spit out: "We are giving that old lady something few people in this life are given and you deem it your moral duty to screw it up."

Brook was silent.

Ives exclaimed, "Well, I will not have it! Do you understand? I will not tolerate your actions."

Brook cried, "I can't be a party to killing."

"You are not asked to, you fool. Do not overemphasize your part in this. You are needed for mechanical expediencies. Do I make myself perfectly clear?"

Brook shook her head.

Ives, flustered with rancor, elevated his squeaky voice to a shout: "You will obey me! You will do what you are told!"

Her chin quivering with hurt, she cried, "I can't and I won't. Not for you . . . not for her . . . not for money . . . ."

He hit her.

It was a slap which connected with her cheek just below the eye. Flickers of white light danced in her vision.

Then he used his other hand and caught her full on the other cheek. There was a ringing in her ear.

He pulled back to swing again and she cowered, ducking back and away from him.

He jumped forward and grabbed her.

A thought sparked in her mind: she could probably lift the runt off the floor and toss him over the desk.

His aggressiveness did not permit such thoughts to become actions. She continued to withdraw from his wrath.

"You slut. You defecation. You worthless piece of garbage. How dare you hinder me!"

He was swinging as if to punctuate each vindictive accusation, but he was distraught and most of the blows missed. Finally, she had been backed into a corner, against a filing cabinet. He stood fuming at her. The green hue glowed in his eyes. He stopped attacking, raised a hand and pointed as if aiming the finger of death.

A chill as cold as ice gripped her. He said, "I will waste no time with you. Coercion is not my usual approach, but

146

this is an emergency."

She felt an unexplainable urge to listen to him. Something focused her attention as he said, "You have taken part in the crime of murder. Once before in your life you committed murder. You will do as I say or you will be taken to the police. That is that." He heaved a deep breath and stepped back.

She had heard each word as if it had been amplified. She did not doubt he would carry out his threat. She nodded assent as he demanded compliance.

Then he said in a placid voice, "I am sorry to threaten you. It is not our style. Let us not carry anger with us. I merely demand that you do as you are told." She nodded again. "Come." He led her down the hallway to his seance room.

As he closed the door, Miss Finney said, "I am sorry to have subjected you to this, Brook, but haste is essential." Brook stood somnolently, as if she had been drugged. Her aunt demanded: "Answer me, child!"

Vacantly, Brook replied, "Yes, Auntie. We must hurry."

The old lady turned to Ives and accused, "You've drugged her!"

Ives shook his head with a temperate grin. "She is merely contrite."

Brook said, "I'm sorry, Auntie. I am sorry."

Miss Finney was angry. "Mister Ives, I do not like what I see. What have you done to my niece?"

"Miss Finney," Ives said stiffly, "I have done nothing to your lovely niece." He moved to Brook and said, "Brook, tell her."

Brook's voice started to recover some vigor, but she was still speaking softly. "I have caused unnecessary problems. I promise to behave, Auntie."

"Look here, Mister Ives," Miss Finney charged, "I expect you to help me in all ways possible, but I do not approve of your destroying my niece." Then, turning to

Brook, she asked, "What has he done to you, my dear?"

Brook smiled lightly, showing the first emotion she had mustered since joining Miss Finney in the room. "I am truly sorry, Aunt Finney. I have had a bad time with what happened last night."

The old lady cast that aside with a quick nod, but then she waved her hand in the air and nearly shouted, "But look what good has come of it. Please, dear Brook, weigh the one against the other. Use some judgement. I am partially well. I can move my hand without the horrible pain I used to have. Weigh that against the inane existence of that worthless gardener who meant nothing to anyone. Compare the two and you can see what a good thing it has been."

Brook opened her mouth to contradict her aunt, but she flicked a glance toward Carlos Ives and knew she had to comply with his demands. She had no choice. She would take part in a fictional killing, but she would make sure nothing went wrong this time. She would control the weapon.

There was a barely audible rap at the door. Ives opened it and Willa stood there, taking in the scene.

She went to Brook, saying, "Thank you, Brook. I am pleased. I am sure Auntie will show how pleased she is."

Brook voiced confusion. "Hey, wait a minute. How could you know I agreed to do it? You have been down in the car."

Willa smiled as she looked towards Carlos Ives. "There never was any doubt that Mister Ives would make you see the error of your ways. He is such a totally convincing person. He has great powers."

Miss Finney lifted her arm again and moved it back and forth to bear witness to Ives' powers.

Ives said, "There has been too much tension and distraction over the 'unfortunate accident' last night."

He went to Brook and, pushing his face close to hers, he said, "You do what your aunt demands. She is a good woman, a woman destined for great things."

Meekly, she nodded submission. Ives smiled. "You, too, might be destined for things you could not imagine."

The question that started to form on her lips was pushed aside by Willa, who bustled in and took charge of her aunt's wheelchair.

The aunt waved her away, saying, "Please, Willa, I am capable of handling this myself. We are off."

Brook wanted to ask Ives the question, but there was no opportunity. The trio moved out of the office and, as Ives was closing the door, he flashed a huge smile and a knowing wink at Brook.

Brook fought against the impulse to respond. She lost the fight and sent back a toothful smile and a friendly nod.

Willa caught the interchange and snidely asked, "Are you taken with him, Brook? Or do you have something cooking?"

The image of an amorous liaison with Ives was too comical to conjure up without bursting into laughter. Willa and Brook roared.

Their aunt did not understand the joke, but she joined in the levity. It was nice to feel better. In time she might feel perfect.

They left Ives' offices in good humor.

6

The automobile was a 1936 Lincoln Brougham, a 12-cylinder luxury vehicle, one of the ten ever made. Miss Finney had purchased the car new when it was offered. If she wished to sell it in the current market, she could realize twenty times the original purchase price.

But the old lady did not buy things for speculation. She had bought the car because it was posh and mechanically perfect. Constant care from the nearby Ford-Lincoln dealer had kept the auto pristine and sound.

There was one drawback: The car was designed for a family with a chauffeur. The open front seat of the Brougham was magnificent for a liveried driver with a black cap. When Willa had let the chauffeur go, along with the rest of the mansion's staff, Brook had become responsible for errands.

She handled the vehicle well and was moving it through the early evening traffic with no problems.

Earlier, when they had returned from the visit to Ives' offices, Miss Finney had refused anything more than a cup of tea. Brook could not determine in her own mind what had been said by Ives that had effected a mental change.

There had been ominous threats that she knew were real. But that really could not have changed her mind; she had been adamant in her plan to leave. She tried to evaluate his violence and his vicious oral attack, but she could not concentrate. She was glad she had changed.

She saw that they were right about Baldwin. He was dead and nothing would change that. They were right that he had been a worthless slug, and that the world was a better place for his departure. Willa and Ives were right, she thought, when they said it would be silly to pass up substantial sums of money just because of the accident with Baldwin.

The incident with Baldwin was now "the accident" in Brook's mind, yet she did not know why she had stopped questioning that the event was accidental.

A plan had been struck by Miss Finney: Her nieces would go out and find another reprobate and bring him back to the mansion.

With an evil gleam in her eyes, Miss Finney had said, "And I will kill him."

"She looked like a witch." Willa was speaking.

Brook snapped her attention away from her driving and looked across the front seat at Willa.

Willa looked over and said, "Well, she did. Dammit, Brook, the old lady could have been standing over a bubbling cauldron when she said: 'And I will kill him!'"

They burst into laughter.

Willa hunched over and pulled her lips back, exposing her teeth and gums, as she bent her fingers like claws and rasped out, "Bubble . . . bubble . . . pot's so tinny. Come and serve our Auntie Finney. Heh . . . heh . . . heh!"

Brook laughed so hard, she was afraid she would lose control of the car. "Stop it," she yelled, "You'll get us killed."

They were moving west on Poydras Street. They had left the French Quarter and cut across on Rampart to Poydras. They had passed the Superdome a few minutes before. They kept driving, looking for a place where vagrants were likely to congregate.

Though she was reluctant to admit it, Brook was glad the tensions and angers had been put aside between Willa and her. There was no reason for them to be antago-

151

nistic. Aside from their aunt, they were the only living descendants of the Finney line. It would be a fearful loss if they forfeited their friendship.

They had gone over the scheme ad infinitum. Finally, they had agreed to stop discussing it. One thing was certain: Brook was to handle the gun. There would be no slipups with blanks and real bullets. They would let their aunt think anything she wanted; they would let her enjoy another mental victory over physical illness.

But this was to be the last of the playacting.

It was dangerous, because they were bringing a stranger, an itinerant, disreputable stranger, into the mansion. They were also contributing to Miss Finney's delusion that she was being cured or made younger. Willa had even agreed there was immorality in letting their aunt fall prey to such self-deception.

So, they would take the next check and then it would be up to Miss Finney. If she agreed to stop the nonsense, they would stay for a time, at least long enough for her to find some caretakers for the property and some nurses to see to the old lady's needs. If she did not agree to stop the foolishness, they would quietly slip out of the mansion one night and leave New Orleans. They would go to some big city where there were lights, life and good times. Brook especially wanted some good clean fun. Willa said she agreed with the plan.

Willa startled Brook by shouting and pointing off to the left: "There! Look!"

They had driven quite a distance after they had passed the Superdome. Brook did not really know where they were. But she could see what Willa was excited about. Across a vacant city block was a collection of railway cars. It was a railway yard. Tradition told her bums always circulated around railway yards. She made several wrong turns before she got where she wanted to go. Once there, she knew it was right. There was a section of abandoned boxcars at one end. The rest of the street advertised that

152

this was the place.

There were two storefront church/missions, a Salvation Army building, a Goodwill factory-store and an assortment of cheap wine and liquor stores.

"This place is IT!" said Willa. She laughed gleefully and poked Brook in the ribs.

Brook eased the car to a halt and leaned forward on the steering wheel as she turned her head and looked at Willa. After studying her for a moment, Brook said, "I have never seen you this way. You are joking and having fun. . . . What's come over you?"

Willa reached out and touched Brook's shoulder. "I have been really uptight about the way you have been acting. I was mad as hell at you about the way you were trying to screw everything up. Now that pressure is off and I am enjoying being with you. You are kin, you know.

Brook nodded, reached up and touched Willa's hand as she said, "We'll make it, cousin. We'll make it together."

Willa snapped them out of the mood jokingly: "Let's go shopping."

Brook dropped the car into gear and moved slowly along the street. She realized Willa's hand was still on her shoulder, but it did not seem threatening.

Both women searched the darkness.

"Stop," came softly from Willa. Brook eased her foot onto the brake. "Over there." She pointed across the street where there was a row of abandoned stores. Some of the windows were broken, some were boarded up. The doorway was blocked by heavy mesh screening. As Brook's eyes adjusted from the glare of the headlights, she could see an alley between two of the buildings. A man was sitting on a garbage can. He seemed to be smoking.

Willa whispered, "There's Mister Wonderful."

Brook started a deep laughing that she could barely get under control.

With a wave of her hand, Willa said, "Go up the street and turn around. Then come back down and stop by him."

Brook followed Willa's directions. As she eased to the curb, she could see the bum look around in panic. Brook guessed he was fearful of the police. She tapped the horn.

The man had had a rough life. His face was scarred, his clothing was thin and tattered. He emitted a halo of dissipation. He stood weaving, probably drunk.

Willa looked at Brook and gave a smile that conveyed both humor and repulsion. She shrugged her shoulders. "Here goes nothing!"

She opened her door.

The bum moved his head back slightly, as if to focus his eyes on Willa, standing there before him.

"You wanna see me, lady?"

Willa completed a silent inventory and decided he was a fitting candidate.

She opened the back door of the car. "Yes! Get in!"

The man challenged her: "Just like that?" His weaving continued.

With contempt, Willa ordered, "Just like that."

He seemed to pull his bent body a little upright as he balked. "Wha'd'ya mean?"

Sucking in a deep breath and glancing with impatience back at Brook, Willa said, "I have something for you. I've an offer to make."

A simpleton's grin burst onto his face and he said, "Well, if it's a drink yer offerin', yer on." He let the top part of his body lean forward and he began a controlled fall into the back of the automobile. Somehow he managed to keep getting one foot in front of him just in time to stop a fall. With a clumsy lunge, he landed on the back seat. Willa jumped in behind him and called to Brook, "Drive!"

The bum demanded, "Hey, where's the drink?"

Willa shoved her back against her side of the car as she desperately tried to put distance between the man and her.

He questioned again: "C'mon. Where's the drink?"

Willa said, "I can offer you all you want to drink, sir. I will also give you a hundred dollars. Are you interested?"

A flash of distrust flickered on his face. "Are you offerin' me a job, lady?"

She beamed a friendly, "Yes."

He dove for the door. "Goodbye!"

She had to move quickly to get his hand off the door. He was ready to dive out, even though Brook was doing better than twenty miles an hour.

Willa struggled with the man, imploring him, "Wait, listen to me, dammit!"

His body had been so abused that he slumped back in the seat puffing, as if he had just run a mile. "Take it easy on me, lady. I ain't well. That's why I can't work. You know . . . . "

She nodded with contrived understanding. She said, "This . . . job . . . is not really hard work."

"Huh?"

"Well, it would only take you about an hour."

"I don't get it."

"It might take even less. And I'll give you a hundred dollars."

"What do I gotta do?"

Willa did not answer. She sat there with a sheepish grin on her face. After a moment, he began to realize the implications of her words and smile. He nodded his head in a knowing manner. "Aw, I get it."

Willa asked, "Do you?"

He reached up and wiped at the stubble of beard on his face. Some dried spittle broke loose as he did. He said, "Now I get the idea."

She did nothing. After a couple of seconds, he said, "It

may take me more'n an hour, lady. I'm kinda outta practice." He gave a laugh that threw off an odor of garlic.

Willa asked, "Do we have a deal?"

He squirmed a bit to find a comfortable position on the seat. With an exaggerated smugness, he said, "Holt is my name." He reached out and laid his hand on Willa's knee.

She figured she could take that; it would only be for a few minutes. Then his hand began to move. She first thought it was heading up under her skirt, but he moved to take hold of her hand. That would be even easier than the knee.

He did not pause. He gave a slight tug on her hand. He was not strong, but he had caught her slightly off balance. She found her hand nestled in his lap. He was forcing her to move back and forth. She even considered putting up with that until she realized there was a dampness to the front of his trousers. Then she realized there was a strong odor of urine in the car. The man had wet his pants.

"Oh, shit," she said out loud.

"Hey," the man quipped, "I kinda like dirty talk, too. You go for that, huh?"

She yanked her hand away and pushed him with the other hand. "No offense, mister, but we're going to wait until we get home. Now, you keep your distance."

Willa picked up the microphone that connected with the driver's section of the car and cried into it, "Brook, pleeeeeze! Get us home! Quick!"

Brook looked into the rear view mirror and nodded her sympathetic understanding.

She leaned on the accelerator and the car sped toward the mansion.

In the parlor, Miss Finney chatted with the drunk as if they were at a church social.

At the far end of the room, Brook and Willa stalled as they prepared him a drink. Miss Finney had insisted they pour him a glass of port.

Willa had kept clowning. She had convinced Brook this was going to be fun, a lark.

"Don't give him so much," Willa jokingly scolded as Brook poured the port into a glass. "He'll wet his pants again."

Brook shuddered. "Oh, isn't that awful. I saw the stain on his trousers when we came into the house. He is a slob."

"Uggh!" Willa made a face. "I touched that thing. Oh, don't remind me."

"Willa, please promise you won't leave me alone with him too long, will you? Please? Promise?"

Willa folded a sisterly arm around Brook's shoulders and squeezed lightly. "Don't you worry. You get him into Baldwin's room, and we will be right behind you. As soon as you see us, you get off the shot and I'll whip Aunt Finney away. She'll think you did the killing and we'll get another check."

"He'll go for it, Willa, don't you think?"

Willa gave a confident nod. "I am sure. I know his type. He needs money to buy his wine. He is probably right, you know, he probably could not perform if you wanted him to . . . sexually, I mean."

Brook's look of disdain said what she was thinking. She made a vulgar noise with her mouth.

Miss Finney called, "Come girls, where is Mister Holt's glass of port?"

The two women went to the sitting room where Miss Finney sat with Holt. He looked uncomfortable; he obviously felt conspicuous.

Willa urged him, "Drink up, Mister Holt."

He tried to act suave but did not pull it off: "I'm hurrying. But something tells me I'm gonna need my drink . . . and maybe more."

The three women watched. It did not occur to him that they did not join him. He finished off the port and smacked his lips. "Ah, now . . . that tastes like . . . more!"

Brook took his glass, went to the small wet bar at the far end of the room and began pouring. Willa was beside her saying, "Let's get going."

Brook nodded, tensely. "I'm ready."

"The gun?" Willa asked.

Brook patted a patch pocket on her skirt. "Right here. Loaded with blanks."

The pouring was done. As they crossed the room, Willa whispered, "Good luck."

Brook whispered her reply: "Just get there . . . fast!"

Brook walked to where Holt was sitting. Standing over him, she said: "Follow me, Mister Holt. I will carry your drink."

Brook turned and moved gracefully toward the door. Holt gave a confused glance at Miss Finney and Willa, then moved obediently in Brook's wake.

When he came out of the parlor, Brook was already at the far end of the hall, ready to exit the mansion. She called, "Come, Mister Holt."

Like an eager-to-please puppy, he hurried toward her.

They were standing outside, looking at the night, before he spoke. Holt asked, "When do I get my hundred?"

Brook smiled. "My cousin was right."

"Huh?"

"You are only interested in the money. You will do anything for money."

"Hey, babe, don't get me wrong." Holt moved closer to her, she took a step back. "Don't get me wrong at all: I like dames like you. I'm ready."

Brook walked away, forcing him to follow her across the lawn area towards the servant quarters at the back of the property. She talked as they walked. He had to quicken his pace to keep up. "There has been some misrepresentation," she said.

He grunted another: "Huh?"

Brook stopped and shoved the glass of port at him. He took it and drank. When he was through, he tossed the glass away. It shattered on the concrete sidewalk.

Brook was furious. She shouted, "You animal! That was good lead crystal!"

A bit sheepishly, Holt said, "Gee, I'm sorry. I'm used to drinkin' outta paper cups. You know."

Exasperated, Brook spun away and walked. "Come!"

He followed. They entered Baldwin's former room and she left the door open.

Her stomach turned flip-flops as she looked around the room; the sight inspired graphic, gory memories.

Holt walked in and looked around. He observed, "Kinda nice. This where we gonna get it off?"

Brook replied with impatience, "That's what I was telling you: We are not going to 'get it off' anywhere."

"Hey, I came here for a hundred!"

Brook glared at him as she announced, "You are going to get two hundred!"

"Two?"

"Yes," Brook explained, "but you will have to play a little game with us."

"Game?"

Faking concern, Brook said, "You see, Mister Holt, my aunt has a problem up here." She pointed to her head. "She likes to see people . . . well . . . she likes to see people killed."

Panicked, Holt looked at the door. He was ready to bolt.

Realizing she had not handled it well, Brook forced herself to go to him, calm him, and stop him from fleeing. She came close enough so that she could reach out and cup his face in her hands. It seemed as if she might kiss him.

But she continued talking, "I am sorry, Mister Holt, I

put that badly. What I meant was, she likes to *think* she sees people killed. We do this frequently for her."

Holt had calmed. He asked, "You mean she gets off that way?"

Brook shook her head. "I do not know if it is sexual or not, Mister Holt. I only know it gives her pleasure and she will pay you two hundred dollars to take part. Will you?"

His breath, as he spoke, carried an odor of cheap wine. "I'm glad about the two hundred. But I was kinda planning to have some fun with your cousin. You, too, if you like. But I really need a piece of ass."

Brook was angry. She began to hate this person whom she knew nothing about.

"We will see about that, Mister Holt." She played with his ear lobes. "Will you go along with my aunt?"

He asked how they would playact.

She took out the gun and handed it to him. "This is the weapon. I will act as if I am shooting you. You fall down and play dead. My cousin then wheels Auntie away and that's all there is to it."

He said, "That sounds simple to me. How about a fuck after?"

She probably could have handled the vulgarity, but she became violently angry when he leaned forward and tried to kiss her. She shoved clear of him.

"Two hundred dollars!" she shouted.

He stopped, trying to get himself under control. He was breathing deeply. "Shit, I got the hots for you. I think I'd do it for nothin' if you'd get into that sack with me right now. How about it?"

She was struggling to control her anger and beginning to wonder if they would be able to get rid of him when the charade was over.

"I will talk to my cousin about it," she said sweetly.

Placated at least for a moment, Holt looked down at the revolver in his hand. He opened the cylinder and popped out the bullets.

"They're blanks, all right. You can shoot me all day with this." He handed the gun back to her.

With the situation somewhat back under control, Brook began setting the scene. She told Holt where to stand, then she positioned herself beside the bed. She was less than five feet from him. He made a mock move at her and she tried to keep him in good humor by jabbing the gun at him and shouting, "Bang, bang!"

He leered at her, saying, "I'll 'bang bang' you, lady."

She smiled enough to let him think he had been cute. To herself she thought, "Maybe it would be a good idea to use real bullets."

Looking past Holt, she could see her aunt and Willa coming toward the bedroom. They stopped a few feet from the door.

Holt sensed their arrival. He turned around and looked at the old lady. Turning back to Brook, Holt gave a wink and yanked at his shirt. He exposed his hairy chest and said, "Okay, lady, go ahead and shoot. I got it comin'."

He moved closer to Brook as she took the gun out of her skirt. She pointed it where she thought his heart would be. He kept coming. He blocked out her view of Miss Finney and Willa as he stood about two feet away.

He whispered, "Hold it!"

She wanted to look around him to see if Willa was ready for her to begin. She couldn't move enough to see behind him. She was angry with Holt for delaying. She said, "Stop it!"

An ugly grin was on his face as he pleaded, "Hey, really. You gotta stop. You gotta give me a break."

She was flustered. "Don't be silly."

He said, "I ain't kiddin'! I gotta take a leak. Real bad."

She pulled the trigger. The noise was overpowering, but still she heard: *Th-waang th-thump.* Holt lurched backward for an instant and faked the recoil of being hit by a bullet. Then, in the next part of a second, the upper part of his body snapped forward. An invisible hand seemed to grab at his face, twisting it into a grotesque shape. A small stream of blood trickled out of the corner of his mouth. His tongue suddenly pushed out between his teeth and emitted a large blob of foamy red liquid.

He fell forward, his hands searching for support from Brook. Some of the bloody spittle hit her face as she tried to jump back. His hands reached her, clasped her arms, and pulled her to him. She did not know what was happening. Everything was going wrong.

He had not made a sound. There was only a gurgle as he fell into her. His head bounced on her chest and slid down the front of her skirt. His mouth left red smears on the contours of her body. She looked down. It was a full second before she screamed. An arrow was imbedded deeply in Holt's back. Brook looked up, startled into silence. Just outside the door, Willa stood holding Brook's bow. Their aunt was reaching out, touching the bottom of the bowstring.

Willa looked at the form of Holt crumpled on the ground and said, "We will bury him tonight."

Dazed, losing all sense of reality, Brook dropped the gun to the floor and ran wildly out the door, shoving Willa out of the way.

Brook remembered collapsing on her bed before she passed out. She knew there had been no attempt to sort out events: their scope was overwhelming. She did not want to handle any overwhelming problems. She did not want to handle any problems at all.

She wanted the peace of oblivion.

7

Her hand reached out, tentative, cautious, aware. Miss Finney was testing. She had sat in her wheelchair for countless hours—she did not care how long. Anticipation had her on an emotional rollercoaster. How many times had she stated that night: "That's two. They are mine!"? She had lost track.

Ives swore the cure was real, and that her body would actually shed the years and their accompanying infirmities. Now, in the dark of night, she was demanding her payment. She sent her commands out into the night, hoping they would reach him, and that he would not fail her. She was desperately hoping the killings were worthwhile.

But nothing had happened.

Willa had made sure her aunt was safely in her room. Then the niece had gone to dispose of the body. Funny. The thought of a corpse on the mansion grounds did not matter. Nothing mattered. Only the promise of Carlos Ives mattered. She slid her hand down under the coverlet which lay on her legs. She felt her thighs. They seemed stouter, but that could be her imagination. It could be the familiar arthritic swelling. In the past eight or ten years, her thighs had shrunk so that it was actually possible to see the outline of a bone in the upper part of her leg. She could also see the curve of a hip socket. It was all disgusting to her. It was no better when the whims of her illness dictated that she retain water; the swelling was as repulsive as the shrinking.

Her knees were different; she could tell by touch

whether they were encased in excess fluids or fleshing out.

She explored a kneecap. Quickly she yanked at her dress. She pulled it above her knees with both hands. Hope. More than hope, now. Something was different. She tossed off the blanket, leaned forward, and let her hands slide down the calf of each leg. The ankles were trim. They were not tender to the touch. A cry slipped out between her lips. She was torn between turning on the light and enjoying the sensation of touching her legs. To the touch, they were better. The pain had slipped off into the night; the size was normal. But turning the light on may shatter the illusion. She did not want to throw away the moments of ecstasy she was experiencing.

"Oh, Carlos Ives. Is it really happening?" She scolded herself: suppose the girls heard her? Talking to herself. Like an old hag. But that was changing, too. She could feel a metamorphosis of her mentality. She was not thinking old. She was not feeling sorry for herself. Something was happening! Her hands left her legs and, without command, came up to the armrests of her wheelchair.

The strength in her arms now seemed even stronger. She took hold of the chrome tube and lifted. Her body rose and she leaned forward, forcing her weight onto her legs. They held. She gave a final push and she was vertical: standing on her own legs. She had not stood in more than ten years. She stepped. The legs held her. She was moving. Another step. It worked!

She cried out loud, "Carlos Ives, I could love you!" She felt no shame now. She did not care if Brook or Willa heard. She wanted the world to hear.

Seven steps took her to the open window. She leaned out, her hands resting on the sill. "Hear me, world! I am back!" She laughed. There had never been a laugh like that in the Finney mansion. People who heard it smiled; it was a perfect expression of joy. People in the French Quarter liked to hear joyful sounds.

Miss Finney's explosion of happiness drifted out into the New Orleans night. None could guess what had inspired such a sound.

The sound that came from Brook's room slightly after dawn was a very different sound, a sound which might have come from the dead. Those who heard it thought of calling the police, but they were few, and they felt better not interfering in other people's business. Brook's scream was cut off by her Aunt Finney's voice: "Brook, child, you will wake the dead!" Miss Finney stood over Brook, looking down with a happy smile.

Brook did not move; she could not remove her gaze from Miss Finney. "You . . ." Brook started, then tried, "I don't . . . . " Nothing seemed to work. She was totally amazed.

Miss Finney's voice was even different: softer, easier, more vital. She said, "Dear Brook, you do not, cannot know what you have done for me. I am a new person. Maybe I should say I am an old person, the person I was."

Brook fought to complete a sentence: "But . . . you are so . . . Auntie, your face. It is. . . ."

Miss Finney cut in: "My face merely reflects the happiness I am feeling. I am standing, Brook. I am walking."

Willa ran into the room, noisily bumping into the door. She let out a shout of amazement: "You are standing!"

Nodding, her aunt said, "Brook and I were just talking about that. I feel . . . . "

Willa blurted: "I don't believe you are walking!" Miss Finney did not try to talk. Brook had stopped screaming, and the two young women exchanged exclamations. She let them chatter. Brook rolled over and rose. She was wearing clothing from the night before. The blood was still there. Willa was in a nightgown but her hair did not seem mussed from sleeping. Each woman expressed her amazement. Finally, their aunt was able to get them quiet.

"Now, Willa, good morning. I frightened poor Brook and obviously woke you."

"Now, then," Miss Finney stated, "It seems that something is happening to me. I do not know what it is. Possibly all I needed was for you girls to fuss over me; maybe I needed the attention." She motioned for Willa to approach. Miss Finney sat down on Brook's bed.

She said, "Now, no matter, dears. You have both been through much more than you should go through and so I have decided to reward you as we discussed." She handed each of them a check.

Willa said excitedly, "This is for twenty thousand dollars, Brook! Look!" Brook suddenly let a morose expression slip onto her face. A look of horror followed.

Miss Finney patted Brook's hand. "Now, dear, look at your check. It is for twenty thousand dollars. It is my token of appreciation."

Brook cried, "For murder!"

The silence was heavy in the room. Willa moved to Brook and said, "He did not die, Brook."

Brook was furious. She struck out at Willa, crying, "You lie! I saw him! We killed him!"

Willa's face begged Brook to listen. Her voice pleaded, "Brook, please. Listen. He did not die. I promise."

"Promise!" Brook challenged. "You promised that he would not be hurt. But I saw him. I saw the arrow." Then, looking down at her clothes, she pointed to the stains and said, "These, this blood. Is that all imagination?"

Willa grabbed Brook's face roughly and hissed, "I tell you he did not die. Get hold of yourself!"

Before Brook could erupt again, Miss Finney said, "Tell her, Willa. Tell her the truth."

Willa was concerned. She could not speak. Brook watched the two women.

Miss Finney purred warmly, "I spoke with Carlos Ives

by telephone less than an hour ago. He told me. He explained the whole ruse."

Willa was flabbergasted: "He told you?"

Brook was not yet caught up. "But we killed two men."

Willa was incredulous: "He told you what we were doing?"

The old lady nodded and said, "You girls must love me very much to do such things for me."

Brook repeated, "But we killed him."

Willa said, "He did not die. It was a trick arrow, Brook. Ives gave it to me."

Brook retorted, "That's a lie! You would have told me."

Willa was feeling her way. She seemed put off by the news that Ives had exposed the trickery. Still, she tried to calm Brook, hoping not to jeopardize the gimmick with her aunt. "Brook, if you had just waited for a minute, until Auntie had gone, you would have seen. The man did not die. It was all an act."

Silently, Brook jabbed at the bloodstains on her blouse and skirt. Willa declared, "Theatrical blood. All a gag."

Brook was not able to assimilate that; there were too many questions.

Miss Finney had other ideas. She was feeling her age . . . and then some.

She ordered, "Now, ladies, we must begin our day. I want you dressed and downstairs in just a few minutes. No dallying around. There is work to do." Neither girl moved. "Up, up, girls. There is much to be done!" She flitted out of the room.

Willa sat down on the edge of Brook's bed. She took her cousin's hands in hers and said, "Brook, I am sorry I lied to you."

Brook had a vacant gaze on her face.

Willa continued, "There was no way I could tell you. There was the chance of you letting the secret out. You might have slipped to Auntie, or you might have said something that would have cued in the others. But, dear

Brook, she knows now, so I can tell you: It was all acting. None of them died. I was going to tell you last night, but you vanished and I had to get rid of Holt. I might add, dear Brook, he expected me to perform some impossible sexual act with him. He said he'd use some of the money to satisfy his lust. I wish you had not promised so much; I nearly had to deliver. That would have been ghastly."

Brook tried to accept the news. It was difficult to think. She was struggling up through a labyrinth of emotion which had settled over her the night before.

Suddenly, Brook decided it was unnecessary to clarify each little morsel of data. She reached out and grabbed Willa. They enjoyed a sisterly embrace and Brook released a deluge of tears. Shortly, they were laughing like children. Gibberish came from Brook. Willa cooed. It would have gone on longer, but there came a demanding shout of orders from the first floor: Miss Finney expected them downstairs, quickly!

Willa ran to her room while Brook saw to an abbreviated morning toilet.

They were downstairs within ten minutes.

The old lady was in the breakfast room, puttering about, walking because she could walk. She was still using a cane, but she was not an invalid.

"Now, girls," she stated as they came into the room, "We must get at some type of a schedule for today."

Brook and Willa poured cups of coffee. Miss Finney brought them glasses of orange juice; she was enjoying being able to fuss.

"Now," the old lady charged forward, "I want you two to go to the bank and put those funds in your own name. Lord knows I might drop dead at any moment. Those checks would be worthless."

Brook and Willa scolded her for having such thoughts. She kept walking, as if each step delighted her. She said, "I know what is best. I am, or was, a good businesswoman in my day. You will cash those checks today. Also," she plunged onward as if she could not stop, "we have a neighbor whom you girls have met but I have not. He has been on our property this morning, snooping around. I do not like that type of behavior, but I would rather have him where I can see him than to have him lurking in the dark. Willa, you will see that he becomes friendly."

Willa asked, "What should we do about Mister Brown's snooping?"

Miss Finney said, "We shall figure that out later. I think for now, we will become good neighbors. Make friends."

With that, Miss Finney moved out of the room, leaving Brook and Willa with a final demand: "And I wish to go to Mister Ives' offices later."

She was gone to some other part of the house. Willa and Brook looked at each other.

Willa observed, "She is quite a whirlwind. I'll bet she was a terror when she was young."

Brook asked pleadingly, "What has happened to her? Her face is younger, her hair even seems different. And the walking is incredible. What is it, really, Willa?"

Willa shrugged. "Ives swears to me that it is entirely a trick played by the mind. It seems there are some things about the body that are still quite unknown. Such as adrenaline. Massive doses of hormones from the adrenal gland can make a person superstrong, violently powerful. Ives' magic, if you want to call it that, is to get certain hormones and enzymes flowing in the right direction at the same time. Auntie is getting a chemical boost from her own body that tells her she is feeling younger. It is all very complicated, yet very simple. All that is necessary to keep the hype going is that she believe something good is causing her to prosper. She is a hope junkie. She hopes; it happens; she is high."

"Where does it all lead?"

Willa pointed an index finger, snapped her thumb and said, "Bang! It goes on a bit and she explodes. At least her head explodes. Then the aging is twice as fast."

"But . . . ."

Willa nodded: "But, when that happens . . . *finish:* she's gone."

Brook shook her head, trying to fit all the pieces into place.

Willa said, "But I've told you most of this. We are on a one-way ride out of here. Getting to the bank today will be a big step; we need the cash."

Brook worried, "But what about her?"

Coldly, Willa said, "Screw her. She's due to die anyway. We're just making her final days a bit nicer. Don't you worry, dear cousin. She is on her way out. All we have to do is humor her with a couple more performances and then we . . . ."

Brook was on her feet, protesting. "Oh, no. Not me!"

Willa spoke firmly: "Yes, you, dear cousin. I need your help."

Brook said, "But it is all an act. You said that. You don't need me for that."

"I will decide that, Brook," Willa said, "and I have decided. We do another one tonight."

Brook was near tears as she begged, "Please let me out of it. Look, Willa, we each have thirty thousand dollars. Why don't we just forget about the whole thing? With that much money we could be out of here today. We could go to New York or L.A. She won't live long. Let's go!"

Willa began to sound nasty: "I have a deal with Ives and I can't go back on it. You have a deal with us, too, Brook. Now you just make sure you see it through and everything will be just fine. If not, there could be trouble."

Then Willa eased her tone and spoke warmly to Brook: "Now look, kid, don't make me go back to those threats. I don't want to do that again. We're having fun. We had a really great time yesterday. So do what you're told, and we will have some good times ahead of us."

Meekly, Brook nodded.

Willa restated, "We do another. Tonight!"

Brook did not answer. She sipped her coffee and wondered if there were some way out of the whole thing.

"Raymond Oxford Brown the Third" was a mouthful, but that was the name the man gave. He was wearing an outfit that looked like it was stolen from a tintype photograph from decades before. White oxford shoes and white trousers. A tennis sweater tied with sleeves around the neck. An ascot stuffed in the neck of a cotton shirt. A newspaper ad for tennis rackets, circa 1920. But his manners were up to date: exuberant, not stuffy. He looked as if he fit back in the rear area of the mansion, puttering in the gardens. Even Willa looked part of the picture in a summery off-the-shoulder dress and thong sandals.

"They look nice," Miss Finney said.

Brook looked out the kitchen window and said, "Yes," but that was all. She had wanted to speak to her aunt, but there had been so much gabbing about things Miss Finney wanted to do—like washing dishes, which she was doing—now that she was feeling better.

Brook, taking the plunge, said, "I want to leave, Auntie."

Miss Finney turned from the sink and studied her niece. "I guessed you were troubled. I did not know you felt so."

Brook said, "I can't take it. Murder is too much for me."

Her aunt laughed. "You silly child, your cousin told you it was all a ruse. There have been no murders. It is all a scheme."

Brook charged, "Do you realize Carlos Ives is a

171

confidence man who is trying to bilk you of money? That Willa and I have been part of a scheme to get money out of you?"

Miss Finney was drying her hands as she said, "Now, Brook, it is not quite as bad as all that. Mister Ives has explained some of the mystical concepts to me and I have accepted them as my gospel. There are some extenuating things that must accompany my own ritual, but that has nothing to do with you. I will admit to you that Willa should have been more gentle with you and not put you through such a traumatic experience, but that is behind us. There will be no more trauma for you, my dear. I will see to that."

Brook said nothing. She did not know what to do.

The old lady looked out into the back garden again where Brown and Willa sat. They seemed to be deeply involved in serious dialogue.

Absently, Miss Finney observed, "He seems like a fine young man. Very attractive."

Brook cried, "You don't need me, Auntie. Willa can manage for you. I want to leave."

After some moments of consideration, Miss Finney said, "Well, then, so be it. I will let you leave—and take the money with you—tomorrow."

Brook became excited and ran to her aunt. Before she could make contact, the old lady added, "After we do one more exercise tonight."

Brook froze. A chilling stab of anguish punctured her elation. She was trapped.

Her aunt said, "When I was talking to Mister Ives this morning, he told me it is critical for me to evoke another sacrifice."

"But there is no 'sacrifice'," Brook protested.

Miss Finney replied haughtily, "I like to think there has been. That is all that is important." She continued, "And I will expect you and Willa to contribute again to my well-being. I demand it."

Brook charged, "You are insane!"

"All the more reason to humor me . . . one more time."

Brook cried, "No one will die?"

"Right," the old lady replied, "no one will die!"

Brook sank into resignation. "One more . . . just one more . . . and we . . . we will pretend."

Her aunt touched her cheek, "There is a sweet girl."

Brook asked, "And you will pay me? And I will leave?"

Miss Finney gave Brook a hug and said, "Now, dear, such virtue. Such moral eminence. And all coming from a convicted murderess. At least the men we have been pretending to kill were strangers. You killed the man who loved you."

Brook snapped, "He did not love me. He was evil!"

Miss Finney gave Brook a hug and said, "Now, dear, do not get excited. That is all behind us. We will do well this evening and then we can be about our own lives."

The reminder of her past made Brook feel grim. She wanted to do what was necessary to get away from this present so that it would become the past, to be forgotten.

Brook was about to say something when Willa came bounding into the kitchen. She seemed to have the litheness of a happy young dancer.

"Hello . . . hello . . . hello," she chanted lyrically as she spun around the kitchen.

Miss Finney let go of Brook and called, "Easy, Willa, you will damage something. Why so excited?"

"It is a lovely day," Willa chirped.

"Does it perhaps have anything to do with Mister Brown?"

Willa laughed. "Not in the way you might think. But he is a part of the whole. There is a great part yet to be discovered."

Sternly, Miss Finney accused, "Willa, have you been drinking?"

Jokingly, Brook said, "Or is your Mister Raymond

Brown a supplier of good grass?"

Teasingly, Willa replied, "You will both have to wait and see what I am referring to. You will know soon enough."

Miss Finney asked, "Did he accept the offer I told you to make?"

"Well," Willa replied, "after he planted a lovely rose-bush, which was his idea of a peace offering, I asked him to come this evening, just as you instructed. He accepted."

Pleased, Miss Finney said, "Well done." Then she added, "Your cousin wants to leave. She no longer wishes to satisfy the whims of crazy old Aunt Finney."

Brook protested, "I did not say that!"

The old lady quipped, "You did not have to. I know what you think! I want both of you to know how important this all is to me. I am going to make you both rich. I have an offer so big that you will not consider leaving without helping. Just see me through to the end of this and I will give you . . . a hundred thousand dollars . . . each!"

Thoughts of other things subsided in Brook's mind; she was about to become independent. To anyone who has ever been through—or could imagine—the horrors that Brook had experienced under the control of others, independence seems the one thing in the world worth having.

8

Brook was impatient to the point of anger. She wished Willa would hurry; she was taking too much time. The car was parked less than two blocks away from where they had found the first derelict. This locale offered less promise because it was near the railway yard, but Willa had insisted it was best to change locations.

Brook tapped the horn lightly two times. Off in the dark, she could see Willa waving acknowledgement. The wave seemed to say, "You can wait." Brook waited. Near a couple of abandoned Southern Railway boxcars obviously being used by transients for temporary living quarters, Willa was, in fact, enjoying her repartee with the bum she had selected as the next victim.

He was saying, "Now, why would a nice-lookin' broad like you offer me a hundred bucks?"

Willa snapped, "Why would a nice stud like you worry where a hundred bucks is coming from? Can you really be so selective?"

In a move that made him look as if he were swaggering as he stood in one place, he said, "Madam, no member of the clan O'Hara is anything less than selective. Dat's why I drink only the best dollar-a-gallon wine."

She laughed. It was easy to be easy with O'Hara; he was an easygoing type. He did not seem as filthy as most of the vagrants in the skid row area. His clothing did not have the typical baked enamel crust of collected dirt. Even the baseball cap had only a minor stain of sweat around the beak.

Willa finally reacted to Brook's impatient horn-tappings. She demanded, "Seriously, Mister O'Hara, would you like to make a hundred dollars?"

He quipped again: "Would I like to hit five hundred for a season?"

"Baseball?" Willa asked, forcing politeness.

"Yep," O'Hara responded, "the Dodgers, 1961."

Politely again, Willa asked, "You were a star?"

"Naw," was O'Hara's embarrassed reply, "I only tried out. But they liked me."

He was a pathetic soul. He looked like a dissipated ex-athlete: his face was haggard from too much booze, and his body was paunchy from eating starchy foods and avoiding exercise. A piece of social flotsam and athletic jetsam.

With the command, "Follow me," Willa turned and began walking briskly toward the car where Brook waited.

O'Hara hustled to catch up. His beer-belly joggled and he breathed heavily with the effort.

At the car, Willa yanked the back door open and gestured for him to climb in.

He hesitated. "Hey, really, what we gonna do?"

Willa snapped, "We will talk."

"Really," he responded, "a swell broad like you paying a hundred bucks to talk to me. You a baseball fan?"

Willa, masking her impatience, affected slyness: "Well, one word leads to another, and before you know it . . . ." She paused, then pressed him: "You want the job or not?"

With a slovenly imitation of a military salute, O'Hara slurred back, "I'm on the payroll as of now. My name's O'Hara and I'm at yer service, lady." Then, sneaking a leprechaun expression onto his face, he squeaked, "But, I'll be telling ye this: I don't go fer whips nor black boots nor German helmets. Do ye understand?"

With an exaggerated hand gesture, Willa said, "Now

be getting inside of the car before I box yer ears!"

As he elaborately climbed into the back seat, he lolled his head back and forth saying, "A woman after me own heart!"

She slammed the door shut and jumped in front next to Brook. "Drive, Brook! Let's go see our dear aunt."

As she began moving the car onto the street, Brook asked, "How come you're not riding in the back?"

Willa burst out laughing as she said, "Our Irish Eros back there fancies himself to be the answer to woman's need. If I had a dollar for each time his hands *accidentally* touched one of my private parts, he'd owe me the hundred . . . and more. He is quite a romantic."

As Brook drove the car through New Orleans to the Finney mansion, their latest acquisition enjoyed being chauffeured in a regal automobile. He bounced around and was full of levity. He also made obscene and suggestive movements with his hands and body. Willa, laughing at his antics, warned Brook not to look in the rearview mirror.

It was not until they were in Miss Finney's parlor that Brook decided to look at the man. She saw the remains of a wasted life. She felt compassion for him. She was glad he was going to get a hundred dollars. She decided she would throw in another hundred as a gift to their final actor.

Miss Finney, in contrast to her prior cheerful mood, seemed distant and preoccupied. She never directly addressed O'Hara. She chose rather to communicate via her nieces. She told Brook, "Get some port for Mister O'Hara."

Willa had anticipated the instruction. She walked to the man and handed him the drink with a coquettish fluttering of her eyelashes. "Your drink, dear sir."

"Oooh, I do like this setup," he said. Then, raising his glass, he cried, "Here's to Reggie Jackson!"

He gulped down half the glass, then, looking at his

hostesses, he asked, "What'd'ya think of them Yankees? Not as good as the Dodgers . . . but still one hell of a team. Right?"

Willa said she thought they were neat. He dropped baseball. He was suddenly weaving. He tugged at his collar and knocked back the remainder of his drink, then said, "Hey, it sure seems warm, huh?"

Willa went to him and took his glass. She placed it on a small table and took his arm. She began steering him out of the room.

"Come with me, Mister O'Hara."

He repeated, "It's warm." Then, leaning precariously backward, he said, "Whoops . . . gotta be careful." He looked blearily at Brook and, after appraising her, he asked, "What about her? Is she gonna get some, too?"

Willa mumbled, "Yes, whatever you want. Come with me!"

With a dizzy lurch, he started moving as he said, "Aw, what the hell . . . It's the World Series! I'll take 'em all on."

Willa led him out into the hallway and pointed him toward the door to the basement stairs. She left him and ran to open the door. His weaving became jerky; he seemed about to fall. He slurred, speaking almost unintelligibly: "I ain't used to drinkin' nothin' with a label on it." He hesitated, unable to move.

Willa quickly unbuttoned her blouse and opened it wide, exposing her slip. He could see her bra and the ample size of her breasts. "Oh, boy," he gabbled, "I gotta get me some of this stuff before it. . . ." He had made it to the open door. He had stopped talking, because the look on Willa's face was icy and hard. She was buttoning her blouse. He was unable to stop weaving. He spoke weakly: "I need . . . a little . . . just a little air."

She raised an eyebrow and pointed down the stairwell. "There is fresh air down there."

He looked. He was having an impossible time trying to

bring his eyes into focus. He pleaded, "I . . . don't know if I can make it down . . . down there. I feel . . . suddenly I feel . . . . "

Willa reached up and took firm hold of his shoulder. She turned him so that he was facing down the stairs. She told him, "Go on down, O'Hara. You'll feel better. It's cooler in the basement."

He leaned forward. He was precariously close to falling. He said, "I've never been like this before . . . been drunk . . . but not fuzzy . . . I . . . I'mmm. . . . '

She reached up and shoved him. His arms moved in a reflex action to stop the fall. He grabbed at the walls too late and with too little force; he did not stop until he slammed into the concrete floor at the bottom of the stairs.

Quickly, with agility, Willa ran down the stairs and untangled the mess of arms and legs. She felt his limbs, probed his chest and stomach, then checked his heartbeat and respiration. Satisfied that he was simply knocked out from the drug in his drink and the fall, she left him on the floor.

Back in the parlor, as soon as Willa walked in, her aunt asked, "Is he? . . . Did he?"

Solicitously, Willa crossed to her aunt and said, "He is out cold. Nothing broken, nothing damaged. Those drops in his drink should keep him out for two or three hours."

Miss Finney nodded. "That is all we need."

Brook took in the exchange. There was something going on that was beginning to bother her, but she could not put her finger on it. She wanted to say something, to ask for assurances, to try and get them to tell her . . . .

The doorbell rang. All three women acted guilty at the sound. Police? It was as if they had been caught in their crime: furtive glances flew in triangles.

Nervously, Willa said, "I'll get it."

Brook moved to Miss Finney as if to join forces against

an impending threat. Miss Finney reached out and touched Brook. "Don't worry, dear Brook . . . we will just pretend. You just trust Willa and me."

Brook started to reply, "Something just came over me . . . . " She was cut off as Willa walked back into the parlor, Raymond Oxford Brown, III, in tow.

Willa announced, "Our guest has arrived early."

It was possible to hear the sigh of relief that came from Brook. Miss Finney breathed a modest "Oh," of surprise.

The man walked up to Brook and extended his hand. "Er, your name is Brook, am I right?" She nodded. "I'm pleased," he finished.

She said, "Yes, it's Brook. You are early. I had planned dinner to be . . . . "

He cut her off: "Do not fret, dear Brook. I will not impose." Then, turning to Miss Finney, and with a gaudy exaggeration of bravado, he bent into a bow and took her hand. With an elegant kiss, he said, "And this must be the illustrious Miss Alcorn Finney."

She was not flustered. She said, "In our circles, Mister Brown, the hand kiss is properly reserved for the married woman."

He straightened himself and said, "Can it be that such a lovely lady has never wed?"

With aplomb, she replied, "If it is any of your business, it is possible for the likes of me not to marry. But it is not your business, young man. I need not explain my marital status."

Unthwarted, Raymond asked, "Could it have been a sad romance in your early life?"

Miss Finney used her cane to stand a little more erect. Disdainfully, she said, "Your boldness approaches crudity, sir. Do not misconstrue our neighborly gesture as an invitation to shun good conduct."

Nodding his acceptance of the rebuke, he said, "Do not think me presumptuous, Miss Finney. It is just that I am pleased to meet you. I have always had a warm spot for any pretty girl called 'Goldie'."

She was startled and showed it. She had a difficult time maintaining a proper tone as she asked, "Where did you hear I was called by that name?"

With mild confusion, he shrugged. "I don't know, really. I must have heard it from Willa."

Willa shook her head, not knowing what to say.

Raymond seemed to be toying with them. "Hey, listen, Miss Finney. I am sorry if it is some kind of secret. I promise not to tell anyone else."

There was a distinct change in her attitude. She was still socially correct, still civil, but she was vexed. "It is no secret, Mister Brown. But . . . only a very few people know that name."

With convincing contrition, Raymond said, "I am truly sorry, Madam. I did not mean to transgress into private areas. I was trying too hard to be friendly."

Miss Finney softened somewhat. "Then we shall let it be."

Tension had built in the room. Willa seemed distressed that the get-together was marred. She tried to bubble some life into the group: "Well, now! What will we do to dampen this levity?"

Everyone was slow to smile. Miss Finney was the last to submit. When she had, Brook made the extra effort of taking drink orders. Conversation began to displace the tension.

While they waited for Brook to bring the drinks, Miss Finney said, "And now, Mister Brown, it is my turn to display some inelegance. You would not mind, would you?"

Taking a seat next to Willa on the divan, he said, "I would appreciate any crudity you might care to extend, Miss Finney."

All laughed.

Miss Finney was the first to stop. She observed, "You have a caustic wit, Mister Brown. Not many people

181

nowadays have such keen senses. Not many . . . . " She seemed to drift off for a moment. She caught herself: "I am sorry. I was remembering."

Raymond nodded understanding. "Remembering is the offspring of notable moments. We are granted the gift of remembering in payment for taking part in great events."

Miss Finney chided, "You seem to be a flatterer, Sir."

Brook was placing drinks beside everyone. She sat next to her aunt on the other divan. The fire seemed to warm the spaces between them.

He ignored the chide. "You were going to offend me," he said.

"Ah, yes." Miss Finney sipped at her drink, then went on, "Yes, I did say that. I was merely wondering, Mister Brown, why a young man like you would think of buying the property next door. It is not the best setting for an active young person."

Raymond nodded. "I am not offended and surely do not feel you have transgressed in kind, as I insulted you. It is a natural question. The property is an investment for the future. I have been overseas most of my life; I have only one major tie to the United States. But there have been family investments that have done well and, if I choose to take the profits out of the country, I must pay a heavy tax. So, I will leave the money here, in the form of the property next door, and I will have a nice place to visit. And, I must add, I will have very nice neighbors." He paused, looked at the three women, then asked, "Does that explain my eccentricities?"

Brook asked, "Do you live alone, Mister Brown?"

Miss Finney gasped. "Really, Brook! I thought I was graceless, but that question is in poor taste."

Brook blushed. She felt bad and was only saved from total shame by Raymond saying, "Another quite reasonable question. I am happy to respond. I will be living alone until I can be with the girl I love."

182

Brook, now ignoring the possibility of another rebuke from her aunt, asked, "Have you found her, or are you still looking?"

With ease, so that none of them felt contrition for Brook's forwardness, he said, "Oh, I have found her. I am pleased you asked. I hope she will be with me soon."

Speaking for all, Willa said, "That will be so nice for you."

Brook's curiosity was satisfied. She finished off her drink and said, "I'm off to the kitchen. Dinner will be ready very shortly."

As Brook flitted out of the room, Willa stood and said, "Well, Mister Brown, how about a tour of the mansion?" She used his proper name, but there was a hint of familiarity in her voice that made it sound ludicrous for her to call him "Mister."

He seemed elated. He was boyishly excited as he popped up and said, "I'd love to. I'm fascinated by architecture."

Something snapped in Miss Finney. "What? What did you say?"

Willa said, "I'll show Mister Brown . . . . "

Angrily, Miss Finney hushed Willa. "No! What did he say? I must know!"

Raymond and Willa looked down at the old lady. They did not reply. In a moment, she pulled herself together and said, "I am so sorry. It was just something you said, or the way you said it. I am sorry. Please, please go look at the house. I am quite embarrassed."

Raymond smiled at her and said, "You should not rebuke yourself, dear lady."

At Willa's urging, Raymond followed her out of the room.

Miss Finney sat staring into the fire.

"Auntie, did you hear what I said?"

It was Brook's voice intruding into her aunt's thoughts.

"Auntie!"

The intrusion was complete. Brook was standing there, a look of concern on her face.

Miss Finney shook her head as if to shake matters into order.

Brook was there, wearing an apron, looking pleased, yet concerned. "I was frightened, Auntie. Your eyes were open, but otherwise, you looked as though you were sleeping."

Miss Finney was irritated. Brook had no right to intrude into her privacy. "I was thinking."

Brook knew there was more to it. She started to talk: "But you were . . . . "

Miss Finney replied coldly, "What do you want, Brook? Is dinner ready?"

Brook was hurt. She was merely trying to be considerate.

Miss Finney, especially since she had made that journey back to that hurtful moment in her life, wanted no one to show consideration or any other emotion. She was totally satisfied with what she carried inside of her. She needed no more.

The old lady struggled a bit getting to her feet. Once standing, she saw that Brook was deeply hurt.

As a sop, the old lady reached out and stroked Brook's cheek as she said, "You must forgive an old fool, dear niece. We have many problems that come with age. Cantankerousness is one problem. Just the same feisty manner that afflicts youngsters. Remember Uncle Allen's adage: 'Once an adult, twice a child.' "

Brook was relieved. She wanted to stay in her aunt's good graces because she wanted to get away from the Finney mansion and begin a life of her own. She accepted the gesture with happiness.

Brook said, "Dinner is ready."

Miss Finney asked, "Is the coffee set with the drug Mister Ives gave to Willa?"

Brook nodded. "It is. But why do we have to put Mister

Brown through this silly stage play? He seems like a nice enough neighbor."

"True," her aunt agreed, "but, because we will be merely pretending, Mister Ives said we must do two. So, we will pretend to kill Mister Brown after we have pretended to kill that dreg you have down in the basement."

Brook nodded. It was all beyond her. All she wanted was for this night to be behind her, and to be done with the Finney mansion. She had earned her pardon. There was a cashier's check for thirty thousand dollars and two thousand in cash in Brook's purse. There were promises of much more money after tonight's effort. Then Brook would be gone. Away from the mansion, away from New Orleans, away from the craziness of the past couple of days. She would begin a new life.

She looked at Miss Finney. There was another reason Brook wanted to flee. Willa had said their aunt's physical changes were caused by chemicals that were being released throughout her system. But the chemicals were being released on an emergency demand. If Willa was correct, the demand would soon reach a limit. Miss Finney would have a chemical reaction that would accelerate the aging processes. The results would be catastrophic.

Miss Finney's face had lost many wrinkles and her hair had less gray in it. She looked fiftyish. Brook could imagine the hideous things that would happen to the appearance of her aunt. And it would happen so quickly.

Brook did not want to be around when the change began.

"Do call Willa, my dear. We must have dinner."

Brook went to the hall door and called loudly.

A sound came back that sounded like Willa acknowledging the call.

Miss Finney walked with Brook into the dining room.

Raymond Brown pushed himself back from the table

and did a poor imitation of a stout man patting an over-stuffed stomach. Brown's abdomen was perfectly flat. His sincerity came across, though, as he said, "Miss Brook, you have a magic touch when it comes to preparing food. The excellence of the fare is in concert with this beautiful mansion. I am quite pleased with this evening. Thank you . . . all."

Brook was touched. The compliment was nicely delivered and well accepted. Brook nodded her thanks with modesty.

Miss Finney spoke: "You enjoyed the guided tour that Willa gave you, Mister Brown?"

"Indeed," he said, "I am an avid student of architecture. There is real heritage in this fine building; you should be proud."

Miss Finney quipped, "We try to avoid pride, Sir, because pride demands a showing of assets and that is not an interest of mine. I am selfish and do not like to share with others."

Brown replied, "You shared with me."

The aunt smiled, saying, "You are a different matter, Mister Brown."

Willa said, "We surely think you are special."

She moved to the sideboard. "Coffee?" she asked. All indicated interest.

As Willa poured, Brook cleared the table. Soon they were all seated again.

There was a session of prattle that lasted for a couple of minutes. Finally, Willa interrupted Brook: "Isn't anyone going to drink coffee but me?"

Raymond gave a smiling look at Willa and said, "I hadn't noticed you drinking, Willa."

Willa lied, "But this is my second cup."

He picked up his cup and smiled. He held it halfway to his lips and looked at his dinner companions. He asked, "Now, am I to be the only one to drink Willa's coffee?"

Brook picked up her cup and said, "We will, Mister Brown. Please drink up." But she did not move the cup to her lips.

Raymond brought the lip of the cup to his nose and he gave a quick sniff. "Ahh," he said, "It is mountain coffee with just the right amount of chicory." Willa nodded appreciation. Then he placed the rim to his lips and took a tiny sip. They looked at him.

"Hmmmm," he said, "It seems to be ester of barbituric acid. If I drank only half this cup I would pass right out." Willa sucked in a breath. It was audible throughout the room. Raymond smiled and continued, "And if I passed out, you'd probably do away with me, as you did with those poor creatures out in the back garden." He narrowed his gaze and replaced his cup in its saucer. "I think I'd better not have any coffee tonight, thanks."

Crash! Brook dropped her cup onto the table. The cup broke and the liquid splashed over everything. Droplets of coffee ran down her face.

Raymond was quickly on his feet. He moved to Brook, using his napkin to dab away the coffee. She pushed away his hand and toppled over her chair as she jumped up. "No!" she cried. He took hold of her shoulders, strongly locking her where she stood. He made to clean her again as he said, "Messy, messy, Brook. Are you angry that I was right? The two in the back garden and the one in the basement. Right?" Brook fell to the floor in a dead faint.

He had broken her fall and, as he looked down at her, he said, "I must watch what I am saying. Every time I mention those fellows, something happens to poor Brook, here."

He invested a few moments in reviving Brook, who came to but hid in a refuge of startled lethargy. When he helped her up, she allowed herself to be reseated. With a casual manner, he went back to his chair and picked up his half empty glass of wine. "I am glad you drugged the

coffee and not this fine wine. I'd rather this than coffee."
Then, with mock civility, he said, "Thank you, anyway,
dear Willa."

Willa sat stonily.

With humor, he said, "I am really afraid to say
anything, now!"

Miss Finney asked with an accusatory tone, "Why have
you failed to report us?"

Without forced effort, he replied, "Well . . . it's none
of my business, is it? I mean, just so you don't try to add
me to your collection." He pushed the cup of coffee
symbolically away from him. "As far as I am concerned,
you may do away with the entire French Quarter if you
like!"

Silence crowded the room.

In a near-whisper, as if she did not really want to
speak, Brook asked, "Don't you care about what we are
doing?"

Immediately, Raymond replied, "No!"

She continued, "Aren't you angry that we tried
to . . . ." She pointed to the drugged coffee.

In an unconcerned manner, Raymond replied again,
"No. Of course not."

In a voice so low that it could barely be heard, she
asked what she did not want to have answered: "What are
you going to do now?"

Almost too casually, Raymond said, "I am not going to
do anything. Live and let live. That is what I always say."

From the other end of the table, in her steady, even
voice, Miss Finney said, "We have nearly finished what
we must do, Mister Brown. Tonight could have been the
end of it."

With noticeable sarcasm, he said, "Well, I apologize
for lousing things up. But, you see, I am not ready to die
yet. My life is not complete. Now I have a life to live; all
my debts are paid."

He looked at the women individually. Then he rose,

folded his napkin neatly on the table and said, "It's late . . . and you still have work to do. Thank you for the dinner. I'll let myself out."

Miss Finney stopped him at the dining room door: "Mister Brown! Would you believe me if I told you I had decided during dinner that no harm would come to you?"

Without looking back, he replied, "Yes, Miss Finney, I'm quite confident of that."

He moved out of the room toward the front door.

Willa, dazed from the turn of events, jumped up and ran to the hall. She watched as Raymond left. She came back in saying, "He's gone. What a shock!"

Brook said, nastiness creeping into her weak voice, "We're in a fine mess now. He has us where he wants us!"

Willa asked, "What do you mean?"

Brook explained her view: "I mean, tomorrow or the next day he's going to present us with a deal. He will threaten to expose our silly games with derelict bums and make us the laughing stock of the Quarter. We will not be able to live with such a shame. He could bleed us dry."

Willa asked, "Blackmail?"

Brook nodded and Miss Finney said, "You are wrong, Brook. He will do us no harm."

Brook snapped venomously, "You are crazy, aren't you, Aunt Finney? We've got to get that bum out of the basement. We've got to get him out of the house before our neighbor decided to call the police." Then the import of Raymond's words finally settled in. "He really thinks we have been murdering people. We must stop this foolishness."

Willa, showing some degree of control, said, "We've got to get ourselves together." She nudged Brook and said, "Let's get some coffee that we can drink." Willa stood and took the drugged coffee cups off the table. To Brook she said, "Come on with me. There's still a pot of coffee in the kitchen." Turning to her aunt, she said,

"We'll be right back."

Like an automaton, Brook followed. She did not look at her aunt.

In the kitchen, Willa busied herself getting fresh cups. Brook got the glass pot from the afternoon's coffee, whining, "Why did I ever get involved in this mess? Why did I go along?"

Willa, coming to the table, said, "Hey, listen, Brook, we've got a little problem. But remember, you went along because you wanted to be rich! We are rich; don't forget that. We can go wherever we want to."

Brook lashed out, "We can go to jail for the rest of our lives! That's where we can go . . . to jail!"

Anger burst onto Willa's face. She was almost yelling at Brook as she said, "Well, if you're so damned pure, then call the police!" Willa grabbed at a wall telephone and waved it at Brook, "Take this damned thing and call them!"

Brook did nothing.

Willa shook the telephone again. She said, "I'm telling you, there has been a law broken: Murder . . . kidnapping . . . drugging . . . SOMETHING! Call the police!"

Brook did not move.

Willa said, "Okay. You must make a choice. Either you stay in this with me, taking the money and having your freedom, or you call the police. Now. That's the deal. You are in or you are out. You must decide."

Brook felt shattered, beaten. She could not call the police; they would send her back to the insane asylum. They had done wrong, but they had not murdered, Willa had promised that. They had broken the law, and Willa was right: if any law was violated, Brook should have called the police. Murder—which they had not done— was only a worse degree of crime.

Brook knew she would not telephone the police. She was committed to seeing the scheme through with Willa;

she wanted the money more than she wanted to call the police.

She sadly stepped toward Willa and said, "I'm sorry. I will not call the police."

Willa shrugged, smiled, and led the way back into the dining room.

When they got there, Miss Finney was not there.

Brook felt an ugly presentiment coming into her mind. "Where is she?"

"Calm down," Willa ordered. "Did you ever think she might simply have gone to the bathroom? She has a right."

Brook did not enjoy the humor. There was that bum down in the basement, and Brook felt he should be gotten out of the mansion. She did not trust her aunt.

"We can't just sit here, Willa," Brook urged. "You're taking all this too calmly. You don't realize the trouble we are in."

Willa said, "I tend to agree with our aunt: Brown will do us no harm."

Brook said, "I don't know how you can be so damned sure. He is a total stranger and he knows we have killed two men . . . . " Her words slammed back into her as a fist would slam into a stomach. She had admitted the unadmittable, she had faced the unfaceable. Brook knew deep down that Willa had lied to her. Willa was sitting there, sipping coffee. She had an evil smirk on her face.

"No!" Brook pleaded, mostly to herself. "I didn't mean to say that!" Willa did nothing. Brook's lower lip trembled and she sobbed, "I was wrong. We didn't kill anyone. Willa. Willa! You promised we were only pretending. You told me!"

She was accelerating out of control. Willa seemed not to care. An iciness had formed on Willa's eyes. Their coldness penetrated into Brook's awareness.

A loud, uncontrolled scream came from between

191

Brook's taut lips. She was slipping over the edge of insanity. Willa rose and walked to the hallway. She stood there and waited. Brook convoluted her scream into an agonized cry. She rose out of her seat quickly and bumped into a chair as she ran to Willa. Brook grabbed hold of her cousin, grasping tightly, burying her head against Willa's chest. "Please, I need to know, Willa. Please tell me we did not kill them. Oh! P-L-eeez!" The sound was primeval. It came from deep within Brook's chest. She felt like a trapped and injured animal.

Willa roughly reached up and took hold of Brook's head. Brook thought it was a gesture of affection. She allowed Willa to rotate her head in the direction of the hall. There, entering through the basement door, was Miss Finney. The woman leaned against the door jamb, shoulders stooped, head hanging, hair unkempt. The sight that triggered the blackness surging into Brook's consciousness was the butcher knife hanging limply in Miss Finney's right hand, dripping blood. There was blood on Miss Finney's stockings and some had splattered onto her face. The last thing Brook saw was the sticky glob of dripping blood that slid down the knife blade and splotched onto the floor.

Her hands grabbed at Willa, but she could not clutch. Brook fell to the floor. Blackness carried her away from the grisly horror.

9

Miss Finney lay propped up in her bed. Her hair had been brushed, she had applied a bit of make-up, her peignoir was draped carefully in place.

Willa came into her aunt's bedroom carrying a morning tray. She approached the bed, stopped and studied the picture framed by the fluffy, pink-cased pillows.

"I don't know," Willa said in a serious voice, "It seems some, but nothing dramatic."

Miss Finney gave an emphatic nod. "I am quite disappointed, dear Willa. Quite disappointed."

Willa moved forward and lowered the tray into position as she said, "I guess our last victim simply did not have that many years left. That is too bad."

Miss Finney agreed: "I wish there were some positive way to tell how many years a person has left so that we could better predict what will happen."

Willa, stepping back, asked, "Have you guessed that Brook is gone?"

Miss Finney stated, "I have guessed as much."

Willa asked, "And you're not concerned?"

"I have a pretty good idea of where she will go," the aunt said. "She can do us no harm."

Willa smiled. "It is good she has that insanity background. That lessens any threat she might pose."

Confidently, Miss Finney agreed. "To be sure. I have thought about what she will do and I know what that will be. No need for us to worry."

Willa stepped back and took another studied look at Miss Finney. The niece said, "I don't know if there is *any* noticeable difference, Auntie."

"There is some, I know that." Her aunt began to spread jam on a muffin. She spoke before she took a bite: "I must say I was disappointed. But, Mister Ives warned me that such an event was possible, even probable."

Willa sat on the edge of the bed as she said, "The age left is really a problem, isn't it?"

Miss Finney nodded. "Apparently, this O'Hara person was really in poor physical shape. Probably cirrhosis of the liver, the way he drank. There was little benefit for me. Too bad."

Willa nodded, "Too bad."

10

For the first several hours of the night, it was not difficult for Brook to drift around the French Quarter. Life in the Quarter is most vibrant after midnight. She floated along with the ebb of people until places began closing, then she became a little obvious.

She had been propositioned a dozen times and, for a fleeting moment, she thought it might be a good idea to go with some man to a hotel and spend the night. She would not be found that way. But she was not able to compromise her morals for the sake of expediency; she would find some way to survive and evade.

Survival was made easier by the amount of money she was carrying. That aspect would be no problem.

Evasion was another matter. She felt certain that her aunt and Willa were searching desperately for her; she tried to keep out of sight as much as possible. Bourbon Street was a natural because of the crowds packing the street, but there was a major drawback: she was a woman alone. In the nicer places, she drew attention. That would make it easier for Willa to track Brook's moves. If she went to the seedier places, the people there would assume she was out on the make. There was the fear that she might be arrested as a prostitute. Bourbon Street had been good for only a couple of hours. A polite bouncer at one of the jazz clubs told her of a place, just a couple of blocks away, where she could sit for a long time and not be noticed or hassled. It turned out to be a fine jazz room that charged a fifty-dollar cover. That steep ticket kept out all except the serious jazz buffs. It gave Brook a haven until it closed at five a.m.

She was back out on the streets.

Dozens of small restaurants deal in dawn breakfasts for merrymakers who need nourishment after a night out on the town. She treated herself to a huge meal and idled over coffee until well after six. Then, that place closed, too.

Back to wandering the sidewalks, she was beginning to feel the danger that might pop up at every turn.

There was one fact on which to base hope: Willa could not drive a car. Any pursuit would be either by taxi or on foot. That gave Brook an edge, a slim edge; she knew what to look out for.

But roaming the French Quarter, especially at that time of morning, was the best way to draw attention. Not many people strolled about just after dawn.

She left the Quarter.

She was able to pass nearly an hour wandering around the Culture Center across from the Municipal Auditorium. Then she took a brisk walk up Saint Ann Street, all the way to the Interstate, where she perched on the grass and watched the morning rush hour traffic begin to build. She was jealous of those people who were living normal, stable, secure lives. They would get up and go to work each day; they would come home each day; they would share with their loved ones each day. They lived comfortable lives. She knew such a life would eventually bore her, but better to be bored than to have a hurricane of emotions and horrors swirling through her life daily.

Peace. How she longed for peace. A predictable day, uncomplicated people, common enjoyments.

She would have to escape. She would escape.

She knew she was doing the right thing. The plan had come more easily than she thought. She had begun to formulate it when she realized she could not simply go to the airport and catch a plane out of New Orleans. Her aunt and Willa both knew Brook was carrying the large cashier's check and a substantial amount of cash. The airport was the first place they'd look for her.

She would catch the Amtrak train and buy a ticket for Chicago. She would take a Pullman roomette. She had never felt the luxury of a train trip, and she had heard people say how nice it was. She would leave the train at St. Louis and then catch a plane to either New York or Los Angeles. Whichever plane was leaving first. Damn! What a great feeling. What freedom. But there was one thing she must do before she could finally be free. She needed an answer, one answer. Then she could flee. A clock on a billboard advertising a savings and loan company told her it was eight-thirty. Now she could go and get her answer.

It was after nine o'clock and the sun was beating down hotly when she went into the sidewalk telephone booth at the corner of Orleans and North Rampart. She dialed. After only one ring, Carlos Ives answered.

"I must see you," she demanded with no salutation.

"Brook?" Ives asked.

"Yes, I must see you!"

"What is the matter, my dear?"

She smiled. If he had known what had happened, he would not be asking if anything was the matter. Willa had not contacted Ives. Brook answered, "There's plenty the matter. My aunt . . . it's impossible, what is happening to her. I . . . ." She faltered and was silent.

"Brook!" Ives called, "Brook! Are you there? Tell me what has happened!"

She said, "I . . . I can't . . . I can't talk like this . . . I'm at a telephone booth."

Brook heard Ives' words as soothing, comforting, understanding: "I want to help, Brook."

She paused, thought, then pleaded, "Can I come to

your office and see you? Now?"

He replied, "I have some people with me, appointments, you know. But you sound so distraught, I will reschedule what I can. Come right away."

She hung up and stood looking at the telephone. She could call the mansion and find out if Willa and her aunt were there. Then they would not be able to accidentally show up at Ives' offices.

She shook off that idea. Ives had sounded sincere; he would keep them from her. She would talk to Ives. Then, after she had resolved the questions that were oppressing her, after Ives had helped her clear up the confusion in her mind, she would be gone.

It took her twenty minutes to make the walk. By the time she entered the elevator in Ives' building, her dress was sticking to her body; the inner frock from the night before was not designed to be worn on a long, hot morning walk.

During the ride up on the elevator, she patted some of the sweat from her face and tried to organize strands of moist hair into some presentable order on her head.

She rapped at the door and let herself into the reception room.

A woman who seemed to be older than Miss Finney was sitting on one of the chairs. The woman could have been a porcelain statue, except that no artist would create such an ugly face and twisted body.

The woman gave a smile that announced she was missing several of her front teeth. The smile vanished, as if it were too difficult a posture to maintain for more than an instant.

Brook worried that the woman was possibly one of Ives' other customers, one like Miss Finney. But that could not be; the woman in the chair was dressed poorly and showed no sign of dignity or breeding. She could have no money; she could not be a customer of Ives.

Brook was about to make a polite greeting to the

woman when the door to the seance room opened and Ives came down the hall with still another woman. Brook noted that the fortune telling business seemed to do well, even in the early morning in the French Quarter.

The woman with Ives was saying, "You are so kind, Carlos, so very kind."

Brook could hear Ives' velvet voice, "It is dedication to my profession that brings me to help those in need."

He walked past Brook and opened the door for the woman to leave. "Until Thursday." Ives gave a formal bow. The woman smiled and said, "Yes, Carlos. I will see you on Thursday. *Adieu.*" The door closed.

Ives made a motion for Brook to go into the seance room and, in an officious tone, said to the woman in the chair, "I know you were next, but this shan't take long. It is an emergency. I am sure you understand." Brook looked back to see the woman meekly nodding her submission. Ives walked Brook down the hall and took her into his room.

With the door closed, Ives stood there, looking at Brook.

She was more nervous than she really had expected to be; she was free of the mansion, free of all the turmoil that was erupting there, yet she felt tense. Looking at Ives, she wondered for an instant if she had done the correct thing. He was wearing his white suit and, while it was a fairly comical getup, it was not offensive. Brook noticed again that she was a full head taller than he and reminded herself that she could probably outmuscle him if it became necessary. His long blond hair, while stylish, did seem on the edge of being foppish.

She knew why there was a tinge of regret about coming to him when she got to his eyes. That was the strength of Carlos Ives: his gaze. As she looked at Ives, she convinced herself that she had done the right thing; she had to convince herself. She gave credit to his eyes. A man with eyes like those was wise about life, and he would help her. She was glad she had come.

The visit went well, at first. He asked, "What is wrong? You seem quite upset, Brook."

She wanted to answer, but she also wanted to let this man pour his understanding and kindness over her body. She waited. He disappointed her immediately.

A razor flowed out with his words, cutting right to her vulnerability: "Does murder disturb you?"

Her affection for him was lost in an instant. Okay, she thought, to hell with you. I need answers and I will get them. If it cannot be nice, then it will be nasty.

She was angry.

"Yes!" she spit out, "Murder disturbs me. But there is more."

He moved around to his customary chair and sat. Once seated, he instructed her: "Go on."

Brook leaned forward, her hands on the green felt-table cover, her head nearly touching the crystal gazing ball. She spoke haltingly. "She's . . . she's growing younger. Younger, Ives . . . just like you told her she would. Either that . . . or . . . or I'm going mad."

Ives paused, looked at her and said, "I never lie, Brook!"

Her voice rose slightly in volume and considerably in tension. "You never lie? What the hell is that supposed to mean? Our plan was to get as much money from her as we could and . . . ."

He flipped up a halting hand gesture. " . . . I told you, if you remember, that if she killed, she would grow younger. Our 'plan,' as you call it, was just to fool her. You made it real . . . you started killing people."

In loud defense, Brook pleaded, "No! They made me . . . ."

Ives shook his head. "No one made you do anything, Brook. Face it, you are a greedy woman . . . and a murderess!"

She pulled back, as if struck.

He eased the tension slightly when he said, "Don't be alarmed. You see, I quite approve of what you started." He let a smile glimmer on his face.

Brook tugged at the conversation; she wanted it back where she could get answers. With answers she could leave this man and this city. She charged, "You'll never make me believe it. It's a trick. Some kind of a trick. She's not growing . . . younger. She's NOT!"

Ives shrugged. His voice was cynical as he replied, "You think we would go to such lengths to trick you, Brook? You place a great deal of importance on yourself. That is quite conceited."

He leaned forward, "And let me make you aware of something, my dear Brook. My pact with your aunt stipulates that no harm shall come to you!"

"Pact . . . ?" she cut in.

He nodded. "Yes, 'pact.' After the first murder, she gained the use of her hand. She called me to say the spirits were working for her. It was then that I told her of the facts . . . the facts of . . . death!"

He reached out his short arm and took hold of Brook's hand. He lowered his voice for effect as he told her: "Don't get in my way, Brook. There are worse things in life than death."

She was slipping. She felt herself falling into an abyss of fear and anxiety. She could not think why she had come to this man. She pleaded, hoping to find answers that would release her from doubt. "You don't make sense," she said. "You . . . you wanted her money."

Full of rage, Ives flung her hand away and stood. He was shouting: "*I want no money!* We need no money. We have Willa. . . . We have Miss Finney. . . . We have Raymond Brown. There are thousands more. Why do we need money?" He struggled and brought his passion under control. He moved around the table and came close to her. Her took her hands in his, looked at her with those penetrating eyes and said quietly, "You could be with us, Brook. Think of that. You too could belong."

Only one word stuck. "Belong?" she asked, "What do you mean? What could you mean?"

Mistaking confusion for interest, Ives squeezed her hands and said eagerly, "How old do you think Willa is?"

To Brook, the question was silly. The answer was obvious. "Willa is about twenty."

Ives moved his head from side to side. A knowing, arrogant smile appeared on his lips. "She was seventy-four when she first came to me."

Brook threw his hands away from hers. She tried to step backwards but was frozen there by his eyes. "No!" she cried, "You're insane!"

He ignored her insult and continued, "She is not your cousin, dear one. Her name is Margaret Norwood Brown. She is your neighbor, Raymond's sister."

Brook cried, "You lie!"

He went on, beating her down: "She went to live with you and your aunt at my direction. It was done so that she could send your aunt to me."

Exasperation overcame Brook as her voice began to crack. Too much confusion was being jammed into her mind. "Why? What purpose? Why would you do all of that?"

Ives' eyes were glowing again. The green hue radiated out. "It was Raymond's wish. He has come back to live with his love . . . . He has returned to Miss Finney."

"Returned," Brook's anger was giving way to desperate uncertainty. "He did not return to her. He is a neighbor. You LIE!"

He tried to hold her back, but now she had mustered the strength to step away from him, to break the strong will of his gaze. She spit out, "You are lying to make me think I am crazy!"

Ives' hands, eyes and voice pleaded: "That's not true. I am trying to offer you the same gift. The same gift that I gave to all of them."

She scoffed: "Life!"

His voice boomed, "Life eternal! All you have to do is kill . . . now and then. Just like your aunt Finney."

Brook's mind shattered like a piece of glass dropped to the floor. *"No . . . No . . . Not! It isn't real . . . you are the devil!"*

She twisted from his grip and spun away, running out of the room.

She was possessed by panic. She could sense him following quickly behind her. She burst into the reception room and made for the exit. The old, dirty, toothless woman who had been there before was standing, blocking Brook's escape. Brook tried to dodge around her, but the woman grabbed Brook's shoulders. The old woman's grip was stronger than one would expect of such a decrepit soul.

The woman's voice squeaked, "What's the matter, dearie!?"

Brook was screaming, *"Let me go . . . let me go!"*

The hag's screech was louder than Brook's scream. She offered, "I just want to help."

"NO! NO!"

Brook whirled violently and managed to spin loose from the woman's grip. Brook's eyes swept the room and she spotted a large vase on a wall table within her reach. She grabbed at the vase and began pummeling the head in front of her. The woman fell heavily to the floor. Brook straddled the woman, still hitting her.

Red began to mix with the white hair. Brook stopped. She stood there, looking down at what she had done. She hated herself. She hated Carlos Ives. She hated life. Everything was too much to bear. She wanted to cry, but she could not bring the sobs or tears. There was only an evil churning inside of her, a conflagration that she could feel but not identify. She dropped the vase and looked up. Over the wall table, where the vase had sat, was a mirror.

When Brook saw her own reflection, she tried to let out a scream. She wanted to let the whole world hear her anguish. She wanted to wrench her very soul out of her body and show it to the world.

She wanted to die. The scream would not come. In the mirror she saw something that she could not understand, but had to accept. Her fingers came up and gently touched the skin of her face. There were age wrinkles where her skin had been smooth. Under her eyes, where the color had been a fresh, vibrant pink, there were now the black worry sacks of a haggard person. Her hair, which had been soft and blond, was now wiry, and a prominent gray streak grew from the cowlick at the middle of her forehead. She had aged, she guessed, about fifteen or twenty years. She turned to Ives with terrible fear on her face.

His eyes narrowed into two corrupt slits, his lips drawn tight across his teeth. He said, full of vitriol, "You challenge me, Brook, and you will pay. My promise is a two-way proposition. Kill for me and you will have the remaining years given to you; kill against me and you will have the remaining years plucked from your life."

She looked back into the mirror and saw herself as a middle-aged woman, a pitiful sight.

Ives did not speak. She could not scream.

She ran out of the office and fled the mystical horror that had trapped her.

Brook thought: Sleep, dammit, sleep! Go back to sleep!

She fought to keep her eyes from fluttering. It was hard to be awake and not open her eyes. She could not be sure where she was. It was easy to tell she was not in her own bed. She was not in any bed. Her face could tell she had been sleeping on leather. A leather couch in the police station.

"She's really pooped," a male voice said. She worked extra hard at looking as if she were still sleeping. She did not want to face the police again.

Another male voice said, "You got anything out of the computer on her?"

The first voice said, "We ran a 'Wants-and-Warrants' on her: Nothing. Nothing in Missing Persons, either. I've got Records looking for something. They'll take about another hour to pull a clean check. I doubt if they'll find anything, though. She seems like a decent broad."

Brook felt that she was among friends, or at least not enemies. She opened her eyes.

She recognized the one man; he was the one she had talked to when they had first brought her into the station house. She had been pensive about the police, but they had picked her up as she ran through Jackson square. They had grabbed her just as she was about to run across Decatur Street. She probably would have been hit by a car. It was best, she admitted to herself. It was time to stop running.

"How ya feeling?" the detective named Gale asked her.

She gave a slight nod; she was not sure how she felt. She knew her body felt like it had been the test track for the Olympic relay team. She ached.

The detective named Gale said, "You sit up. I'll bet you'd like coffee." She nodded and pulled herself into a sitting position. Gale left the room.

It was just what a detective office in a police station should be: functional, no personal touches.

As Gale left the office, the other detective said, "I'm Detective Scarne. Gale and I work together. You okay?"

She nodded and adjusted her clothing. Then she ran her fingers through her hair and moaned.

"What's the matter?" Scarne asked.

She said, "Nothing." But there was something; her hair was a reminder. It was coarse and stringy. Her hair had always been soft and flowing.

So all of it had been real; it had not been a vile dream. And here she was, back in a police station, and ahead of her . . . . She could not, would not, let that terrible thought continue. She concentrated on trying to act normal; that was vital. She offered Scarne a big grin.

He asked, "How you feeling? Better now?"

Brook said, "I don't know . . . it's all a nightmare!"

"Hey, now." Scarne took a chair and brought it over to the couch. As he sat, he said, "Listen, we're here to help. You don't have to live any nightmare. I'll guarantee that."

She studied him. He was handsome. He was the type of man who would appeal to her if she were looking for an appealing man. His features were well-defined: alert eyes, manly nose, full mouth, jutting chin. His hair was cut in a modest, becoming style, his clothes were not trend-setting, but they were not shoddy, either. He put Brook at ease.

But he had the manner of a detective, too. He said, "Okay. Now that you've calmed down, I'd like you to run through what you told Detective Gale. He asked me to give him a hand with you."

Gale came back into the room carrying three cups of coffee in styrofoam containers. They sipped, then Brook spoke: "I've calmed down, but my story is the same."

Gale, being just a bit more officious than when they had been alone, said, "You said you killed a woman!"

Scarne asked, "You don't want to change that?"

Her hand shook: she spilled a drop of coffee. She said, "I have killed a woman . . . and I have killed two men."

"Tell us again," Gale instructed her. "How did you kill the men?"

Brook began to dislike this whole thing. She looked back and forth between them as she replied, "I shot one . . . with a gun . . . and . . . and the other . . . the other man, I killed with . . . with an arrow."

Gale looked at Scarne. Scarne kept staring intently at Brook. Gale asked, "With an arrow?" Brook nodded.

Scarne asked, "And the woman?"

Weakly, Brook admitted, "With a vase."

"A vase?"

She snapped and yelled, "Yes! A v-a-s-e! I beat her to death with a vase!"

Scarne reached out a hand and rested it on her shoulder. His touch was immediately calming. She looked up at him and he seemed to be a person who could understand. His eyes offered comfort. He asked Brook, "Can you show us where the bodies are? We really need a corpus delicti . . . from a legal point of view, that is."

She said, "Yes."

Gale said suddenly, as if Brook was not in the room, "She says she's from the Finney Mansion. You know we. . . ."

Scarne silenced his partner with a raised hand. He said drily, "You don't have to give me a history lesson on the Finney family. I know they're an old line; I know they give a lot of money to charities—like our Benevolent Association. So don't brief me."

Looking at Brook, Scarne asked, "Are the bodies on the Finney property or in the mansion?"

"The men are at the house, buried in the garden." She returned his gaze.

He asked, "And the lady?"

"I can show you that, too." Brook's voice faltered. "I killed the woman not more than a couple of hours ago in the reception office of Carlos Ives. He's a fortune teller. He's a phoney mystic who is helping them make me think I am crazy. They're all trying!"

"Hey, take it easy, Brook," Scarne was calming her down, "You keep that up and you'll work yourself into a bad state of paranoia. Where you think everyone is out to get you."

Brook replied coldly, "I know the term. And they are trying to get me."

Gale asked, "Why is this Ives person trying to do anything to you?"

Brook said with a flare of anger, "Because he is after my aunt's money and he wants me out of the way!"

Scarne asked, "Why did you kill the woman?"

Brook cried softly, "She tried to hold me . . . !"

Scarne kept an even tone of voice, "Hold you?" Brook nodded, then he asked, "What about the men, why did you kill them?"

Brook's voice became eager; Scarne seemed really interested. "It was Carlos Ives' idea. He made my aunt think she would grow younger if she . . . killed!"

Scarne corrected her, "But you said that *you* killed them."

Brook nodded. "She is old . . . was old . . . she was always there. She controlled the killings. It was as if she had me do it and she got the credit. So that she could grow younger."

Gale said with noticeable sarcasm, "Did she grow younger?"

Brook did not answer; she seemed afraid to answer.

Gale probed, "Well, did she?"

Brook nodded. Then, barely audibly, she said, "I . . . I think so."

Gale shook his head in disbelief. Again, as if Brook was not in the room, he said, "She's really into something, Scarne. What do ya think?"

Scarne ignored Gale. He asked Brook, "You said this Ives is a phoney. Right? Then . . . how come your aunt is growing younger?"

Brook dropped her head into her hands and sobbed out an answer: "I . . . I don't know!"

He reached out again and patted her on top of the head. He gave a nod to Gale and the two men moved to the other side of the room. Scarne said, "She's really spread pretty thin. She seems on the verge of mental collapse. I think we'd better get her home and let them get her to a doctor. I'd hate to be responsible for pushing her around the corner. She could crack anytime."

Gale asked, "What about this Ives guy?"

Scarne nodded, "Yeah, we'd better check him out, too."

They moved back to her. Scarne eased Brook's head up from crying. He stated, "Okay, Miss Brook. We'd like to take you home. All right?"

Brook exploded, "NO! You don't believe me! You think I'm crazy. That's just what they want!"

Scarne said, "We do not think you are crazy, Brook. We think that you are under some kind of a terrific strain. We will check out everything you have told us. But I think it is important for you to get home, quickly. Detective Gale and I are going to take you there, now."

Brook answered with calm determination: "I'll go with you. But first we stop at Carlos Ives' office. Then you'll see."

Gale, in an aside to Scarne, said, "There's been no report of anything about any Carlos Ives."

Brook said indignantly, "I won't go home if we don't go by Ives'."

The two detectives exchanged glances. Scarne said, "I'd like to see what he's up to, anyway. We might just hurt Brook more by forcing her to go home first. We're getting too many fortune tellers in the Quarter. Okay, Brook. We'll see what we can do. We'll stop by Ives' and let you show us anything you care to. Okay?"

As they came out of the elevator on Ives' floor in the building, Gale said, "I think I'll get with the building inspector and department of health. This place ought to be shut down. It ain't safe or healthy."

Scarne chided his partner, "Hey, are you going to act like a uniform cop all your life? Forget it. We've got Brook's problems to worry about."

Brook appreciated Scarne's attitude. During the ride from the police station, he had been kind and gentle. He seemed to want to get Brook taken care of properly and he did not poke fun at her. Gale had jibed a couple of times; Scarne seemed more mature and considerate.

Brook shoved the door open before Gale could knock. The two detectives were startled, because there was the technicality of illegal entry. They waited outside the door; Brook stood inside.

Ives came hurrying into the reception area. Looking out into the hall, he said, "Hello, gentlemen, can I help you?"

Brook cried near hysteria, "Let them in!"

Ives, talking smoothly and moving between the detectives and Brook, was saying, "Brook, why are you here today, my dear? Your appointment is for tomorrow."

She was loud: "I have no appointment!"

From the hall, Scarne said, "I'm Detective Scarne, this is my partner, Detective Gale." Both men flashed their badges. "We'd like to come in. Will you invite us in?"

Ives hesitated for an instant. It seemed as if he knew he had rights which were about to be violated unless he cooperated. Then, with an exaggeration of open hospitality, he said, "Please . . . please come in. I am so sorry. It is just that I am surprised at Brook being here a day early for her appointment."

Brook screamed again, "Dammit! I have no appointment!"

Ives gave an arrogant shrug of his shoulders and asked Scarne, "Is there anything wrong?"

Scarne made a quick study of Ives. He made a special effort to avoid insulting the small man standing there. He hoped Gale would be circumspect; there was enough going on. He said, "Mister Ives, Brook, here, is having a difficult time. She has come to us and now claims to have committed, or been a party to, the crime of murder. This is a serious position for a person to take. She has done this of her own free will."

Ives, feigning concern, replied, "I have nothing but good will towards Brook, gentlemen. But how does her problem bring you to my offices?"

Scarne stated, calmly, "She said she killed a woman here earlier in the day."

Ives' jaw dropped. He was almost too good as a theatrical performer as he gasped, "Brook . . . Brook . . . Brook. You said that you would not say such things again. You promised." The tiny man was trying to look imposing. He turned back to Scarne and said, "Brook has . . . well . . . she has a problem with a vivid imagination."

Brook lunged at Ives. Reaching down, she was able to snag his shoulder. Gale slipped easily forward and grabbed Brook. He held her still, but he could not stop her from screaming: "He lies! I killed her. I killed her right here. And when I did . . . my hair . . . . "

She stopped herself, gasping, looking at Ives. The mystic was cruelly quiet in his tone as he asked, "What about your hair . . . ?"

Sadly, she reached up a hand and abstractedly stroked the grey streak. She whimpered, "I . . . it . . . it changed."

Ives, beaming a smile of satisfaction said, in a voice laced with charity, "She really should be put away, gentlemen. But the family is bravely trying to prevent that sad option." Then he said to Brook, "Why don't you go home now, my dear? I am sure these gentlemen are willing to make sure you get there safely."

Brook raged. "He's trying to make you think I'm crazy! I killed her right there where he's standing!" She waved a frantic hand down the hall towards the seance room. "She must be in there. He put her in there!"

She broke away from the men and ran down the hallway. Scarne was after her fast. He caught up to her just as she flung the door open. Scarne grabbed Brook and prevented her from going through the door.

Indignantly, from behind them, Ives shouted, "Really, gentlemen. I am insulted. I'm in the midst of preparing a reading. I must ask you to leave and take Brook with you!"

Gale had come up beside Ives. All four of them were looking into the seance room. There was a smallish looking, ancient woman seated in a chair, facing away from them. She seemed to be totally concentrating on gazing into the crystal ball.

Scarne wrapped an arm around Brook and eased the door closed as he said, "I am sorry, Mister Ives. We surely did not mean to be disruptive."

With hostility, Ives said, "Quite! I think I have been most patient!" Then he said in a milder voice, "I think it should be clear to you what you are faced with, officers."

Scarne nodded understanding. They had overstepped the bounds of a polite invitation to enter on a person's property. It was time to get moving or to start thinking about civil rights violations.

"We will be going," Scarne said to Ives, and he made a motion for Gale to get hold of the other side of Brook. There had been enough excitement. They went out and Ives closed the door behind them. As they stood waiting for the elevator to come up, Brook was in a daze; she was unable to speak. The two detectives looked at each other and shook their heads; it seemed they were dealing with a sad mental case. Too bad.

Back inside his offices, Ives took several deep, calming breaths. He then walked down the hall and entered the seance room. With an evil smirk, he walked around the table to his chair. As he began to sit, he said out loud, "I am sorry for that little disturbance. She was such a nice person. Too bad."

He looked across the table at the blood-splattered face of the old woman. There was a cut in her forehead where Brook had pounded with the heavy vase. The cut was separated and a fissure in her skull revealed the yellow mass of her dead brain.

12

The detective's car was parked by the front entrance to the Finney mansion. Neither man had reached for the handle to open the door.

Gale said, "I just don't like going in there like this."

Scarne asked, "Ever been in the place?"

Gale shook his head.

Scarne said, "Me neither."

Gale said, "They could get mad as hell about this. We ought to take her back down to the station and let the family come for her. We could let the booking desk handle the whole thing. That way we'd stay out of it."

Brook, who had not spoken since the scene in Ives' office, said pleadingly, "Yes, let's do that. Make her come there. Then you can arrest her."

Scarne turned and spoke to Brook in the back seat: "Now listen, Miss Brook. We are on your side. We will let nothing happen to you. I had to get you out of that fortune teller's place because you were right in the gray area of breaking the law. I don't want to see you in any legal problems."

Brook's eyes widened in disbelief. "I've killed, Detective Scarne. I think that is pretty legal and pretty problematical!"

He smiled. "I'm glad to see you're getting yourself under control. I know when things go wrong, it is easy to lose control. You are handling yourself great right now.

Let's keep working on that, huh?"

She said, "I'll try."

Gale repeated, "I think we'd do well not to go in, Scarne. This is the bigtime and I'd hate to get the old lady pissed . . . . "

"Hey!" Scarne said angrily. "Watch the language."

Brook offered, "Please, gentlemen. I want to go back to the station with you. Please."

Scarne pleaded, "Look, Brook, the best way to solve a problem is to face it."

Brook urged, "I'll face it at the police station. Okay?"

Scarne was patient. "No," he said, "It's no good to run. You are a bright lady and you know that. Now, there is something going on that must be cleared up. I know, you claim you killed some people. Let's get it cleared up now."

She was reluctant. She looked to Detective Gale as if to find support. He had decided to let Scarne handle the situation. She nodded. They climbed out of the car and mounted the stairs.

There were several persistent knocks before the door opened and Willa, showing pleased excitement, shouted, "Brook!"

"I'm Detective . . . . " is all that Scarne got out before Willa plunged on with her enthusiastic welcome: "Brook, we've been worried to death. We searched for hours." Then, to the detectives, Willa said, "Oh, thank you, gentlemen, for bringing my cousin home . . . . "

Brook jammed in, "We're not cousins!"

Willa feigned shock. "Dear Brook, I don't understand?"

Scarne raised his voice to garner attention: "I am Detective Scarne, this is Detective Gale."

Willa nodded, then asked, "I don't understand . . . . Has she done anything . . . wrong?"

From behind Willa, Miss Finney came into view. She was the epitome of confidence as she said, "I heard you say you are detectives. I see my niece has been acting up again. My name is Finney. Miss Alcorn Finney."

They all felt it at the same time. It was as if a charge of electricity had bolted out of Brook. In near shock, she shouted, "You're . . . young!" Then, dazed, but quieter, she said, "You've grown younger. I can see it."

Miss Finney looked distraught at her niece's behavior.

Scarne asked, "Could we talk for a minute?"

Miss Finney said in a kindly voice, "Certainly. Please come in."

Willa escorted them into the formal sitting room across from the parlor. The room was furnished with a valuable collection of Victorian pieces set in a period environment. Miss Finney indicated that all should sit at the massive, carved oak table in the center of the room. It provided a meeting-room atmosphere.

As they adjusted themselves, Miss Finney asked, "Where did you find her?"

Willa was seated beside her aunt. On the other side of the table, Scarne and Gale flanked Brook.

Gale answered, "She sort of found us. Down by Jackson Square."

Miss Finney nodded without comment.

Gale said, "This is involved, Miss Finney. Do you think we can talk alone?"

Brook snapped angry glances at Scarne, "Don't spare my feelings: say it here! I'm crazy because I said I killed three people and I did . . . . " Brook threw an accusing finger at Willa, across the table. "You were there! You tell them! *Tell them!*"

Miss Finney tried to ease the tension: "Please, Brook, dear."

Brook redirected her anger towards her aunt. "Don't 'Brook dear' me, you witch! You killed that man last night. Right in this house! Right down in the basement!"

Scarne touched Brook again. The contact had a soothing effect and Brook's voice became moderate as she said, "He must still be down there. Go and look!"

From Miss Finney came an offer: "Why don't you make a check, officer. It might help things. Please go down and make an investigation."

Scarne gave a nod to Gale. Willa left to show Gale the way. At the door to the basement, Gale told Willa, "That's okay, miss. I'll go down on my own. If you don't mind. I'd just as soon do it alone." Willa did not argue. Gale went down the stairs. The lighting was good. The basement was not cluttered. Gale distracted himself a little by wondering how such a huge house could have such a well-ordered basement. It reminded him he needed to clean out his own cellar on his next days off. He wandered around, detecting. There was nothing to detect. The floor showed no sign of blood; there was no place to hide a body! the whole thing was silly. He studied the contents of the area and they were diverse: sewing forms from back in the days when women made their own clothing, tricycles and rocking horses from a day when children lived in the mansion, trunks packed with personal mysteries. None of it was the business of Detective Gale.

He walked to one wall where shelves had been built and he noticed stacks—hundreds—of *National Geographic* magazines. He knew that the collection had to have a considerable financial value; copies went back into the 1890's.

As a friendly gesture, he wiped some cobwebs away from the magazines. It made him feel as if he were helping to preserve the treasure. He turned to go back upstairs and, at his feet, he saw a baseball cap. He picked it up because it was litter in a litter-free basement. He looked for a place it might have come from, but he could not find a logical place. For an instant he wondered who might have been the fan, then he placed the hat on the protruding neck of the sewing body form.

He went back upstairs. While he was gone, the others had waited. Miss Finney chose not to speak; Brook was apparently waiting for damning evidence to be found by Gale; and Scarne was trying to figure out how to get away from the mansion without getting a reprimand from his department for harassing a community stalwart.

Willa walked into the sitting room with a tray containing glasses of iced tea, which Miss Finney had deemed proper for a policeman to drink. Taking the glass offered him, Scarne asked, "How did you know that iced tea was my favorite drink, Miss Finney?" She, with a charming flutter of her hand, replied, "Noblesse oblige, dear Sir."

Scarne sipped, feeling better. Possibly he would not face a reprimand.

Gale walked in at that instant, just as Brook shouted, "You are a wicked woman, Aunt Finney. They will find out what you have done!"

Trying to ignore the jibe, Miss Finney said, "Now, Brook, drink your tea."

Gale was sorry he had not been a couple of steps into the room when Brook grabbed her glass and sent it crashing against a wall. She screamed: "You'll not poison me!"

Scarne, too late, grabbed Brook's hands. He too felt he should have been more alert toward Brook. He said, "I am sorry she did that, Miss Finney. It was careless of me."

Miss Finney replied, "Don't chastise yourself, officer. We have had to handle Brook's actions for quite some time. We are quite used to them." Then she asked Gale, "Were you able to find anything in the basement, Detective Gale?"

"No, Ma'am, not a thing."

Miss Finney noted, "Naturally."

Brook, frustrated and hysterical, said, "The back garden! They buried him already. He is in the garden with the others!"

Brook struggled to stand; Scarne held her down.

Brook pleaded, "I'll show you. You must look! I'll show you where they buried him!"

Scarne looked at Miss Finney, who put up her hands in resignation. Scarne said to Gale, "Go with Miss Brook. See what she has to show. I want a few words with Miss Finney."

After Gale had left with Brook, Scarne turned to Miss Finney and asked, "Can you look after her? Do you take the responsibility if I leave her here with you?"

Miss Finney was patient. "Oh, yes. She will be all right. We are doing all we can for her, short of putting her away. That would grieve us, wouldn't it, Willa?"

Willa nodded and said, "We will call her doctor just as soon as you leave."

Scarne asked, "Is there any chance of her becoming . . . dangerous? She did toss that glass with a pretty hefty arm."

"Heavens, no," Miss Finney quipped. "She just lapses into fantasies; she imagines she has killed someone. We have been assured that she is quite harmless."

Scarne stood up and said, "Could we go out where they are? The other officer and I had better leave now."

Miss Finney rose and moved toward the door, saying, "I am sorry to have put you to all this trouble."

As they walked, Scarne looked around the mansion and grounds. At one point, he said, "This sure is a lovely place." Immediately, he felt the words were inadequate.

She felt his unease and politely offered, "You must come back. At a time more conducive to visiting."

They walked to where Brook was standing with Detective Gale. She was pointing to the garden with frustrated gestures. Work had been done in the flower beds. The plants were gone and full-grown grass had been sodded into place. There were a couple of bushes that looked as though they had been planted there during the Battle of New Orleans in 1812. Brook was talking with a feeble voice. "This is where they were buried. Yesterday. Last night!"

Gale responded, "It looks awfully undisturbed to me, Ma'am."

Unable to cope, Brook whimpered, "They did something. Really . . . they must have."

Scarne asked Brook, "When did you say they buried these people?"

Brook's eyes widened in confusion. She did not attempt to answer.

Scarne looked, shaking his head helplessly at Miss Finney.

From around the house, the neighbor, Raymond Brown, came walking, carrying an article in his hands. It was a rosebush.

He came up to the gathering and said, "I must admit my curiosity got the best of me; I saw the police car in front of the house."

Miss Finney spoke to Scarne: "This is our good neighbor, Mister Brown, officers. He is aware that Brook ran away last night. He helped try to find her."

As Brown was handing the rosebush cutting to Miss Finney, Brook erupted in anguish: "Him! Ask him! He knows all about it!"

To the policemen, Brown said, "Hey, ask me anything. I'm only too glad to help. Is Brook in trouble?"

Gale offered, "The lady said she thinks there are some bodies buried here."

"Buried!"

Brook pleaded, "Tell them, Raymond. You know we killed those men and buried them here. You said so last night at dinner, *You know! Tell them!*"

Gravely, Raymond said to Scarne, "I think she is really serious."

Gale said, "She is!"

Brook forced out words between sobs as she accused, "Ives said you were one of them, Raymond." Then, she said to Gale, "Don't you see what's happening . . . . ? They're all in it together. That's how they stay alive . . .

they keep killing people!"

Her aunt came forward and reached out to touch her niece. Brook's shoulders sagged, her head fell forward, lethargy took hold of her mind and body.

"Brook . . . dear . . . ." Miss Finney said. Brook stood silently.

Her aunt said, mostly to Scarne, but to all those who were standing there, "There is a limit beyond which we must not extend this with Brook. These gentlemen have been most patient. But I must tell you, Detective Scarne and Detective Gale, our Brook has had major problems in her life. I will not bother you with the sad details, but several years ago, Brook killed her husband. She was sent to the state asylum and then released to me. We have lived quietly with no difficulties. Brook has frequent debilitating dreams that cause her great anguish and sometimes there are uncontrolled fantasies. This is the first time she has run away and caused such turmoil. I am sorry."

Scarne said, "I appreciate you telling us, Miss Finney. We would have found out shortly. Our Records people would have dug up the file on Brook. Thanks for telling us."

"It is a sad situation, Detective Scarne. We should have done better and not let it get so far out of control."

There was a poignant pause, then Miss Finney added, "We will take better care of her now. Thank you for your concern." And, with her masterful take-charge manner she started the others all moving: "Willa, please see these gentlemen to their vehicle; I am sure that Raymond will help me get Brook up to her bed. The poor dear looks like she needs some rest."

The detective, Scarne, said, "I hope it all works out, Ma'am." Then he turned to Brook. "You'll be all right, Brook. We'll look in on you in a few days. Okay?"

Absently, Brook replied, "Yes, yes, I'd like that. Please come back. Soon!"

With a stern quality to her voice, Miss Finney said, "That will not be necessary!"

Scarne gave a knowing wink to Miss Finney and nodded agreement. As Willa led the two policemen away, Raymond took firm hold of Brook and began steering her toward the back door of the mansion.

The departing detectives could hear Brook rambling: "I'll never kill again . . . You won't make me do that again, Auntie."

The police were out of earshot when Raymond half carried Brook up the back stairs into the kitchen. As they moved through the house, Miss Finney observed, "My, my, your hair looks different, Brook. You look . . . older." Miss Finney smiled. "Are you ready to join, Brook?"

Brook cried weakly, "Never!"

Moving beside Raymond, Miss Finney said to Brook, "Strange indeed, Brook: When I kill, I grow younger; When you kill, you grow older!"

Mournfully, as if she had heard nothing, Brook sighed, "I'll never kill again. And I don't want your money, do you hear me? I don't want your money!"

They were nearing Brook's room as Miss Finney said, "We will see, dear Brook. A warning to you, though; Carlos Ives demands that no harm come to you. However, I could grow weary of you if you continue to be a bore. I would like to remind you that I am a strong woman. Remember that I will break my promise to Ives if you continue to obstruct our activities."

They were in Brook's room. Raymond lifted her and placed her on the bed.

Suddenly, with no warning, Brook sprang from the bed and ran to the front window of her bedroom. Before she could be stopped, she flung the window open.

Scarne and Gale were just getting into their car and Willa was saying a few parting words.

Brook screamed a hideous, high-pitched wail:

"Noooooooo! *I want to leave. Save me! She is going to kill meeeeee!*"

The detectives looked up, startled. Miss Finney forced her way to the window, pushing Brook back, out of sight. Raymond clapped a strong hand over Brook's mouth. He easily wrestled her to the floor. Miss Finney called down, mustering all the casualness possible, "Thank you, gentlemen. We will have everything under control soon."

To Willa, Scarne said, "We'll be going now. Sorry."

Willa nodded as the men climbed into their car. As they pulled away from the front entrance, Scarne asked Gale, "What the hell do you think about all of this?"

Gale said, "It's spooky."

Scarne paused for a moment to consider and then said, "Don't get me wrong. I don't mean I believe any of that girl's story, that's all nonsense. But you're right; it's spooky. That house, those people, that mystic, Ives. If I were going to write a story about witchcraft, I'd use the whole shooting match." He paused, reflecting, then asked, "You know something else?"

Gale gave a knowing laugh, "Yeah, I know 'something else'; you'd like to check 'em out, but you're afraid I'd laugh at you.

Scarne laughed and Gale added, "I was going to check them, anyway!"

Scarne nodded, "I thought so."

The car was well out of the front gate before Brook had stopped struggling on the floor with Raymond. By then, Willa had come running into the room. She was holding a hypodermic syringe in her hand. Willa sped to Brook and plunged the needle into her cousin's arm. In a moment, Brook was stilled by the drug. Raymond picked Brook up and placed her on her bed again. He said, "Hopefully, she will stay put this time!"

Miss Finney said, "The shot Willa gave her will last eight to ten hours."

Willa said caustically, "I should have doubled the dose.

That would have gotten rid of her for good."

Miss Finney said, "Ives wants her. We must do what he has ordered."

Willa smiled her agreement and said, "I know that better than you might think, Auntie."

Miss Finney said, "I am sure you do, Willa."

Willa walked out of Brook's room with Miss Finney and Raymond. As the door closed, Willa beamed a sly smile at Raymond and asked, "Well, what do you think?"

Miss Finney showed some confusion.

Raymond smugly replied, "I think things are just fine."

Willa asked, "How does she look to you?"

Raymond studied Miss Finney and said, "Almost right, I'd say."

Miss Finney was flustered and she asked, "What are you two chattering about?"

Willa said, "Auntie, dear, I think that right now is the time for me to leave you alone with Raymond." Willa slipped down the hall toward her own room. As she went, she added, "There is a lot for you two to talk about!"

Miss Finney was puzzled. She looked at Raymond. It took only a few seconds for a new look to start replacing the puzzlement.

Miss Finney's mouth flew open in a most unladylike manner, and joy poured forth.

13

Since Brook had killed her husband on their wedding night, she had been plagued by a recurring mental aberration. It had happened to her three days before in her bathroom as was drying from her shower. That was how the wickedness had always come to her: in the daytime, when she was alert and active.

Despite the scar on her soul left by the killing of her husband, she had never been subjected to nightmares. She had never had nightmares in her entire life, not even as an imaginative and sensitive child. For that reason, it was difficult for her to realize she was having a horrible nightmare. This nightmare was too real. The first thing that came to her was the awareness that she was not securely in her bed where she had been placed after Willa had given her the injection. She could not figure out how she had been transported out of her bed in the Finney mansion.

But she had been moved. No question. She had been moved to a field, an open field far out in the country. It was bright daylight. Suddenly, with a gift of knowledge that she wished had not been bestowed upon her, she realized that this was not a dream. This was actually happening! It had to be happening, because she could feel the dampness of the grass under her back and sense the air drifting coolly over her body. She was naked! She went to reach a hand down to check and make sure she was at least wearing underwear. Her hand would not move. She tried to kick a leg and thrust herself into a sitting position; the leg would not move. She looked and saw that her wrists and ankles were tied to stakes driven into the ground. Her arms were spread wide, her legs pulled embarrassingly wide apart. Above her, she saw the distorted faces of her Aunt Finney, Raymond Brown, Willa Hawk and Carlos Ives. They leered down at her body. Saliva dripped from Carlos Ives' mouth and splattered onto her breasts. She could not speak to them. Hate had struck her dumb.

She twisted her head, hoping that when she looked back they would be gone. She saw in the distance a sparse oak tree incongruently perched by itself atop a small knoll. The tree was an obscene object standing there twisted and bent out of shape. The sky was not the sky of a good or bad day. It was the ominous sky of foreboding.

Her head snapped back. A voice—belonging to Ives— was incanting, a deep, sonorous utterance: "Awake, ye powers of hell, the wandering ghost who once was Clyteninestra . . . . Arise. Immortality be upon this one if she accepts you as master and offers in return her soul to do your bidding."

Looking up, Brook saw the four of them turn toward the oak tree. She followed their line of sight. Thunder came, but no lightning. A cold wind blew from the invisible flames of a hidden fire. From her angle, she could not see well, but there was a movement, as if the humped shape of the tree was coming to life. But the tree remained still as a form moved into full silhouette. There was another horrendous explosion of thunder, and the black form moved towards Brook. She wriggled her body, trying to free herself. She felt the wet grass on her back, and then it was between her thighs. It was wrong; nothing was allowed there. The grass caressed her and fondled her and touched her privately. She was revolted. She yanked her head and looked back at the four hovering over her. She was furious that they were looking at her nakedness and she could not stop them.

They were gloating. They cried in unison: "He is here! He is here!"

She wanted to look away, to be free from this indignity, but a force she could not combat kept her eyes there on them as they bent down and petitioned: "He is waiting to take you. Give yourself to him!"

Reacting without thought—she did not need to think—she shouted at them: "NO!"

They chanted at her, "Let him take you!"

Brook hurt her throat with the scream: *"No! I will not accept him!"*

Ives knelt down, bringing his cherubic face inches from hers, and said: "We will bring his beauty to you. Bring him closer!"

Ives' companions waved and pleaded: "Come closer. Come closer. See your gift!"

Brook screamed: *"No! I will not accept him!"*

He stood over her. No fright had ever been so intense, no anguish she had ever felt could match this anguish. From the waist up, he looked to be an extremely ugly goat. Hair on all the surfaces, face full of pus-filled bumps, drool caked dry to the whiskers of his chin. His lower half was that of a man, unclothed. She writhed, trying to get free. The form knelt down before her, preparing to enter her body. She emitted a moan of fear.

Ives chanted, begged, "Share the sun's everlasting light and the eternity of darkness. There will be no danger of death. He will keep you forever. Say you will submit to him!"

Brook prayed that she might pass out, but her prayer was denied. She could only scream: "NO! . . . NO! . . . I WILL NOT!"

Her aunt, not ugly but with her face twisted in anger, screeched at Brook: "You must. Give yourself to him!"

"YOU ARE DOOMED TO HELL," Brook screamed back at her aunt, "I WILL NOT JOIN YOU THERE!"

Ives implored Brook, "You must do as he commands."

She could not yell any more; her throat would only let out a rasping whisper, "I will die first . . . . "

Carlos Ives, with contempt burning in his eyes, said, "You fool . . . . "

The bestial figure that was poised between her legs pulled himself to his feet and, without another gesture, it moved to the oak tree and vanished. The wind, still cold, blew over their knoll. She sensed rather than saw Carlos Ives placing a ceremonial cloth over her face. She was blinded. Then there was a noise that could not be identified by her senses until she felt the shovelfuls of dirt landing on her stomach, breasts, legs and face. They were burying her . . . . She would . . . .

Suddenly, a hand came loose. Somehow it was free of the stake. She swept the hand at the cloth to remove the suffocating dirt. It was a pillow. Only a pillow that had fallen over her face. She reached down to feel her body. It was fully clothed in her nightgown; she was safe in her bed. Except. Her body was drenched in perspiration. Brook sat up, trying to remember and forget at the same time. The nightmare had been too real, too savage. She wanted to cry, but crying had done no good over the past few days. She must get her life under her own control. She was in her own bedroom and that was a blessing.

She could hear voices coming from elsewhere in the house. Perhaps it was the detectives come back to save her. She climbed out of her bed and eased to her door. With it open, she could hear voices from the first floor. She tiptoed down the stairs, ever so careful not to make a sound, on guard not to be seen. From the second floor landing, if she stood exactly in the right spot, it was possible to see more than half the front parlor through the double sliding doors of the entrance foyer. Brook located her spot on the landing.

She could not tell if the chill came over her body because the nightmare had caused her to sweat or because of what she saw in the parlor. Her aunt, Willa and Raymond were there, and they had another derelict in the room with them. The poor man was a sorry sight; Brook's heart went out to him. She must stop them. The man was tipsy. He wore tattered clothing.

Miss Finney was asking, "You say your name is Kosko . . . ? Is that Russian?"

The man spoke with a heavy accent: "Polish! I wanted to be a concert pianist." He flexed his fingers with their dirty nails and grime worked deeply into the skin. "Good hands! But I went into the coal mines instead."

Willa asked, "Why?"

He moved a hand to his face and rubbed, as if to wipe away the dirt there. He told them, "Just for a little while, I thought. Then one day, I looked around and I was thirty-five, and I ordered myself: *Now!* Now is the time! So I left Stupsk and came to America."

Raymond asked, "And how old are you now?"

Proudly, the man answered, "I am now fifty-five. I am going to begin my music studies any day now. First I must get onto my feet. You know, save the money so I won't have to work. It is not too late."

Raymond said aside to Willa, "Fifty-five. That could be exactly right!"

"It sure could be," Willa replied. She asked the man, "Another drink, Mister Kosko?"

Politely, the man said, "Yes! Your wine is good. Not so good as I remember having in Pozan. But it is a good wine."

Willa went to the bar and Brook saw her put some white powder in the man's glass.

Willa approached the man and handed the drugged wine to him. "There, you may have all you want, Mister Kosko."

He had sipped and was preparing to finish it off when Brook screamed.

The scream brought the glass crashing down, and the

people in the parlor jumped up.

"RUN!" was the beginning of the scream, then Brook pleaded, "*Please! Run while you can!*"

Miss Finney shouted at Willa: "Where's the nurse? Dammit! Where is she!"

All were shocked; Miss Finney had cursed.

Brook, hunched by the railing of the second floor landing, spun around just in time to see a hulk of a woman in a white uniform running toward her.

The man, Kosko, had moved out of the parlor into the entrance foyer; he was confused.

Brook jumped up and yelled at the top of her voice: "*Don't drink! They'll kill you!*"

Brook was hoisted in the air by the powerful arms of the nurse. She had never felt so defenseless; the woman was as strong as two people.

Seeing the man backing towards the front door, Brook implored him: "Get out! *Run for your life!*"

A broad, antiseptic hand clamped over Brook's mouth. But she could still see: the man had sipped enough so that he was not able to escape. He slid to the marble floor of the entrance foyer; the drug had taken hold. Brook was carted back to the bedroom and tossed onto her bed by the nurse.

Brook hissed venomously, "Who the hell do you think you are?"

The nurse glared coldly at Brook. She did not reply.

Miss Finney came barging into the room and demanded of the nurse: "Where were you?" The monster of a woman towered over Miss Finney's petite figure, but the nurse was cowed by authority. She answered, meekly, that she had gone to the bathroom and left Brook unguarded for only a few minutes. Miss Finney slapped the nurse, who accepted the abuse.

Looking at Brook, the aunt said, "Time is running out for you, Brook." Brook had been plopped down in an ungainly position. With effort, she pulled herself into a sitting position and declared: "I will see you destroyed. I don't know how, but I will!"

Miss Finney sneered, "Soon you will know how impossible that might be."

Behind the nurse, Willa came into the room and displayed a syringe. She handed the instrument to the nurse and ordered: "Give this to her. And stay on duty!"

The nurse hulked over Brook.

In the squad room, Detective Scarne worked his way through a pile of folders that were in need of clerical attention. The French Quarter had recently lessened its crime problems by imposing a teenage curfew. But there were still persistent, perennial violations: purse snatching, pickpocketing, drugs and prostitution. Scarne wondered—for the millionth time in his career—if all law enforcement jobs involved such extensive recordkeeping. He looked up as Gale came into the room.

Gale closed the door and asked: "How old would you guess Miss Alcorn Finney is?"

Scarne flipped a folder closed and lit a cigarette as he gave careful consideration to the question. After adding a few years that might be covered with make-up and then a couple more that a well-tended figure might camouflage, Scarne answered, "I'd put her at forty . . . forty-five."

Gale nodded and said, "I'd have guessed the same. I might have gone a bit younger and said that, since she has money, she's aged a bit from fast living. But I was not willing to go below the upper thirties."

Scarne asked, "What'd you find out?"

Gale replied, "According to the records, a daughter was born to Mister and Missus Bernard Finney in that very house. . . ."

Scarne waited while Gale paused. Finally, Scarne said, "Okay. When was she born?"

Gale continued: ". . . 1896."

Scarne blew out a stream of smoke with a long whistle

before he challenged: " . . . 1896?"

Gale moved to his own desk and said, "That is correct, Detective Scarne. Our Miss Finney, that 'almost-lovely-chick' should be eighty-five years old. But she's not! We have seen that!"

Scarne offered, "Maybe there are two Alcorn Finneys!"

Gale scoffed, "Born in the same house? Quite a coincidence, wouldn't you say?"

Scarne nodded. "An impossible coincidence!" Then, after a moment's thought, he added, "Do you suppose the old lady is dead?"

Gale picked up on the thought and continued, "But the relatives are keeping it a secret so they can live on her money?"

Scarne smirked. Then, in a conspiratorial tone, he speculated, "Maybe they even killed the old gal off."

Gale laughed and quipped back, "Well, we solved that case. Now what do we do for the rest of the day?"

Scarne said, "I don't know what we're going to do about that case. But hold off on sending your report to headquarters, okay?"

Gale asked, "How come?"

"Think it through," Scarne said, "I don't want it to look like we were taken in by a bunch of loonies."

"It won't," Gale protested.

"I know," argued Scarne, "But it is something to think about. Listen, do you want to dig into this? Just for the fun of it?"

Gale asked, "You mean check on skid row and see who is missing? And have a long talk with Miss Finney and especially her niece, Brook?"

"Take it easy, wise guy," Scarne checked Gale's humor, "Do what has to be done. But hold onto the report until the very end. Deal?"

"Deal!"

Scarne rose from his chair and said, "Let's take a ride."

"Where first?"

As he put on his jacket, Scarne said, "Skid row."

Skid rows in any town—every town—have a bush telegraph that signals when the police are on the prowl. Scarne and Gale had set the New Orleans bush telegraph tingling and, after questioning a dozen destitute souls, they came upon a man who had obviously not gotten the message that the law was afield. The bum was caught completely unawares as the detectives walked into his alley haven. Scarne was, by that time, tired of conversing with bums who thought it was cute to harass the police. Scarne began, "No crap now. We're looking for two men."

The bum slurred, "Wud dey do?"

Scarne snapped back, "They didn't do anything. They're just missing. Are any of your chums missing?"

"Everybody's missin' down here, Chief."

Gale, more patient, probed, "Actually, we are not sure if they are even missing or not. Maybe they didn't even exist."

The bum scrunched up his face and said, "Gowaan with ya! You puttin' me on, ain'cha?"

Gale backed off. He could feel his own patience wearing a little thin. "We are just running a routine check," he said flatly.

The bum asked, "You been drinking hair tonic, too?"

Gale laughed and said, "Nope. Just looking for some help . . . Mister?"

"Wha'da'ya gotta know my name for?"

"Forget it," Gale sighed. "Do you know of any men that might have been picked up by women lately?"

"Ha," the bum scoffed, "that happens fifty times a night."

Scarne reentered the frey: "The difference this time is that the gal had a car and she was an uptowner."

The bum snapped back, "That just means they charge more money. That's all."

Scarne gestured to Gale that they should leave. The detectives turned and began walking away when the bum stopped them by saying, "There was one funny thing last week."

Anxiously, Gale spun around: "What was that?"

"Well," the bum began, "There's two guys that hang out together a lot. Down by the yards. Well, I seen a car pull up and them talking to a gal that got out of that car."

"Who?"

"Let's see . . . Morgan and O'Hara. That's their names." He paused, struggled to get his memory working, then went on, "Well, this gal gets out and she is talking to them. Then it looks like Morgan is sent away. O'Hara talks a little more and then he gets into the car. He rode off with them."

Anxiously, eagerly, Gale pressed, "Where do we find this Morgan and O'Hara?"

The bum replied coyly, "I . . . I can't tell you that!"

Gale pleaded, "But this is important!"

"Naw," the bum resisted, "I don't know where they are. I can't tell you anythin' like that."

Gale was flustered. He was trying to find the right words when Scarne edged past and took out a five dollar bill. He held the bill up for the bum to see as he said, "They haven't done anything. We think they may be hurt."

The bum was shaken at the sight of the money.

The bum snatched the bill out of Scarne's hand and said, "They're down by the train siding . . . in that wrecking yard. You'll find them sleeping in a blue Chevy. The one with the hood off."

With that, the bum scampered away.

Gale asked, "Does that always work with these guys?"

Scarne replied, "It has so far. They need money to buy booze. Simple."

It took the pair less than fifteen minutes to locate the Chevy wreck. The bum, Morgan, was asleep inside.

Scarne picked up a hubcap filled with rainwater. He tossed it into the back seat of the car.

Morgan shouted and sputtered, "What the son-of-abitchin' hell. . . ." He spotted Scarne. "You tormentin' bastards. You got some nerve."

Gale flashed his badge and ordered the bum, "Police! Get on your feet."

Flustered, Morgan scrambled out of the car. Weaving, he tried to get his mind to wake up with his body. He begged: "Whatever it is, I didn't do it! Read me my rights . . . I forget them!"

Gale smiled, "That won't be necessary. We just want to talk to you."

Morgan, realizing he was not in trouble, became hostile: "You break my ass, almost drown me, then all you want to do is talk? What do you jerks do when you're serious?"

Scarne stepped in and shoved a pack of cigarettes at Morgan who said, "Naw, thanks. They're bad for your health."

Scarne asked, "Are you Morgan or O'Hara?"

"I'm Morgan. Right."

Scarne stated, "Last week you were standing with O'Hara when a gal came up in a car."

Vaguely, Morgan stirred around in his memory. "Last week . . . last week . . . Yeah! I remember."

Gale asked, "What happened?"

Morgan replied, "Well first, it was two gals. It weren't hardly anything. They parked out on the road, then one of them comes out and starts talking with us."

"Then what?"

"She said she only wanted to talk to one of us. So O'Hara gives me a look and says, 'Beat it.' So I beat it. Then I see them go over. He gets in with her and they take off."

Scarne asked, "Did you get a good look at the women?"

"Enough."

Gale asked, "What about their hair. Each one."

"Yeah," Morgan replied snidely, "they each had some."

Gale said impatiently, "Do you remember if either had a gray streak through the center of her hair?"

The bum shook his head. "Naw, they weren't that old."

Scarne asked, "Where can we find O'Hara?"

"Hey," Morgan seemed to be startling himself, "you know, I ain't seen him since then. He must'a got a good bunk, or somethin'."

The detectives looked at each other.

After a pause, Morgan asked, "Is it okay if I go back to sleep? You sure as hell made my bunk a mess. It'll take half the day for it to dry out."

Scarne took out another five dollar bill and handed it to Morgan. Scarne offered no advice; Morgan offered no thanks.

Scarne said, "One more thing, Morgan."

"Yeah."

"How can we spot this O'Hara?"

Morgan laughed, "That's easy. Just look for the guy wearing the Dodgers baseball cap. That O'Hara wouldn't be caught dead without his baseball cap."

The detectives were grim. Gale said, "Thanks." Morgan climbed back into his wrecked-auto sleeping quarters.

As they approached their auto, Scarne said, "I think it's a dead end, Gale. It's the wrong girls. Too bad."

Gale stopped walking and took a deep breath. Scarne listened as Gale asked, "Remember when you sent me down into the Finney cellar to have a look around?"

Scarne replied, "Sure."

Gale bit the inside of his lip before he answered. "Well, when I was down there, I found a Dodgers baseball cap lying on the floor." There was silence for a moment.

Then Scarne gave a couple of quick nods and said, "You know what we're going to do, Gale?" Gale waited anxiously. "We're going back to headquarters and check out another vehicle for you to use. Then I'm going to have a long talk with that Carlos Ives character . . . and you are going back to the Finney mansion and pick up that baseball cap. I'll meet you there!"

Gale asked, "What about the report?"

Scarne smiled as he said, "You don't worry. I'll file it."

14

The room was full of mist, a fleeting, obscure mist so wet you couldn't light a match. Through the mist, Brook saw a figure outlined in a shaft of light. The figure's voice called her name and offered something; she recognized her name, not the offering. A force made her rise from her bed. She stood wondering, frightened.

It was Scarne! The detective, Scarne. His voice was saying, "Brook . . . come with me. I'm going to help you . . . come. You must escape . . . . "

Brook knew she must escape and she was glad Scarne would help her. He seemed a nice person. By now she knew it was another dream; a house does not fill with mist in real life; a detective comes to a crime, not a rescue. But it was a nice dream: He threw a cloak of safety around her. She surrendered to Scarne's imperative. He led her. In the hallway outside her bedroom, the mist took on a different quality. It was there, but it was possible to see through it, to penetrate the fog.

Scarne held her hand. His was warm and comfortable. She followed with no more urging. He did not speak. They descended the stairs and entered the foyer. The front entrance was a few feet away: freedom at last!"

A sound came from the sitting room. She looked and it was dark in there. She leaned toward the front door, but Scarne tugged with a gently coaxing pull. "No," he whispered, "this way . . . we have friends . . . . " She trusted. As they moved inside the doors to the sitting room, a thought began to take form in her mind. She looked painfully at Scarne, but he had turned his head away. She tightened her grip on his hand, pleading that he turn to her. The thought sped towards completion. Silently, she screamed at Scarne to look at her so she could stop the evil thought that was forming. The thought arrived: She would not know she was dreaming if she were really dreaming! The doors behind them slammed shut and the noise was loud and echoing. The room was in total darkness save for a shaft of light which beamed down on them.

She wanted to let Scarne know the thought that had come to her. She pulled his hand. He turned. It was Carlos Ives. Scarne had turned into Carlos Ives. She was permitted a scream. Lights flooded the room, more lights with each new gasp from her mouth. As the lights came on, she could see that the room was empty of furniture. At the far end was a large mass of stone: an altar. Beside the altar stood Miss Finney, Willa and Raymond.

Brook would not stay in the room. She turned to run. The wall where the door had been was solid. There was no way out. There were others in the room, people she had never seen before. A movement by Carlos Ives caught her attention and she started to beg him to let her out of this place. She had come to the room in error. She did not want to interfere. She would leave.

Ives motioned to two men. They came to Brook in an easy manner. As they took hold of her, Ives approached her and said, "There is nowhere to run, Brook. You should feel fortunate. Some of us would have destroyed you long ago, but He considers you to be special." The men held her firmly. She did not respond to Ives. He waved his hand and the two men led Brook to the other end of the room.

On the altar there were symbols, jagged signs that meant something, but not to Brook. None of what was happening meant anything to Brook. She felt numb. All she could feel was fear. The men's hands moved over her body, taking off her gown, stripping her of even her underwear. She fought the hands but was no match for their strength. She was naked. They lifted her up onto the stone altar. She thrashed and twisted, but each effort to resist was countered by an overpowering force. Her hands were chained, her arms spread wide. She was on her back. Her legs were shackled in a way that forced her knees in the air and her feet flat on the stone. Her pubis was toward the congregation.

Vilely, they looked at her nudity and she cried in shame. She lifted her head, searching for a clue as to what would happen to her. The people in the room were lined up, as if they were a congregation in a church. Ives came to her and stopped close in front of the altar. She watched him through the 'V' of her legs. He leaned forward, bringing his head down.

She closed her eyes and emitted a mournful, agonized cry.

She stopped.

Ives had not made contact. He was chanting. With tears of pain on her cheeks, she looked at Ives. A devilish cherub. His face angelic, his words satanic: "Emperor Lucifer will see and hear." Ives offered a ceremonial bow and brought his face close to her body. He stopped before touching, then he continued his litany: *Shabrir . . . Xilka . . . Besa . . .* His witnesses from the lower regions . . . *Bael . . . Agares . . . Botis . . . Lilith . . . Valefar."*

The congregation moaned a supportive incantation. Then, with a blaze of passion in his eyes, Ives snapped himself erect and shouted: "Bring forth the sacrifice!"

Brook raised her head to see. Two men, different men than those who had placed her naked on the altar, came forward dragging the limp form of a man between them. Brook could see. It was the old Pole, the man she had urged to flee. He had not been able to flee. He was bloodied. One eye was bloodied. One eye was swollen closed from being struck; gaps showed in his mouth where teeth had been knocked out. But the blood surging out of his mouth was too much to be coming from tooth damage. The surge of blood was offensive; it came with an unearthly sound, a sound that seemed to come from the man's soul.

As the man was being pulled up by chains, Ives told Brook, "He cannot speak. He has no tongue. Look at the power of Satan, dear Brook." Then she could see what Ives had told her, the blood was pouring out of the man's mouth from a red blob in his throat. The blob was all that remained of his tongue. She wanted to look the other way, but an evil fascination held her.

Ives nodded to Miss Finney. Brook looked pleadingly at her aunt, begging her to let her escape this horror. Miss Finney and Willa wore black robes. Hoods covered their heads. On a signal from Ives, Miss Finney extracted a long daggar from the deep folds of her sleeve. The knife came up and was poised at the chest of the man stretched up off the floor.

Ives looked down at Brook and asked, "Will you save him, Brook?" Brook did not want to know what Ives meant because she knew what Ives meant. She blocked comprehension. "Don't fool yourself, Brook," Ives said with a chill in his voice. "You know what I mean. You can save Master Kosko here, if you will submit. Will you submit?"

She could not do it. She did not answer. From high beside her, where the chains had elevated him up for the sacrifice, a sound came out of the gap in Kosko's face: "Save . . . me . . . Brook."

Her head snapped toward the bloody mess. Her eyes grew ugly with anger and hate. She yelled, "You cannot speak!"

More blood accented his plea, "Save me . . . please . . . save me!"

With more anger, more hate, Brook spit out, "Shut up!

You cannot speak!"

Ives looked at Miss Finney; the knife was poised. Ives began: *"Astaroth, Asmodeus, Bael, Belial,* we beg you to accept the sacrifice of this human which we now offer You, so that we may receive the things we ask. Master of slanderers, dispenser of evil, steward of voluptuous sins and monstrous vices . . . Satan . . . it is you we worship!"

The congregation moaned, repeating three times: "Satan, it is you we worship." The last time, the moan rose to a passionate plea.

Ives intoned: *"Sanguis eius super nos et filios nostros* . . . His blood be upon us and upon our children. . . ."

Kosko's bloodied voice pleaded through the chant, "Brook . . . save me . . . . "

Brook's voice was barely audible: "You . . . can't . . . talk . . . . "

Ives nodded emphatically to Miss Finney. The knife plunged into the chest and blood erupted as if from a fountain. The blood gushed out and down onto Brook's body. She could feel the sticky, warm slime flow across her skin. On a signal from Ives, the congregation moved to surround the altar. They moved their hands over Brook's body. They spread blood onto each surface, into each crevice. She commanded her eyes to shut. When they refused, she begged them not to watch the offense that was being done to her. Men and women alike participated in the blood anointing of her body. Hands coursed sensually across her breasts, fingers ushered blood into her orifices. A carmine luster glowed as the hands massaged the fluid on her.

The urge to vomit had passed with the first splash of Kosko's blood landing on her lips; she was beyond revulsion. The worst had happened to her. There could be nothing more! She was wrong. Submission was ahead. A deafening clap of thunder signaled. The participants in the ritual retreated and Brook could see that a thing, a vulgar form, was approaching her. Her efforts to cope with the horror were futile. She experienced total revulsion.

The form's skin was covered with open sores that dripped a gray mush. In places there were rough scales; in others there were mats of kinky hair. It was a large form, bigger than a man. It came at her bearing an odor from the bowels of the earth. It was nearly on top of her now. She could see that it was naked from the waist down. Its member was erect. It came closer. All senses within Brook collapsed. The collapse brought blackness. She escaped into a limbo, crying, "No . . . no . . . no . . . ."

She awoke in her bed. She lay there, struggling not to reexperience the sensations that had just surrounded her. She looked around her bedroom. There was no mist. There was no noise from outside her door.

She reached over and snapped on the light. As the darkness retreated, a comfortable calm came over her. It was a dream, all a dream. Aloud, she said, "It was a dream!" She felt joy.

Then she wondered why she felt joy at not feeling horror. Had things been so bad with her that joy was the exception, horror the rule?

She raised her hands as if in a hallelujah and cried out, "It was a dream. I will not surrender."

The words took on an acid taste; her arms froze painfully in midair. There were bloody lacerations on her wrists, as if they had been chained.

Slowly, knowing what was coming, she lowered her arms and, with shaking hands, removed the bed covers from her body. Her fingers went to the front of her nightgown and pulled the bows loose. The gown fell away from her body. Her skin was covered with caked blood.

15

Detective Gale sat at the front entrance to the Finney mansion. He did not want to go in.

A warning, not tangible, came to him from a source that he did not understand. It told him to leave this place, forget the Finneys and their madness.

He censured himself. He was a cop and a good cop. Cops do not listen to flakey ideas. He climbed out of the car and went up the front stairs. He must have been expected: the door opened before he could rap the knocker.

She was a beauty. Gale had not seen her before. She looked eighteen, maybe twenty. Her figure was dazzling and well displayed in the tight, low-cut dress she wore. Her face was a tad more delicate than a piece of Dresden China.

Her voice poured softly, like real maple syrup. She could charm.

Charmingly, she asked, "Could I help you?"

Miss Alcorn Finney had lied; the last thing she wanted to do was to help Detective Gale. He was a threat to her, but she had to play the game because if he ever guessed she was the person standing in front of him, trouble would be manifold.

Gale asked, trying to sound official, "Is . . . is Miss Finney at home?"

Miss Finney would have enjoyed toying with him, but there was danger in this detective. She would have to be very careful.

"I am sorry," she said, "but my aunt has had to go away. I fear she will be gone for some time. I am her niece, Goldie."

Gale studied the woman—girl—standing in the doorway, then said, "The resemblance is quite remarkable!"

With overt coyness, Miss Finney said, "I will take that as a compliment, sir. I think my Aunt Finney is beautiful."

Gale stuttered as he realized he had neglected to identify himself. "Hey, I'm sorry. My name is Gale. Detective Gale from the New Orleans Police. I was here before."

Miss Finney acted out her part and, with great reluctance, she said, "Of course, Aunt Finney told me about you. Please come in."

She conducted him into the front parlor.

She gestured towards one of the divans and sat on the other.

"Please sit, Mister Gale. Can I offer you a drink of something? Some refreshment?"

Gale shook his head, "No," he said as he looked around. He added, "There were two other girls here . . . ."

Miss Finney nodded. "You must mean Brook and Willa."

He agreed, then questioned: "How is Brook?"

Miss Finney replied, "Aunt Finney was really worried about her; that is why I am here. Brook and I are quite close. You might say I have a calming effect on her."

Gale observed, "Your aunt has quite a few nieces. You were out yesterday when we were here."

"Yes," Miss Finney did not like the course of the conversation, "I returned last night, right after you left. I was shocked at Brook's condition."

The detective showed real concern as he said, "It could develop into something serious, you know. Having an illusion that you have murdered indicates a dangerous mental disorder."

Then, when she did not respond, he asked, "Is Brook better today?"

She replied that Brook was much better.

"Is she here, then?"

"She is asleep in her room. I hope we do not have to wake her. She has been through a great ordeal."

Gale said, "I understand. I don't think that will be necessary at this moment."

Miss Finney nodded, "She is so tired."

Brook's exhaustion had been subjugated to an urge for survival; every fiber was enlisted in the effort to escape. She had cast aside the thought of going out the window. It was too far to the ground and she was so weakened she might slip and fall to her death. Death! Maybe death would be better than the life she was experiencing. No! Life was all that mattered. Life was good and could be better. If she could just escape. Getting out of her bed, Brook realized she was almost too weak to stand. She used furniture as support to get across to the door. The nurse! Back in the jumbled memory of events, she remembered there had been a nurse. A big, powerful woman who looked as if she possessed the strength to kill with her bare hands. The nurse would have to be avoided. But where was she? Where would a nurse stay when not with a patient? The hall outside the door. Surely, the nurse would be in the hall. The hall would be impossible. Brook turned. She did not realize how jellied her muscles were; she bumped into a table and a lamp crashed noisily to the floor.

The door flew open before the tinkling of glass had stopped. The bulk of the nurse loomed; Brook staggered backwards.

The nurse came forward, lumbering like a massive machine of death. The nurse spit out, "You worrisome shit! You have caused me enough trouble. I'd like to kill you!" Brook had lived through worse abuse. The nurse's vitriol did not scar; it did not even touch. The nurse came close and the white uniform sleeve flew through the air as a big hand caught Brook in the face. The blow flung Brook to the floor. A white nursing shoe with a thick rubber sole darted into Brook's stomach. The rubber did not soften the impact.

A place in her mind or heart flashed a danger signal: there was trouble, this was not a small matter. The nurse was so strong and Brook so worn down from her trials that the right blow in the right place could finish Brook's life. In a series of connected, urgent moves, Brook rolled, kneeled, dived, and grappled. The nurse went down. The two women rolled on the floor. Another table, a night-stand, fell and spilled its contents on the floor. A weapon lay there. As Brook's hand and fingers folded tightly around the long scissors, there was no doubt in Brook's mind as to the outcome. The sharp point plunged several inches through skin, flesh and muscle until it stuck on some gristle and bone. En route, the points had cut blood vessels and severed nerves. The nurse convulsed in agony and was still.

Brook was grateful. She felt she had no time for anything other than getting free of the mansion. But she was mentally sound enough to know that she must be more prepared, more ready to escape. She would take the moments necessary to insure success. She sat thinking. Unaware, she also allowed herself the detached pleasure of watching blood flow from the nurse.

Gale and the rejuvenated Miss Finney stood in the hallway. She was hoping he would lose interest and head out the front door. He wanted to go into the room across the hall, but the big double doors were closed. Gale wanted to go all over the mansion and probe in dark corners. If there was ever a place that would reveal skeletons in closets, the Finney mansion qualified in Gale's mind.

But this was the Finney Family and they were people of consequence in the French Quarter and in New Orleans Society. Considerable sums of charitable contributions came from the Finneys. The property value made for a sizeable tax payment. No, the Finneys were not to be tinkered with by some young detective. But he could not resist trying to see what he could see. He was determined to get upstairs and peek in on the girl, Brook. First, he would go for the baseball cap that Scarne had asked for; that would be important, too. Working without a warrant was hell; you had to be so hesitant.

He asked, "Would you mind if I went for another look in the cellar?"

The pause on her part was infinitesimal, but he caught it. She said, "I am sure Aunt Finney would not mind. She is forever telling me how important it is for us to support our police. Please, help yourself."

He tasted that moment of hesitation as a stalking predator tastes blood; she was hiding something. As Gale went down the stairs into the basement, Willa and Raymond came out of the sitting room where they had been waiting for the detective to leave.

Willa was angry. "What should we do?" she asked her aunt.

Miss Finney replied, "Nothing. The cellar is clean. He will leave and we can then go about our business.

Raymond came to Miss Finney and took her in his arms. She looked up and said wistfully, "I have waited for you, John. It has been so long. It has been so long."

Her lover from sixty years before looked at her and said, "It has been too long, dear Goldie. But now we are together."

Wanting more contact, Miss Finney held his hand. He spoke quietly, close to her ear: "All this has been done so that we could be together. When I met that old man in

France and he asked me: 'Would you like to stay young forever?' I said I would give my soul for that so long as I could be with you, the one I love. And now, the promise is fulfilled. We are together."

Willa said with force, "You two have earned what you have. But you have an eternity ahead of you. Right now, we had better do something or you might get to watch each other through the bars of a jail cell."

They pulled apart. Willa demanded, "What are we going to do?"

Miss Finney's love said, "I'll not have anything come between us again. I'll kill Brook if I have to."

Willa cautioned, "That is forbidden. You know He wants her. He has plans for her."

Miss Finney questioned, "What if he does not win her? Suppose he fails?"

Willa stated: "He never fails!"

The trio went silent as the door from the basement opened and Detective Gale came into the hallway.

"Ah," he said, "I see we have company."

Miss Finney said, "I am sure you remember Mister Brown, our neighbor, and my cousin, Willa."

Gale shook hands with Raymond and smiled at Willa.

Willa asked, "Where is your partner, Mister Gale?"

Casually Gale responded, "Oh, he'll be along. But I'll wait for him outside. I've troubled you enough already."

Miss Finney said, "Now that is silly, Mister Gale. You have been no trouble at all."

Contradicting her own words, she moved to the front entrance. They all moved with her.

She asked, "Did you find what you were looking for?"

He was studying her, fingering around in his mind for a fact that he could not pin down. He replied, "No. Not really. I must have been mistaken earlier." Then, without a pause, he asked, "When do you expect Miss Finney back?"

Miss Finney replied, "I do not really know. I will have

her call you."

"No," Gale said, "I'd just like to see her in person. I'd like to see the two of you together." A slight pause in his statement had accentuated the word "together."

Not too coyly, Miss Finney asked, "What on earth for?"

"Just a friendly chat. I'll want to see Brook, too!"

Miss Finney retorted, "You do tend to build intrigue, Detective Gale. Of what do you suspect us?"

"I'll tell you. When I see you . . . together." That time there was no missing the accent. Then he asked, "You say that Brook is feeling better?"

Miss Finney said, "Better than when you saw her in the back garden."

Snapping at the mistake, Gale barked, "How did you know that? You were not here yesterday!"

Nonplussed, Miss Finney let damning seconds pass before she recovered and said, "Why, Mister Brown told me, didn't you?"

Anger at Gale showed on the neighbor's face. He nodded his corroboration of Miss Finney's claim.

Gale nodded. They all knew he did not accept the explanation. He said, "Sure. Of course you did."

He started toward the door. Then, halting himself, Gale said, "As a matter of fact, I may never leave this place. I might just sit out there with Detective Scarne until Miss Finney returns."

With arrogance, Miss Finney asked, "And if she does not return?"

Above the foyer, on the second floor landing, Brook could not hear Gale's reply: "Then I'll find out why!" All Brook heard was the arrogance of her aunt, scoffing at being caught.

Well, Brook would see that aunt Finney would not escape punishment. Brook would see to that herself.

Brook had not been able to comprehend what was happening to her, and she did not really care; she had resigned herself to a disastrous end. After she had killed the nurse, she had sat there on the floor of her bedroom and watched the flesh disappear from beneath the skin of her hands. Faster than she could register in her mind, wrinkles appeared. Nasty brown liver spots showed up. Fingernails cracked and broke.

She had stood. There was a muscular discomfort: legs, arms, back. All feeling tired, aching, . . . old! In the vanity mirror she saw wrinkles, drooping pockets under the eyes, cracks on her lips and a crown of pure white hair. She opened her gown and let it fall to the floor. For some reason the blood had gone, but a new agony was there. Her breasts were sagging, misshapen pouches; her stomach was a series of folded skin with no form. There could be no question: the years remaining to those she killed were being taken away from Brook's own life. Rapidly, violently, ruthlessly the years were being subtracted from her years. Brook knew she must get away.

She had dressed, not really worrying about what to wear. Just something to cover her ugly skin. Stealthily, she moved around the bedroom and was ready in a couple of minutes. She would need a weapon. She went to the gruesome body of the nurse. The scissors still stood there, stabbed deeply into the flesh. Brook could not bring herself to extract the makeshift dagger from the body. She would need something else for a weapon. Her bow and arrows. She took three of the hunting arrows from the quiver and slipped out into the hall.

The voices floated up to her. She crouched down to look into the main entrance foyer. Gale had said words that she could not, did not care to, make out. She was intent on only one mission: Her aunt must die!

Those below were too interested in detective Gale to notice that Brook had risen and, weak as she was, she placed the arrow to the bowstring. She let out a slight whimper as she felt the pain of trying to pull the string back. But it came. Raymond had heard the whimper and his head had snapped up just in time to see Brook about to launch the arrow. The projectile was pointed at Miss Finney's chest. Brook let fly the arrow and screamed: *"Die, you devil!"* Raymond reached out and grabbed at Detective Gale. The officer was taken aback and allowed himself to be spun in front of Miss Finney. The arrow plunged into Gale's chest. He was dead before he struck the floor.

Miss Finney, her lover and Willa all looked up at Brook and smiled. She collapsed to the floor on the second story landing.

"This must be hell," Brook thought as she came to. She could focus on the pattern of the rug and she knew she was in her bedroom. It was pathetic; she was more aged, more wrinkled. Her breathing was labored. Her voice was a warbling sound not easily understood.

"They cannot have my soul . . . they will not . . . they will not. . . ." She spoke the words into empty space. She was alone. The feelings in her body made her know she was near death. Strength was slipping away with each moment.

She struggled with her mind for several minutes before she could get a message to her legs. With nearly super-human effort, she got to her feet. Her brain—it was be-ginning to be addled—convinced her that she could never make such an effort again in her life. She whimpered as she realized that she had stood up for the last time in her life. Determination urged her to make the best of her one last accomplishment. She bumped into things as she crossed the room. She nearly tripped over the body of the nurse. That would have been the end; she would not have been able to rise from that fall. The time it took for her to get her hand to close over the doorknob seemed endless. She had not considered what would have happened if the lock had been set; she assumed they knew she was too near death to escape. She would show them.

Each step was agony; joints shot bolts of pain all over her body. She wished there were some way to walk without stepping. At the top of the stairs, she weaved. She would surely tumble down. Again, she thought that death must be a better solution. If she would slip into the blackness of hell, it might be just as well.

Paying a price she could barely afford, she went down, step by step. She was so exhausted when she reached the bottom of the stairs that she was convinced she was standing in her death room. Hanging onto the newel post for support, she gazed around the room. It would be an ignoble place to die. She demanded that her body move out of the mansion. She was determined not to die on Finney property. On the porch of the front entranceway, she relished the victory she had gained over the front door and the steps from the door. It was a sweet victory, but the price had been more energy. She was not in a position to squander energy. She breathed the air. The night air around the French Quarter was always a sea-scented, invigorating gift and she imagined that sucking it deeply would give her the strength she would need for the final leap of her escape.

Why, she wondered, why are they not after me? Would they chase me? Would they waste their time killing the already dead? Down the driveway, she nearly collapsed from the pain in her joints. The ache was sapping her life. She could not give up. She spent invaluable reserves on making her declaration: "I will not surrender . . . . They will not have me!" She repeated the words but they fell into empty, unhearing space. She was alone in the night, alone with her antiquity.

At the main gate to the grounds, she snaked her fingers into the lacework of wrought iron that she had enjoyed over the past ten years. It held patterns, mysterious messages that she had never decoded. She caressed it; she was saying goodbye.

Out on the public sidewalk, Brook leaned up against a

wall and looked at the stars in the night sky. She was having difficulty bringing things into focus. Her sight was failing. Age was taking a rapid toll on her body, but her mind still fought: "They will not win!" She moved with drunken steps, using lampposts as crutches.

It was late; few others were on the street. Those who were, those who noticed the old, tottering woman, those who passed close to her, turned away. People do not like to see what can, what will, happen. Brook knew they could be like her, someday. Grimly, she thought, give them a chance. They will all have the chance.

Her thoughts were rambling out of control. She walked through time; she went slowly, time went fast. She did not know where she was, she did not know why people did not help her. Along streets, across intersections, past the buildings of the French Quarter, Brook straggled. It must be late; she had not seen a person for hours . . . days? She was on a street that she did not recognize. It was quiet and residential.

She felt peace and resignation. She did not want to live old, ugly and infirm. She did not want to lose.

"They will not win!" She was proud of the oath.

There was a man half a block away. She offered a feeble wave as a summons. She did not want to die alone. She waved again; he came toward her. He was cautious at first. He studied the aged woman. With a politeness that she welcomed, he asked: "Are you all right, Ma'am?"

She begged: "Please help me?"

Compassionately, he came to her side and placed a strong arm around her sagging shoulders. He asked: "Are you ill? Do you live around here?"

She looked at him, her eyes glazed. She whimpered: "They will not win!"

Concerned, the man held Brook tightly, offering security. Quietly, he asked, "What can I do to help?"

She gasped, "Call Detective Scarne . . . please . . . Detective Scarne . . . . " She was fading; she could feel parts of her being begin to shut down. Scarne would help her; he would see that they would not win.

"Detective Scarne?" the stranger asked, "You want a policeman?"

Voice cracking, Brook pleaded, "Detective Scarne . . . only him!"

"I understand," he thought he did. "Let me get you safe first." He guided her with ease. They crossed the street and came to a small, well-kept public garden. She had never noticed it before. He led her to a bench and gently helped her sit down. He spoke with tender tones: "You'll be fine here. Just rest. You'll stay . . . promise?" And he was gone from her view.

She was alone for a time that she could not measure. Visions passed before her eyes. She knew she was living out the end of a lifetime. Her head bobbed; she began to accept sleep. She could not sleep! She must wait! She lifted her head. Excitement tried to fight its way into an unexciteable shell of pain and hurts.

A few feet away, she could see Detective Scarne jumping out of his police car and running to her. She felt elation. He came right to her and knelt down in front of her.

"Hello, Brook." She smiled, gratefully.

Then, what remained of her world crashed in on top of her. She was old, wrinkled, twisted and crippled. Her hair was white, her teeth missing, her back hunched. How could Scarne know she was Brook? He knew! She felt mammoth tears begin to well up in her eyes. Oh, he knew, all right. He was one of them!

She looked up. Another person was approaching. They were there. Willa. Miss Finney. Raymond Brown. Carlos Ives. And others. Some she knew were part of it; some she would never have suspected.

With confidence, Scarne reached out a hand and stroked her cheek as he asked, "Are you ready to join us now?"

She whimpered.

She knew.

They knew.

EPILOGUE

Captain Huff was pleased with what he had seen; they would do a good job. He had just been appointed to his post and he felt the men working in his department would make a successful term possible. Especially his Lieutenant of Detectives. They were walking down the marbled hall of Police Headquarters, their footsteps echoing loudly.

"Scarne," the new Captain said, "I am pleased, really pleased."

"I'm glad we seem up to scratch, Captain Huff."

"Hmmm," the Captain replied.

They came to the front door and, once outside, they started down toward the street. With happiness, Scarne said, "Ah . . . there they are."

Huff looked down to the wide sidewalk. Three people waited. Huff grumbled to himself: "Young people!" Huff was feeling his own age because he was so portly and had indulged himself for a lifetime. Scarne was slim, young-looking.

Huff heard Scarne saying, "This is my wife, Brook." Huff offered a polite hand and was annoyed as she placed a soft, warm hand into his rough, blistered mitt.

"Pleased to meet you, Brook," Huff said, mildly jealous that one of his detective lieutenants was married to such a young, pretty thing. Huff suppressed the emotion, marking it up to his old age.

"And there are our friends," Scarne pushed into Huff's thoughts again. "I'd like you to meet Alcorn and Raymond. Our very best friends." Another pair of disgustingly young, attractive people. Huff shook hands.

The woman, Alcorn, was speaking. She had a charm and bearing that belied her youth. She asked, "Would you join us for lunch, Captain Huff?"

"Oh, no." He always patted his extended stomach when he declined invitations to dine.

Miss Finney spoke with a pleading coyness: "Oh, please. We would like that very much. It is my treat and we are going to Antoine's. Mister Alcitoire is fixing us a special Breast of Pheasant Sous Cloche and Oysters à lay Foch."

Huff groaned. He had never been able to afford such luxurious dishes. "No," he hoped his anguish did not show, "I'll have to pass."

With a teasing twinkle in her voice, she asked, "What about stuffed eggplant and Omelette Norvégienne?"

Those Huff had eaten. He was tempted.

But there was more than just food. Huff felt old and this quartet seemed so young. He would be depressed by a luncheon with them. He turned to Scarne and said, "Your lovely friend has a sadistic streak." Then Huff turned to Brook and said, "Now you take this group out for some fun. Don't weigh yourself down with old fuddy-duddies like me."

They understood. Huff turned and walked away; the others shrugged, called "so-longs" to him and headed towards Bourbon Street.

They made a vibrant group, moving lightly along the sidewalks, laughing, springing with vitality. They had gone several blocks, chatting happily, full of the joys of youth, when Scarne spotted an old couple sitting peacefully, prettily, holding hands on a garden bench. The old couple seemed deeply in love.

As Scarne said to the others, "Hey, hold it," they, too, saw the old couple. Miss Finney and Raymond, Brook and Scarne all stood there looking at the elderly couple.

The couple looked back and smiled.